SOPHIE RAM

THE GIRL who sees ANGELS

a novel

Jeffrey McClain Jones

The Girl Who Sees Angels

Copyright © 2020 by Jeffrey McClain Jones

All rights reserved. No part of this book may be reproduced in any form by any electronic or mechanical means including photocopying, recording, or information storage and retrieval, without permission in writing from the author.

John 14:12 Publications

www.jeffreymcclainjones.com

Cover art from Shutterstock.com.

For those who see but dare not tell.

A Bad Idea

Sophie Ramos slowed her escape, grinding the soles of her Doc Martens on the rock-salt scattered pavement. As she reached her hybrid car, she resisted turning back to see them watching her. She hit the remote unlock button on her electronic key, but the car was already unlocked—in an unfamiliar neighborhood. Her desperate hope for this meeting had numbed her brain. Maybe she should be grateful she'd managed to park her car on the driveway and not on the patchy lawn.

This whole thing was a bad idea. A waste of time. But where else was she supposed to go?

Her head down, evading the eyes trained on her from the house, she inhaled cool, damp air as she climbed into the car. The interior still smelled of mold from a water spill on the passenger seat earlier in the year. Diverting to frustration over the moldy air kept her eyes off the view out the windshield.

She snorted at what the old lady had said. "A gift." Really? *Some* gift.

Slowing her breathing, thinning the curling vapor from her nostrils, Sophie remembered a fortune-teller saying the same thing. "The sight is a gift that only a few are entrusted with." Sophie had entrusted *that* lady with fifty dollars. At least the church lady didn't charge for her nutty insights.

As she turned the key in the ignition, Sophie raised her head just enough to view the luminescent pillars stationed by the humble single-story house. They lent an air of golden splendor. She ducked and glued her eyes to the control panel of her Toyota. This was why she avoided church ladies. The world got even weirder around them. Too many shining

The Girl Who Sees Angels

hallucinations. "Angels," the woman called them. This church lady apparently agreed with the fortune-teller on that too. But the notion of literal angels in this digital age was as uncomfortable to Sophie as high-heeled pumps and tight dresses.

She replayed the meeting in her mind. Detta. Seeing Bernadetta Washington had been Priscilla's idea. Priscilla, the token church lady in Sophie's life. "Detta can definitely help you," Priscilla said.

What had Sophie expected help to look like? Not a retired black woman with smiley cheeks and irrational optimism. Sophie needed real help. A rescuer. An antidote.

Angels and spirits? Maybe what she needed was an exorcist.

"But you don't believe in that either." She muttered as she glanced at the usual crowd of stowaways huddled in her back seat. She looked right through them to the dim gray street behind her.

An SUV buzzed past, a flaming light streaking behind it as it crunched over the scattering of salt and gravel. Was it harder now to ignore the virtual reality layer of aliens others swore they couldn't see? Maybe she was still too close to the church lady's house.

She backed onto the residential road and then slammed on her brakes.

A young black man skipped clear of the driveway, onto the safer grass next to it.

Sophie's heart seized and then dropped off the high wall it had just tried to leap. Where had *he* come from?

He must have gotten out of the car parked by the curb. That new coup wasn't there when she arrived fifteen minutes ago. She checked out the "Beam me up, Scotty" bumper sticker. Then the little decals in the rear window—the cartoon alien family with huge ET eyes. The "My child is an honor student at Starfleet Academy" sticker was a bit crooked on the other side of the bumper.

Sophie felt the guy's stare as she assessed his shiny gray car. He was probably just waiting for her to get out of his way so he could walk up the driveway. Was he related to Bernadetta? She ventured a glance. He kinda looked like her in the eyes.

He didn't stop scoping her as he walked past her window. Maybe he was having as much trouble placing her as she was him. She had never met a black guy so all-in on *Star Trek*. Well, except Melvin. But he was ... exceptional. And maybe that was *Star Wars*. This guy looked smart and nerdy, black plastic-rimmed glasses and all. Pretty good looking, really.

Was she sitting halfway in the street crushing on a nerdy guy who was probably related to that loony church lady? "Gotta get outta here." Back to the city was her best bet. She refused to check out the guy again. Church ladies, sci-fi nerds, and glowing giants. To Sophie, glowing giants were the most familiar characters in this freak show. And she was tired of *them*.

A fast-approaching sedan honked as she pulled past the *Star Trek* mobile. Rearview mirrors weren't optional after all.

Sophie swore under her breath. "This was definitely a bad idea."

Who Was that Girl?

Anthony Washington smelled the chocolate chip cookies before he opened the storm door off his mother's driveway. The inside door was ajar despite the thirty-five degree gloom outside. The kitchen glowed warm and golden through the foggy glass. That warmth was probably why his mama left the inside door open. Unless it had to do with that weird chick leaving just now.

"Hey, Mama. Who was that woman leaving your house?"

"Hello, my son. How do you do, too?" His mother's crooked smirk softened her implied rebuke.

"I said 'Hey.' Is that not formal enough?" He grinned in self-defense as he snagged two cookies from the cooling rack.

She lowered her head and glared at him over her glasses. "Who said those were for you?"

"You invited me to dinner. You could not possibly do that and make cookies for a church bake sale or something instead of your loving son."

"Who says?" She shuffled in for a hug, their eyeglasses clicking briefly as she pulled him close.

Anthony chuckled into her poof of light gray hair, trying not to get cookie crumbs on her back. He extricated himself from his mother's strong arms. "So, who was she? She didn't look like someone from your prayer group."

"That sounds like racial profiling to me." She planted her hands on her hips and puckered in mock disapproval.

"Was she? Part of your prayer group?"

"You askin' because you think she was interesting? Maybe attractive?"

"No." He shrugged. "But I guess she was cute, in an angry sort of punk girl way."

"Punk girl?"

"Yeah. Black hair, black eyeliner, nose pierced, black leather jacket. You know." He bit into a cookie. "But you're not answering my question." He turned back toward the door and pried off his right Nike with his left toe.

"You noticed that, did you?" She chuckled heavily. "Well, you're right. She's not part of any kinda prayer group. But Sister Maynard sent her to see me about some angels and other things."

His second maroon shoe parked by the door, Anthony finished his first cookie—warm and doughy, just the way he liked them. "Angels? Were you giving or taking away?"

"Taking away? Like deliverance ministry?"

"Whatever you call it." He pulled out a chair and plopped down at the kitchen table in his usual spot, freeing himself from his down jacket. He grinned at the familiar orange woven placemat and fall leaf paper napkin.

"I wasn't doing any kind of ministry on her. She sees spirits and hoped I'd give her some kinda remedy for a particular visitation." His mother pulled the lasagna pan off the top of the stove and onto the countertop next to it, a long, thin knife waiting on the butcher block. "I don't know if she was thinking about deliverance, but she didn't ask and didn't give me a chance to offer."

"She thinks she sees spirits?"

"I didn't say that. I said she *sees* spirits, all kinds of angels. I'm pretty confident about that. What I can't figure is how she got this far without believing in God, despite all the spiritual activity she's been seein'."

"She's seen them all her life?"

"Umm."

His mother was either too intent on cutting the lasagna, or she was throttling the release of information. Anthony knew he shouldn't push for more. His mother was privy to numerous secrets about all kinds of people. Mostly church people. But he couldn't let it rest yet. He wiped his right hand on his paper napkin and reached for his water glass. "Does Sister Maynard believe that woman sees angels?"

"Sister Maynard wouldn't ha' sent her to me if she didn't believe her. I guess her daughter Priscilla knows the girl."

"What's the girl's name?"

"Sophie Ramos." His mama lifted a pair of heavy Stonecraft plates from the counter. She was still strong and healthy. A bit overweight, probably, but she was moving pretty well for a woman over sixty-five.

"Ramos. Huh. She's Hispanic?"

"Latinx."

"Oh, so look who's all politically correct now."

"Don't make fun of your old mama. I do my best to keep up." She settled the plates onto their placemats.

"Does she speak good English?"

"I didn't give her a college English exam, but she did fine. She's homegrown, I'd say. Probably from around here."

Nodding, Anthony inhaled a steamy promise—cheese, sausage, and spices he couldn't name.

"Are you interested in this girl 'cause you broke up with Dianna?" His mother looked like a harmless someday-grandma and longtime church lady, but she was actually a precision sniper with decades of deadly hits.

"Uh, yeah. I broke up with Dianna. But I ain't gonna go out with some girl who sees demons in her soup."

"She didn't say anything about her soup." His mother sat down across from him, placing the canister of parmesan in the middle of the table. "Are you gonna say grace?"

Anthony appreciated his mother's gleaming gaze for a moment and then bowed his head.

Gotta Pray for that Girl

When her son left late that evening, after helping her move the Thanksgiving decorations down from the attic, Bernadetta Washington kicked back in her plush recliner and sipped tea from her favorite super-sized mug. Anthony gave her that twenty-ounce mug as a joke when he was in college. The trick was drinking all the tea before it got cold. But then, that was why God created microwaves.

"Help that poor girl find you, Lord. You know she needs it." Detta placed the big green mug on the cork coaster near the corner of the end table. She wondered if she needed to forgive Sister Maynard for sending that girl to see her. It hadn't been a pleasant get-together.

"But who else was she gonna go see? She sure is scared about that thing that comes to see her at night." She puckered her lips into what Anthony called her "duck look." "And I kinda think she'll come back to me. As unlikely as that seems." She pushed her glasses up her nose and settled back to listen to the inner voice she relied on for comfort and direction.

"Help my boy, Anthony, while you're at it, Lord. He seems to be drifting—not on fire for you." She sighed and reached for her tea.

Even as she sipped the apricot infusion, she chuckled. "I swear, I have never seen anyone so gifted and so opposed to her own gift. She nearly scared me to death."

She replayed the moment when Sophie looked over Detta's shoulder and then dodged in an effort *not* to see those spirits. It was clear. Detta had felt a wicked presence behind her at the exact time the girl ducked. Yes, Sophie saw something real. Her reaction was real. And it was the reaction of someone who had seen it before and spent lots of energy trying to ignore it. Whatever that spirit was, Sophie had brought it with her. That was sure too.

"I can't say I understand what your plan is, Lord. Why give a gift like that to a girl who's no better than a pagan?" She breathed a laugh. "Only, she said she'd dumped the pagans too, now that I think of it. Can't say I blame her for that." Detta chuckled deep in her chest until it triggered a full-fledged cough.

"Hmm." That cough had been there for a while now. Maybe it was time to go see the doctor about it.

"Mm-hmm."

Augmented Reality

Sophie closed the text editor window on her second flat-screen monitor and did a test run of the new code. Her boss, Janice, hovered behind her chair, close enough that Sophie held her breath against the woman's sickly-sweet perfume. The web app ran as designed, loading the action buttons quickly this time.

"Yes! You got it. Great work, Sophie." A job well done always got a high five or the verbal equivalent from Janice.

Still focused on the pair of monitors, Sophie nodded her acceptance of the praise. Staying locked on her screens helped her block out ethereal distractions. It generally worked, even if it gave the impression she struggled with attention deficit disorder or something. Wouldn't that be a simple problem to have? A more common problem, at least.

When Janice headed back to her corner office, Sophie saved her work and twisted around to see if Sammy was at his desk. She spotted the top of his head bobbing just above his cube wall.

She slid out of her ergo chair and slunk down the aisle to her coworker's workstation. She lifted his extra set of virtual reality goggles from his desk. "Hey, Sammy. What are you working on?"

"Driving through a mall. Virtually driving through a virtual mall." Wearing his usual short-sleeved T-shirt no matter the weather, Sammy's pale arms filled most of the cube, elbows akimbo as he gripped an invisible steering wheel.

She maneuvered the heavy goggles over her hair. "It looks like something more exciting than that."

"Oh, I added some pterodactyls to keep it interesting."

Sophie snickered as she hit the power switch on the goggles. "Did Dave approve the pterodactyls?" She dipped as one of the prehistoric beasts swooped over the Jeep that Sammy drove through the virtual mall.

"Dave hasn't seen all the augmented attractions, of course. And I'm counting on you to keep 'em just between you and me." He grunted when he ran over a bench in his effort to escape one of the big, winged creatures.

"I think the execs might get suspicious when they see you jerking and dodging like that. Ow!" Sophie banged her hip against the real-world counter next to her.

The real world.

She still hoped to get assigned to one of these augmented reality projects. The big marketing firm that employed her was producing more and more of them. She had also sent out resumés to game developers, but there weren't many in the area. No response so far.

For Sophie, augmented computer interfaces such as these goggles were a way to escape the world she had grown up in, a world enhanced by beings that no one else admitted to seeing. No one except an occasional psychic or church lady.

That Detta woman hadn't claimed to *see* a threatening ghoul in her house, but her evasive maneuver had been perfectly synched with its appearance. She must have sensed the creepy thing Sophie was ducking.

The first time Sophie put on goggles, she felt understood. Like she was no longer a lone seer in a land of blind people. Everyone who donned those goggles could perceive the layer augmenting the "real" world.

Sammy bumped into her now, a classic hip check. He juked and leaned into a fast turn, followed by another attack from a Cretaceous carnivore.

"Ahem."

Sophie ripped her goggles off in a move worthy of a firefighter hearing the station alarm. Sammy followed suit.

David Jasper stood at the portal to Sammy's workstation. "Exciting mall our client has designed?" He propped one elbow on the top of the cube wall and cocked his head.

Sammy nodded. "Very exciting."

"I gotta get to lunch." Sophie stooped past Dave and avoided eye contact with Sammy.

In her haste to escape recrimination, she pushed right through a virtual creature hanging off Dave's back. The cold shiver that grabbed her spine was probably just her over-stimulated imagination. She couldn't *feel* these things. Usually. She just *saw* them. But some of them gave her the creeps in the most visceral way.

She was still recovering when she slipped on her jacket by the elevator. She refused to glance back at Sammy's cube. Seeing how he avoided indictment didn't compel her enough to risk another look at that thing clinging to Dave.

When the elevator door opened, the car was too crowded for Sophie. A guy from upstairs was in there with half a dozen of his followers. A virtual entourage.

"I'll wait for the next one." She tried a weak grin.

The pudgy guy in the elevator scowled at her. But he was pretty scowly anyway. And his accompanying specters were not just scowly, they were scary. As the door closed, several sets of eyes targeted her.

The elevator to her left dinged just as Sophie turned to take the stairway.

For the most part, the office was boring, inhabited by drones who carried little spectral baggage. There wasn't too much for Sophie to ignore, usually. But lately—maybe since she met that church lady—she had a harder time seeing through other people's clutter.

Maybe that church lady did something to her. She'd prayed for her. That's one thing she did. That's what she *said* she was going to keep doing. But what difference could that make?

Sophie closed her eyes and held her breath as she descended past the sixth and fifth floors. It wasn't that she couldn't see the spiritual layer with her eyes closed, but closing them sometimes helped her ignore the aliens.

That didn't work so well today. A layer of orange fog crossed the video screen of her mind as the elevator slowed and stopped. A man and woman boarded the elevator, which forced Sophie to open her eyes and *try* to appear normal.

Before today, blocking out the layer of virtual entities had been like ignoring that chip in her car's windshield. Only when someone rode with her did she notice the damage that threatened to branch into multiple cracks.

Was that church lady in her head? Was she using witchcraft or something?

Of course there was no such thing.

Probably.

Harder to Ignore Today

Sophie answered a call from Crystal as she sat in the sandwich shop on Madison Street. Talking around a huge bite of sandwich, she answered. "Hello, girl. You at lunch?"

"Actually, I have that doctor's appointment today." Crystal's voice was muted, probably by fear, not bread.

"A real doctor and not one of those shamans?" Sophie swallowed and plucked a grape tomato from her salad.

"I don't go to actual shamans, you know."

"Whatever. Is this about your throat?"

"Yeah. That lump—knot or whatever it is—just seems to be getting bigger."

"Nodule."

"What did you say?"

Sophie swallowed the tomato. "I think it's called a nodule."

"Oh, yeah. That thing. But it sounds grosser when you call it that."

"I suppose. You on the train?"

"Yeah. You can hear the guy babbling behind me?"

Sophie started to laugh, but a blood-red flash filled her visual cortex and sapped the humor of it. "Don't stand too close. He's got something nasty on him."

"Don't we all?" Crystal's voice trailed off. Then she perked a bit. "But you can see that all the way down by your office?"

"It happens. Only because we're on the phone though. Or at least that's what I think it is."

"You should see someone, Sophie. This is hard to cope with."

"Hard for *you* to cope with?"

"No. For you, of course."

"I have already seen a lot of someones, Crystal."

"Anyone lately?"

"Just that friend of Priscilla's mother."

"What's she? A psychic?"

"No. A church lady."

"Oh, yeah. Priscilla. What did this church lady say?"

"That I have a gift God wants to use to do his work in the world." Sophie lowered her voice, but not before the couple seated down the counter turned their heads toward her.

"God needs you to do stuff for him?"

"Him or her. The lady didn't specify." Sophie had her hand cupped around the phone now, her voice contained.

"Hmm. I wonder if she might be at least partly right. Isn't there some way you could use this to help people?"

"How could I help anyone? I'm too busy ducking. And I have my own problems."

"But you can shut it out sometimes, right?"

"It's hard. Even harder today. Though it's usually impossible when they threaten me at night."

"Sorry. I didn't mean to bring that up."

"You didn't. I did."

"Still, sorry."

"I know. Well, good luck with the doctor."

"Thanks, Sophie. I hope it's nothing."

"Me too."

After they hung up, Sophie leaned heavily on the counter over the remnants of her lunch. How could she help people by telling them the color or shape of the aliens they towed behind them? Most people seemed perfectly happy not knowing.

But that psychic guru, Maxwell Hartman, had suggested something more, hadn't he? He had offered her a sort of apprenticeship. To learn some system for interpreting what she was seeing.

Of course now he was past offering. He had graduated to threatening.

A teenage girl entered the restaurant, distracting Sophie with what looked like a dancing fairy sprinkling rays of light over her. Did that girl want to know about the happy nymph? Or maybe she already knew.

Sophie let the dancing thing drag her focus. Her blinders weren't working anyway. And maybe seeing Tinkerbell wasn't so annoying. Certainly not scary. But when Sophie stood and deposited her recyclables in the bin, the young woman's shiny friend changed. She, or it, grew until it loomed over the girl.

What the ...?

Sophie pivoted toward the door. She didn't need to know more. She would *act* like she wasn't seeing things. That generally helped her avoid the horror-movie eyes she got when someone heard her secret. Even if ignoring the virtual world didn't work, *pretending* she didn't see it was absolutely necessary.

Kept the shrinks away.

Keeping the Shrinks Away

"If other people don't know what you see, then you're not crazy." Sophie remembered saying that during hospital stay number four. She was with the scrawny female social worker with the beige skin and the flyaway hair. At age sixteen, Sophie had been working on loosening her grip on the truth. A *tight* grasp had never served her well. The truth scared her mother. And it sometimes got Sophie admitted to one of those big boxes full of bizarre wildlife.

She could even hear sounds from some of the specters in that hospital. Why was that? Was she headed back there now, since she was hearing those threats from her nighttime visitor? Why was that even happening?

Why had generally not been the key question when she was a girl. *Whether* was the most important question. And *not* was widely considered the right answer. It wasn't a true answer, but it was the lie that got her home to her mother's cooking and her bedroom with the dark red walls.

Today on her way back to the office, she faked a passing interest in the clothes displayed in a department store window. That averted her gaze from the rotten fruit thing stuck to a guy in a business suit.

At age thirty-two, maybe she would see a professional counselor if she could find one who wouldn't commit her, or who wouldn't insist on higher doses of medication. Which one was she on now? Xanax? How much? Not enough to dull her into oblivion, and not enough to render the ghouls invisible.

Or angels. She stomped her feet on the sidewalk at the very idea. Really? Was that what she saw? If not, then what? What was that thing in her bedroom?

Maybe she should go back to that Detta lady. Sophie had probably run from her little house too soon. Maybe there was some help there still, something other than signing up with a church. The church lady seemed way less creepy than the psychics. And Detta didn't have a prescription pad or wrist restraints.

Straining to concentrate at work the rest of the day wiped most of her worries from view. She did notice the sloppy little dude that generally hung out in Charlie's cube next door. "Lumpy" was her name for him. She didn't tell Charlie about him, of course.

She'd driven to work for a change so she could stop by her mother's house afterward. A side benefit of that transportation choice was a break from the circus that rode on most buses and trains. Headphones and a baseball cap couldn't block out all the freaky creatures and odd entities on public transportation. Too many people, too many critters.

"*Hola, Madrecita!*" She dropped her keys on the prim table just inside the front door of her mother's little ranch house—not so far from that church lady's home ... that *other* church lady. Sophie unzipped her leather jacket as she contemplated a statue of the Virgin Mary on a shelf near the door.

"English, my daughter. English, please. I need you to help me with my English." Her mother cruised across the living room and grabbed Sophie's shoulders for cheek kisses. "I depend on my college-educated daughter to help me improve my language skills so I can become more marketable in the ... in the marketplace of commerce."

Sophie feigned a highbrow East Coast accent. "Impressive. Very impressive, Mommy dearest." She tilted her head to avoid the shiny figure lurking in the corner of the living room.

Two other flashes forced her to bow deeper, but they exited as fast as she could flinch.

Her mother lowered her head to meet Sophie's eyes. "You're having problems with the visions again?" She scrutinized Sophie from beneath her muscular brow. She had exercised that brow extensively during Sophie's life.

"No problems, Mama. I'm fine. How is *el gato*?"

"The cat is fine. And don't change the language or the subject on me." She reached for Sophie's jacket. "I know what *fine* means."

Sophie took a deep breath. "I'm seeing them more today." What a relief to speak truthfully with her mother, one of maybe four people in the world she could be honest with ... most of the time.

"It is something you did? You didn't go to another one of those witches, did you?"

"No witches, Mother." She headed for the kitchen, creaking over the hardwood floor between the living room rug and the dining room. "Actually, I think it was a church lady who put some kind of curse or something on me."

"She is not a good church lady if she put a curse on my daughter."

Sophie pulled a cut crystal tumbler from the cupboard next to the sink. The kitchen shelves evidenced her mother's talent for finding treasures at Goodwill.

"I don't know sh— Uh, I don't know *anything* about curses. So don't quote me on that."

"Quote you?"

Sophie shrugged. "Maybe it wasn't a curse. But she prayed for me, which was when I beat it out of her house."

"Beat it out?"

A movement back in the living room alerted Sophie's defense protocol, but it turned out to be her mother's fat black cat with the white shield stamped on its chest. She sighed. "I ran. I told the lady I wasn't interested in her religion and got outta there." An urge to curse in one or two languages surged in her throat, but she extinguished the flame with a sip of water. Who was she mad at anyway? Detta? Or at herself for fleeing Detta's house without finding out whether she could help?

"Was she Catholic?"

Shaking her head from slow to fast, Sophie ambled out of the kitchen. "No. I don't think so." The golden being in the living room held his post, so she settled for a straight-backed chair in the dining room.

"Why do you sit out here?"

"I like it better."

Her mother frowned again.

Sophie glanced toward the kitchen. "Tamales?"

"Of course." Her mother picked up a small stack of envelopes from the dining room table and carried them toward the kitchen.

"*Muy buenos*, Madrecita."

"Yes. Very good, if I do say so myself."

Sophie laughed at her dear mother. But she could still hear that serious concern in her voice. "Don't worry, Mama."

"I am a mother. I worry." She came back and stood next to Sophie, the front of her fleece sweater brushing her daughter's cheek. "You know you can tell me. I'm not going to send you to one of those doctors again. I know they cannot help you. I know that now."

Sophie wrapped an arm around her mother's medium-sized waist. "Okay. I will tell you, especially if there is something to tell. Right now it's just hard to ignore them. Something happened, apparently."

Her mother stepped back to gaze into her face. "That lady prayed?"

"She did. She wanted to put her hands on me, but I wouldn't let her." Sophie ran a finger along the angles of the tumbler. "But I couldn't stop her from getting God involved in our little meeting."

"Maybe God is answering her prayers. Maybe God is showing you something."

Sophie puffed her cheeks. "I wish he wouldn't. I see too much as it is."

"What is in the living room?"

Sophie tested her resolve about telling the truth. Maybe that resolve was just to reveal what her mother *needed* to know. But constantly sorting that out exhausted her. "Some golden, shining person is in the corner." She twisted to peer into the living room. That being now stood luminous and sentinel-like in the middle of the room, as if waiting for something. It pulsed with warm light.

"Golden? Shining? Is it good? Is it evil?"

"Doesn't seem evil to me. Pretty much always here, as far as I remember. But if you didn't invite it, maybe that's bad."

"A trespasser, you think?"

"The church lady said I see angels."

"Not spirits? Not devils?"

"She said that devils are just bad angels. She said I probably see both kinds."

"How does she know?"

"I told her some of the things that appear to me. And I guess she can tell when they're around. She seemed to know when something came up behind her and hovered over us, though maybe she didn't see it like me."

"You said that witch could tell something was there."

"She wasn't a witch. She was a psychic."

"Same thing."

It was no good arguing this with her mother. Sophie switched lanes. "Is supper ready?"

With a nod, her favorite tamale maker ended the interrogation ... for now.

Time to Take a Closer Look

Detta rested her head on the exam table. A pillow would have been nice, but the point was optimal access to her innards. She shifted her attention to the water stains on several ceiling tiles.

"Take a deep breath." Doctor Gandhi leaned over Detta, her stethoscope chilling small patches on Detta's chest.

Detta tried that deep breath. It caught. She coughed. A twinge like a tweaked nerve ran up her chest toward her head.

"Okay. I want to get an X-ray of your chest. There's something obstructing your bronchial tubes and maybe your lungs. Let's see if we can get a picture of it."

"Too bad you can't just do that with your phone." Detta sat up with a little help from the doctor.

"Yes. Wouldn't that be nice? Maybe that's the next upgrade." The doctor smiled, her teeth white between purplish lips. "You can get dressed."

That was always the highlight of the visit, the best news these days. "You can get dressed." At least it was easier to undo the plastic tie on the paper gown with the opening in the front this time.

When she stood by the counter waiting for the receptionist to give her the information regarding X-rays, Detta's phone buzzed. She foraged for it in her big navy-blue purse and tipped her head back to see the screen. Incoming call. Another buzz followed. Voice mail. She would check it when she got out to the car.

Seated in her ten-year-old Honda Accord, she pulled her phone from her camel coat pocket. A message from an unfamiliar number.

The Girl Who Sees Angels

"Hello, Mrs. ... uh, Detta. This is Sophie Ramos. I basically ran out of your house the other day. You freaked me out with that prayer. But I think I wanna try again. At least to ask you some more questions. Are you willing to see me again?" She huffed a couple times. "Call me back if you do ... are. Uh, goodbye."

"I kinda thought you'd be back. Don't know why. But I suspect you don't know either." Detta had talked to herself for the past thirty years whenever she was alone. An elderly white couple glancing suspiciously in the window as they toddled past reminded her of how that might look. "Blessings to you folks." She waved at their backs and inserted the key in the ignition.

At home, she had her phone to her ear, her other hand holding the white kitchen curtains back. Some chickadees had discovered her bird feeder recently. She pulled that curtain to the right and then reached for the other one. The nervous little black, gray, and white birds darted away.

Anthony greeted her. "Hey, Mama. How are you? How was the doctor?"

"She seemed fine. Maybe a little tired. She works too hard."

"Ha. I *meant* how was the visit for you? What did she say about your cough?" Anthony seemed to hold his hand over the phone to say something to somebody else.

"Oh. I'm getting X-rays tomorrow to see what's goin' on inside there. Bronchial tubes and lungs. Chest X-rays. No matter. I was calling about something else."

"Oh. Okay. What's up?"

"You remember that cute young woman you were admiring in my driveway last week?"

"Cute? Did I say she was cute?"

"I thought she was, anyway. But that doesn't matter either." One of those chickadees dove in to snatch a seed and flitted away. "I was thinking she might be more comfortable if you're around next time she comes over—a generational thing, you know."

"She's coming over again? I thought she ran from your place, like, screaming last time."

"Did she look that scared when you saw her?"

"No, she just looked ... uh, crabby. You were the one who said she ran out of the house like she was possessed."

"I did not. I didn't say anything like that."

"Okay. Maybe not. I forget." He exhaled into the phone. "You think she beat it outta there 'cause you're old, and she'll stick around 'cause I'm young?"

Detta chuckled, restraining it a bit to avoid awakening that cough. "You're young and you're *handsome*."

"Are you using me as bait, Mama?"

"Oh, you're useful for more than that. But that might just work this once."

"Well, she *was* kinda cute. But mad."

"Mad cute?"

"Right. Very hip, Mama. When is this mad cute woman coming to your house?"

"I wanted to check with you first. I haven't called her back yet. I thought dinner when you come over. Maybe she won't hightail it so fast if I feed her first."

"Works for me."

Free food always seemed to work for Anthony. It was better for his pockets than spending twenty-five bucks on dinner like he usually did. Better for his mother too.

Right after they hung up, Detta hit one of those snags in her breathing and coughed for half a minute. That was the worst one yet. Maybe she could at least know what she was dealing with by the time Anthony and Sophie came that weekend. But, then, Sophie might have X-ray vision to see what the devil was doing inside Detta's chest.

"I don't really envy her gifts, come to think of it."

On Friday afternoon, the day after the X-rays, Detta got the call from her doctor. "It looks like pulmonary fibrosis. We should do a CT scan to get a better look."

"How bad is that?"

"It could be quite severe, but it could also be fairly benign. The fact that it's irritating you means we have to look more closely. It's just the cough, is it, and not shortness of breath?"

"Sure. I think so. Though I can't say I'm in the best shape."

"Losing some weight and exercising more is always a good idea. And we can try some medications to slow the progress of the disease. But first let's take another look. I'll have my assistant call you with arrangements for the CT scan."

After hanging up, Detta stood by the window watching a pair of dark-eyed juncos balancing on the birdfeeder. "Consider the birds of the air, Detta. They don't worry. They just do their thing and keep on keepin' on." Sometimes talking to herself was preaching to herself.

"Still. I should look that up." She turned toward the living room and her computer, tucked in the corner. Anthony had set it up on that tall maple end table, built decades before anyone thought of computers.

"Pulmonary fibrosis is the enemy. Let's learn something about this enemy."

Dinner with the Church Lady

When Detta warned Sophie that her son—that *Star Trek* nerd, presumably—would be joining them for dinner, Sophie assumed he was Detta's assistant in whatever kind of magic show the old lady did. But it turned out he was also tech support for Detta's computer. He apparently knew what he was doing.

"It's just an update that got hung up. I can log in with admin privileges and run it for you."

"Okay. Whatever you say," Detta called weakly from the kitchen.

Sophie could tell Detta didn't understand what her son had just said.

"You know anything about those machines, Sophie?" Detta was pulling something out of the oven.

"Computers? I know some. I was a computer science major in college. And I work as a software developer."

Anthony turned in the swivel chair. "Really? What kind of coding?"

She could see his nerd antennae rising above his head—metaphorically. The only otherworldly phenomena around Anthony came and went as brief flashes—green, blue, and amber. Maybe those were echoes of the lights in a computer network room.

"I do Java apps for a marketing company downtown." She stood with her hands in the pockets of her jeans, watching Anthony while leaning on the kitchen doorpost.

"Apps for clients, or for in-house?"

"Mostly client web stuff, but also some in-house projects."

She could hear Detta chuckling behind her.

Anthony studied Sophie until she stared right back. He swung the chair toward the computer table. "I should probably get her a newer PC."

"Maybe a laptop."

"Yeah, maybe. You do computer support for *your* mom?" He clicked at a couple of virtual buttons on the little screen.

"She's still pretty low tech. I don't think she's turned her computer on for a year." Sophie was having trouble even picturing where that computer was set up these days. Maybe she should try to revive it, or at least evaluate it.

"You see her much?"

"Yeah. She lives near here. Next town over, I think." Sophie's map knowledge was entirely pragmatic, getting from point A to point B. She hadn't needed to get from Detta's house to her mom's, but it felt like basically the same area.

Anthony nodded and clicked on more prompts. The operating system restarted with a merry-go-round of dots.

"Did your mom tell you why I'm here?" Sophie expected Anthony knew something, but she didn't like dangling on the edge of wondering what he knew—and especially what he thought about it.

"She told me a little." He turned back toward her as if he had been waiting for a chance to study her again. "I'm not sure what I believe about the whole concept, but I bet my mom can help you if it's for real." He pushed his glasses up his nose. She got the impression he didn't wear them all the time. They looked like a costume prop on him. Maybe he just wore them to his mother's house.

"And if it's not for real, then I should just get better meds, right?"

He nodded, pursing his lips. "Pretty much." He smiled weakly.

"Meds don't help. I still see. I just care less."

"Huh. That's no good." The modest sympathy in Anthony's voice would have sufficed for a crazy old aunt who claimed to talk with her deceased husband. No harm, probably. Just humor her.

Sophie closed her eyes to shut out a fluttering critter like a bird coming to a birdfeeder. It landed on the computer and launched quickly.

Anthony was focused on the computer again, but he was drilling into her experience at the same time. "I guess the only way I can think of it is like another dimension. Like you're seeing the fifth dimension, or something like that."

"You think I'm seeing aliens?"

She could see his cheek tighten, still facing away from her. Was that a grimace or a smile?

He glanced over his shoulder. "Why do *you* get to see them? *I* wanna see 'em."

"You're just not special enough, I guess."

"C'mon to supper now, kids." Detta might have missed most of their conversation.

Sophie sniffed a laugh. "Kids."

Anthony stood up, shaking his head. "Yeah. Still kids at thirty something."

"Is that how old you are?" She let Anthony pass her on their way into the kitchen.

"Thirty next month."

He was a couple years younger than her, but only a couple. She would have believed him if Anthony told her he was twenty-three. Done with college, certainly, but still boyish with his smooth cheeks, dark gray hoodie, and straight jeans. But he was probably like her, working a job that didn't demand pretending to be a grown-up. His mom clearly was in no hurry for him to graduate to full adulthood.

A pair of visitors glowed in the living room, but Sophie didn't bother to turn and study them. Instead, she laid her eyes on the roasted chicken, potatoes, and gravy on the kitchen table. There was just room on that table for their three plates among the serving dishes.

Eating at Detta's house was almost like eating at home, if Sophie had a little brother—a brother who lived to be twenty-nine. Something about Anthony reminded her of Hector, her brother who was killed by a hit-and-run driver when he was thirteen. Anthony was sassy like Hector.

As she considered the tattoo of her brother's name on the back of her right hand, two dark figures rose above Sophie's shoulders during the prayer. A shake of her head chased the interlopers back, at least out of her scope. They were familiar ones. Part of the crew that rode in the back of her car. Not the scary ones. Sad ones, really.

Detta was looking at Sophie, a tip of her head and a serving spoon suspended over her plate. She broke herself out of that stare and dabbed the small dollop of mashed potatoes onto her plate with a click.

Sophie returned the attention. Detta's face was smooth and round, on the jolly side. Sophie could imagine her young and attractive, like Anthony. Her prolonged look at Detta, however, revealed a sort of serpentine thing wrapped around the old woman, its head buried in her chest. Sophie shivered at the grotesque image. She bowed toward her plate to escape the distraction. Focusing on food this good would block most of those distractions. That, and not thinking about her lost brother. She tipped her hand so she couldn't see his name.

"I don't know anything about your family." After eating for a couple minutes, Detta set down her fork and reached for her water glass.

Of course that was a question or an opening for Sophie to tell her story. How much did she want to tell? Maybe the Washington's story wasn't so different than her family's. She saw no sign of Anthony's father around.

Sophie swallowed a bite of chicken as Detta picked up her fork. Her hostess acted as if she didn't mind if her guest didn't tell about her life. That slack felt like safe space.

"My mom lives not too far from here in the 'burbs—a house similar to yours. She lives alone, but I visit her every week. We're close. She's learning English more intensely these days to help her with work."

"Where does she work?"

"She cleans office buildings. She leads a crew of cleaners, but she doesn't own the company. I think she might try to go it on her own next year. That seems to be part of her retirement plan."

"She's gonna retire soon?"

"No. She's not even sixty. And I expect she'll work even after she hits sixty-five."

Detta nodded. "I retired from the Postal Service last year. Retirement is good if the bills are gettin' paid and you have something to keep you busy." She adjusted her glasses, gold wire rims with dark plastic bows.

"I'm thinking about investing in my mother's new business if she starts one. I've got a good income."

"Now that sounds like a promising plan." Detta nodded deeply, pausing to stab some string beans. "What about your daddy?"

A shadow at the corner of Sophie's right eye announced one of those dark stalkers angling for attention. She turned her head slightly to keep her entourage in their place.

"My dad left when I was six. He was a drinker. He went out to a bar one night and didn't come back. We think he might have got drunk and fell in the river or something. We never heard anything since that night."

"Oh, dear. That's a shame." Detta paused as if to allow Sophie to say more.

What else was there to say? A critter on her shoulder was leaning in, making some kind of gesture she didn't want to see. She resisted the urge to brush it away.

"My Thomas was killed in the first Gulf War when Anthony was just a baby. Not many died in that war—not many Americans. But my Thomas was one of 'em."

Sophie snuck a look at Detta to see if her grief summoned one of those shadowy visitors. That serpent in her chest was still there, but no morbid creature arrived to share in the story of her great loss.

"What are you lookin' at?"

At that exact moment, Sophie was poking past the chicken skin in search of more white meat on her plate, but she knew Detta had caught her checking for ghosts around her. How much should she say? Setting down her fork, no more white meat to be found, Sophie sighed. She reached for her water, thirst and the need to decide what to say equally motivating that move. Detta used a lot of salt in her cooking.

Detta just chewed and waited.

Anthony seemed more fascinated by Sophie now. His plate had kept him fully occupied at first. For a skinny guy, he could sure eat.

Sophie relaxed a bit. "I was just checking. Whenever I talk about my dad, I get this little visitor on my shoulder or around my neck. I didn't see anything like that when you talked about your husband."

The turn of Anthony's head was swift, and his eyebrows elevated as if something Sophie said had impressed him. Impressed him as believable? Or as crazy?

"That's good to hear—about me anyway. But what would you say if I offered to get rid of the devil that's doggin' you?"

"Devil?" Of course Detta had already tried to convince Sophie that what she was seeing were angels, including fallen ones. Wasn't that how she referred to them? Fallen angels? Were they devils? Could those little hangers-on really be devils? They were familiar, kind of comfortable. Not like that thing that showed up to threaten her at night.

"What if I don't mind the ones that just hang around me?"

Detta nodded and pushed herself back from the table a few inches. Was she getting ready to stand up and thump Sophie on the forehead like a TV preacher, or was she just going for the peach cobbler cooling on the counter? She didn't get out of her chair. "I know things can get familiar even if they're not entirely good for us. There's that old sayin' about the devil you know being preferable to the one you don't know. But I'm not offering to bring any new ones on, just gettin' rid of old ones."

"You think there's more than one?"

Detta tilted her head side to side. "You would know that better than me."

Sophie waited for Detta's offer to pass like a flight of flaming spirits—something Sophie knew how to do.

Detta didn't say anything more before pushing her chair back a few more inches and standing to retrieve that cobbler.

After Dinner Activities

Generally, when Anthony visited his mother for dinner, it was just the two of them. After dinner they might watch a documentary on cable, but he usually just went back to his apartment after eating, or maybe to meet some friends at a club. No dancing tonight. He had a close-up camera angle on two superheroes. Much better than a documentary. Better than a Marvel movie ... almost.

He had seen his mother in action at church, calling spirits out of a poor soul, crazed by some emotional problem or mental illness. Anthony had seen that once. That was enough. These days he would leave a meeting when it looked like anyone was going to do stuff like that.

He would leave a public meeting if it got weird. A church meeting. But this smackdown was happening in his mother's living room. At least he thought that's what would happen after dinner.

The girl who sees angels versus the mama who can do anything. Well, anything having to do with faith and prayer. He once saw his mama pray for someone with a lump growing out of her neck. When he looked away for a second and looked back, the thing was gone. That might have been the peak of his mother's superpowers, but it was impressive enough.

And he was beginning to believe this girl could really see things. She seemed pretty sane, otherwise. Maybe a bit cocky. But she acted like he might expect someone to act if she was seeing spirits flying to and fro. It was harder to imagine she was faking it at this point.

So Anthony stuck around after the cobbler. He knew his mother wouldn't tell him to leave. She probably wanted to recruit him into her team of super friends, to do the things he had seen her doing. Though she surely knew it was unlikely he would join up.

Seated in the living room, they each sipped something hot. His mother, one of her fruity teas. Anthony, creamy coffee. And Sophie, hot water with a dash of lemon. His mother was the kind of hostess who could pull that off without anyone feeling they had put her to any trouble.

"When did you start seeing spirits on people, Sophie?" Anthony's mother was half reclined in her favorite chair. She started coughing as soon as she finished her question.

Sophie paused, a tightening of her eyebrows.

Anthony tried to recall how long his mother had been coughing like that. She generally didn't seem sick, though maybe a little more tired these days.

"It was from early on. Really, it feels like I was always seeing these colored lights and these shining figures. My dad had to tell me to stop calling them 'the colored people' when I was little."

Anthony laughed hard but pulled on the parking brake when the two women turned to look at him.

A smile was all his mother allowed herself. Apparently this was some serious questioning.

"Sounds like an innocent thing any way you cut it." His mother's voice was a little tight, like she was fighting another one of those coughs.

Sophie frowned at his mother. But maybe that wasn't about what she had just said. This girl flew at her own altitude. She could be responding to all kinds of extraterrestrial input.

"What are you lookin' at now?" His mother's curiosity came with less of a frown than Sophie's.

Raising her eyes as if she had been looking at his mama's chest, Sophie appeared to make a calculation before speaking. "If you can tell these things to leave me, why do you have one that's tied into *your* chest? I think it could be what makes you cough like that."

Recoiling her neck a little, his mother stared at Sophie. "You see something? You see something on my chest?"

"Yes, I do."

"Huh. That would explain that." She nodded. "Okay. Then I want you two to get it off me."

"You two? Us two? What? How?" Anthony's problem was not that he didn't know what she meant. He knew exactly what she meant. What he couldn't figure was how her plan applied to him and this sometimes-hospitalized and always-medicated girl. And he didn't consider himself *more* qualified than the pagan punk girl in this scenario.

"The how of it isn't so hard. I just need a little help with it. I have authority over my own body, so I can say I want it off. You all can be my ministers."

"Really?" Sophie's reply sounded more fascinated than doubtful.

Anthony was still fully doubtful, but slowed by Sophie's hint of willingness. Of course she probably actually saw something. Maybe that made it easier to believe there was something they could do about it.

For his part, Anthony had just scanned the fact that Sophie seemed pretty credible for a young woman with nose piercings and black nail polish who claims to see spirits hanging around. And who was more credible than his mother where spiritual things were concerned? Maybe he should start acting like he believed even if he wasn't fully convinced. The event wouldn't be covered by the news. He wouldn't have to testify about it before a grand jury. Hopefully the police wouldn't get involved.

"How do we do it?" Sophie perched on the front of her seat. The tail of her long gray sweater was stretched over the couch cushion behind her.

Anthony pictured the demon fight he had seen his mother preside over. And he had seen the pastor do some freaky devil thumping a time or two.

While he was pulling these thoughts out of various closets and drawers, Sophie sat up straighter. She might have even trembled.

"What's that, girl? You seein' something good now?" His mother could have been taking heads or tails on whether it was a *good* thing Sophie was seeing.

To Anthony, the girl looked stunned. Good or bad didn't seem clear yet. Was it a good thing when the girl who sees angels looks stunned? Hadn't she seen it all before?

"What?" That was all Anthony got out of his mouth past his spinning thoughts.

"The big ones that guard your house just came into the room. They've shrunk down to fit in here."

Now his mother was shaking. "Thank you, Jesus!"

"Sh—" Anthony just stopped himself from swearing. He was in on the group chills now.

His mother forged ahead. "Okay, girl. You have your reinforcements. You just tell that thing you see to get off my chest."

"But she ..." Anthony hadn't decided which one of his objections should finish that protest. The girl wasn't even a church lady, probably not a Christian. If anything, she was some sort of psychic or something. How could she do this thing his mother's church did?

"She's acting on my authority and on what she sees with her own eyes. She has what she needs." His mother spoke forcefully, clearly excited, and probably not mad at him.

Then Sophie lurched forward, nearly sliding off the couch like something had jumped her from behind.

His mother responded to whatever had just landed on her guest. "You accusers and haters be quiet and leave Sophie alone to do her business. Leave this house right now."

Sophie kept her head down but raised her eyes as if to check with Anthony's mother.

Anthony was checking on both of them. They were sitting across the room from each other. His head bobbed like a Ping-Pong spectator.

"You better do it now." His mother spoke with that authority again.

"What do I say?"

"Tell the spirit of infirmity to get off me right now in the name of Jesus."

Those instructions seemed to freeze Sophie. What had she thought she was gonna say? Was it saying *Jesus* that iced her resolve?

"C'mon, girl. You can do it." Though his mother was looking for her own physical relief, she was clearly focused on helping Sophie with more than that.

Then his mother lowered her eyes and groaned. She seemed to shrink in her chair, crumpling forward and grasping her chest.

"Mama!" Anthony dropped to the rug in front of his chair.

Sophie broke out of her long pause and stood up, brushing past the coffee table on the way toward the recliner. "You snaky spirit of infirmity, get off Detta right now. Let her go ... in the ... in the name of Jesus."

Anthony sat there on his knees, his mouth open, his breath on hold.

Sophie glowered, leaning forward, her hands shaking at her sides. Then she staggered back and looked like a girl watching a rocket launch toward the sky.

His mother sat up straight and smiled.

"You're kidding me?" Anthony would have liked to edit that response.

His mother whooped. "Thank you, Jesus!" And she hooted again. "Well, I'll be!"

The whole room seemed to rock. Anthony almost fell over backward, catching himself on the coffee table.

Sophie and his mother both looked at him. And they both laughed.

Trying to Act Normal

Most of Sophie's life had been spent trying to blend in, to not seem strange. That evening at Detta's was the latest obstruction to doing that. How could she go back to her normal life—as abnormal as it had always been—after an experience like that?

She lay in bed staring at the shadows playing on the ceiling. They were mostly plain old shadows, just an occasional virtual shade fluctuating past her grid. The natural shadows she could only see with her eyes opened. The other kind were fully visible with eyes opened or closed, usually.

Usually. An interesting concept. In computer programming, *usually* was nonsense. Something either worked or it didn't. That was one thing Sophie liked about writing code. Rules. Systems that followed rules.

Those other lights and shadows—the unnatural kind—didn't seem to follow rules very strictly. Unless she just didn't know all the rules. Detta seemed to know exactly what to do and what would happen when she did it. Rules? Maybe. Authority? Definitely.

That snake had come off Detta. Her cough didn't come back while Sophie was there. And Anthony seemed blown away by all of it. But then, he couldn't see the way Sophie and Detta could. Detta had celebrated, but she didn't really seem surprised.

Sophie rolled to her side. She had one waking nightmare that seemed to follow a clear rule. At least it stuck to the clock. It showed up almost every night. When she did see it, the red numbers on her digital clock read 3:33. Was that a rule? Was he following a law, or was he *setting* the rules?

Maxwell Hartman. That was his name. The guy behind the haunting.

The pressure to get some sleep before 3:33 a.m. made it harder to sleep again that night. Even if he didn't appear every night, or she managed to sleep through it sometimes, the fear of Harman's virtual arrival was enough to postpone rest.

Sophie sat up and opened the little drawer in her nightstand. A sleeping pill would help. There was too much buzzing around in her head, let alone the things crawling across the ceiling now.

Was that a giant spider lady? Ugh! She was new.

"Go away!" Sophie landed her water bottle on the nightstand and flopped onto her side again. She didn't really expect that big creeper to scurry away.

Pulling up on the fleece blanket so the edge of it stretched above the cool sheets, Sophie hunkered down. The cozy posture was meant to show her brain that she was serious about going to sleep.

Her tossing mind wasn't buying in.

What made that snake leave Detta? Certainly it wasn't Sophie. Too bad. She would love to send her own nightly apparition away, and not just for twenty-four hours.

Why didn't Maxwell Hartman's floating image show up until this year? This fall? She was back to trying to understand the rules to all this.

What did Detta know? Were other church ladies like her? Sophie's mother prayed a lot and kept one of those golden visitors around. But she couldn't imagine her mother bossing the bad guys like Detta did.

There *was* one similarity. Those guards at Detta's house were like a bigger version of the golden visitor her mother

47

had. Huh. Maybe *that* was a church lady thing. But Detta's guards were more intimidating, giant even. What about that? It sort of made sense. The fight Detta put up tonight fit with those tall brawny guards being her backup.

Makes sense. Another strange concept. Sophie still wasn't going to tell her friends and coworkers what she could see—and sometimes feel. Right now she was feeling a sort of stirring, like her usual escorts were restless, squirmy. Something was up with them.

Sophie rolled to her right side, away from the streetlight slipping past her window shades. Why didn't Detta insist on getting rid of Sophie's squirmy guys? She seemed convinced they were devils. Ugh. That was, like, the worst-case scenario, really. So why wouldn't Detta just attack them?

A kind of convenient mutual neglect ruled her relationship with her flock of stalkers, the ones that traveled wherever she went. How many were there now? Maybe half a dozen? It was hard to count. She could see at least some of them most of the time, but only blurry and obscured. They were slippery, shadowy. Sly. And almost always in the background. Hiding.

What about the one that got aggressive when she was talking about Hector? What was that about?

Seventeen when her little brother was killed, she was only out of the hospital a few months. The house got crowded soon after the accident. Some of her father's relatives even showed up. But most of the crowd were visitors only Sophie could see. Maybe that was when she picked up a couple of her entourage. It was a lonely time. The loss of Hector left a continent-wide emptiness in her life. A few lurking shadows were no substitute for a goofy little brother, but it was better than being alone.

That had been the one time when Sophie thought her mother sensed one of those virtual visitors. Sophie had been sitting at the kitchen table, the maple table her mother had found in an alley. No one noticed that she was drinking beer. She needed it to dull the searing sensation and to dim her awareness of uninvited guests.

She was watching her mother, seated on the couch with one of her sisters and a sister-in-law. Sophie was fascinated by a small creature that was crawling back and forth between her aunts and her mother. Her mother swatted away that critter like it was a pestering bug.

Sitting breathless for most of a minute, Sophie had played it over and over in her head. Not only was her mother swatting at something the other women clearly didn't see, that swat sent it away—back to her sister-in-law and then gone, apparently. Sophie didn't see it again.

She never mentioned this to her mother.

What would her madrecita say about it now? She seemed much less nervous about her daughter's visions these days. That's what she usually called them. Visions.

Not devils?

Aliens, maybe? Anthony's voice in her head.

Sophie passed into a fitful sleep full of struggles and running. Ducking lots of swooping attackers.

Further Testing

Though she hadn't coughed since that Saturday night with Sophie and Anthony, Detta went ahead with the CT scan. If it had been a more invasive test—no dye would be injected—she wouldn't have agreed to it. She was sure her sickness had gone away. But she wanted to be the responsible patient, suitably cautious. She also wanted to hear the doctor explain how the X-ray and the CT scan totally disagreed. She expected that would be the finding, but she wasn't sure how that finding would affect the doctor.

Coasting through the shiny plastic tunnel of the scanner, she breathed easily and held her breath when requested, uninterrupted by coughing spasms. That would have been a problem before. It was a good test. No cough in a tense situation with her breathing restricted. But the doctors were looking for more definitive data, of course.

"All right, we'll send the results to your primary care physician. She'll give you a call."

That was no fun. "Did you take a look? Did you see anything?"

The radiologist was a smallish man with golden-brown skin and black hair cropped very short. "Actually, I haven't looked closely yet. We need to review all the images and then inform your doctor."

"No previews for the patient?"

"Ha. No. No previews. I don't want to tell you something when I'm not certain. Let's just wait for your doctor to call you."

Let's? Detta didn't say that aloud. *She* would wait. She *could* wait. Waiting for good news was easier than waiting for bad news.

When she got home, her sister called. Loretta was worried about her big sister's medical condition. "Well, what did they say?"

"Nothing. We have to wait for my doctor to see the scans."

"That pulmonary fibrosis is nothing to mess with, Detta. And there's no cure. Did you know that? They can't do anything but manage it." When it came to bad news, Loretta was generally willing to deliver.

"Okay. Well, Jesus healed me, so I'm not gonna worry about it."

"Healed you? When did this happen?" She sounded about half skeptical, maybe upset at not getting the news before.

"This past weekend."

"Did you go to a healing service? Was that Bishop Wright?"

"No. It was someone you don't know. She saw a spirit of infirmity on me and told it to go away. I haven't coughed since." Detta sat down on her couch, not sure how long this cross examination would take.

"Oh, really?" There were several ways to say those two words. Loretta said them with the fading timbre that comes marinated in doubt. But she didn't press the point further.

Detta was glad to get out of the conversation without having to explain about Sophie. She noted the uneasiness of keeping a secret from her sister, however, and knew she should talk to someone about the girl. This was next-level stuff, as Anthony might say. She should get some advice for what to do about Sophie.

"Hello, Sister Washington. How are you doing? Have you seen the doctors about your cough?" Word had hopped around the church all the way to the pastor.

Detta switched her phone to her other ear. "I have. And they have an idea about what was causing it, but I'm still waiting for the CT scan results. I'm feelin' like Jesus has healed me since the X-ray, so I'm hoping the new scan's gonna just show the problem went away."

"Well, glory to God. That sounds like a hopeful prospect."

"Yes. And I wanted to talk to you about something related to that. I've met a young woman who seems to have extraordinary gifts, yet she doesn't call herself a believer. I know that happens, but I'm wanting to consult with you on how I should be dealing with this young lady."

"Where did you meet her?"

"Sister Maynard sent her my way. Her daughter is friends with the young lady."

"Priscilla, is it? She's a believer. But her friend isn't?"

"No. I sense that the young woman is open. She came back to me a second time even though I had scared her away by prayin' for her."

"Did she run from the house like the Gadarene demoniac?"

"Not quite that bad, but she did make a hasty exit. Still, she came back. And she even helped me with the spirit that was causing my cough."

"It was a spirit? How did you discern that?"

"Well, that's this girl's gift. She sees spirits and angels."

"Oh. Huh. Well. She sees them? You're certain she sees them?"

"I'm pretty certain. She called off the spirit of infirmity latched onto my chest, which was causing my cough. I told her how to command it away, and when she did, my cough left. Haven't coughed since." She forced more breath out of her lungs, testing for the hitch that used to trigger the cough.

"Well, that is an unusual story. I see why you're reaching out. How to deal with that kind of thing can be tricky. I'm always wary of folks who get too fascinated with angels and demons—though it usually seems to be one or the other, in my experience."

Detta could picture her pastor nodding, maybe one hand grasping his pointy chin.

"Actually, I wouldn't say she's fascinated. More like bothered. It's pretty clear that this is nothing she's looking for. I watched her keeping her head down like she was trying to hide from these things, good or bad. She's completely clueless about what it all means."

"Not fascinated, you say? Not a demon chaser or an angel addict? Well, that's different. Very interesting. I don't suppose I could meet this young lady?"

"Oh, I doubt I can get her to church any time soon. You know I'll be trying. But I'm willing to go slow with her so as not to chase her out the door again."

"That's wise. I understand. So, you see no sign of occult activity, no effort on her part to manipulate the spirits?"

"No. I could tell she was surprised at the very idea that she could send one away. I know she has a few little demons hanging around her that she's not sure she wants to get rid of. And there's something that visits her at night. Getting rid of any of them seems like a new concept to her. She's seen fortune tellers and psychics to try to get a notion of what's happening to her, but she ran from them as fast as she ran from me that first time, I think."

The Girl Who Sees Angels

"Okay. Well, this is very intriguing. Please keep me posted on her progress. And let me know if we need to set up a deliverance session for her—when she's ready."

"Yes, of course. Thank you, Pastor. I'll be sure to reach out when I need some help. And I can see a day when she might bring us some blessings. From what I can tell, she has a sharper discernment gift than anyone I've ever met."

"Well, there's two aspects to discernment, of course. There's perceiving and then there's knowing the significance of what you see."

"Yes. I'm working on that second one with her, that's for sure."

"Indeed. Very good. She's in good hands—yours and God's, Sister Washington."

"Thank you, Pastor. And thanks for your time."

"You are welcome. A fascinating story. I look forward to the next chapter."

"Me too. Goodbye."

"Goodbye, Sister Washington."

That call felt like pulling a string all the way through a loop, the knot tied. Having Pastor Porter informed about what was happening was a well-placed stitch. She might need more from him later. But she was quite sure meeting with a pastor wasn't climbing up the list of things Sophie was hoping to do just yet.

Reading the Signs

Sophie's train to work was late. When she boarded, it was loaded to the ceiling. In the sardine pack, somebody groped her backside. But she couldn't tell if it was the guy with the octopus thing wrapped around his neck or the guy with the spikey imp lodged in the top of his head. Too many suspects and no prosecutable evidence.

On her desk, when she finally arrived at work, she found an envelope. It was a rejection from human resources. No go on the transfer to the virtual reality team. Her boss didn't tell her to her face, relying on HR instead. Even as she tamped down her anger, a tussle started somewhere between her breastbone and her belly button.

The churl who shared Charlie's cube was leaning over the divider, leering at Sophie when she dropped the letter in the recycling.

"What?" It was a rare interaction with one of the virtual beings she saw layered over her real world, especially her work world.

"What what?" Sammy spread his arms and propped himself in the entrance to her cubicle. She could see armpit hair times two up the sleeves of his T-shirt.

Disgusting. She managed to not say that out loud. "Nothing. Having a bad day."

"Did they tell you you didn't get onto the VR team?" He shook his shaggy head.

"They? Yes. HR sent me a friendly rejection letter."

"The letter probably didn't include the part where I threatened to quit if they didn't add you to the team. I even tried the inclusion argument. Woman. Hispanic." He pushed his glasses up his nose, something he did when he was nervous.

"Thanks for trying. Don't quit. Who else will let me vicariously enjoy virtual reality projects around here?"

"Well, maybe they'll pull their heads out and give you the next opening. It's gotta be a growing team from here on."

"Yeah. Probably. Thanks." She stopped abruptly after that last word.

A smarmy guy eased over Sammy's shoulder like it was riding piggyback—a darker and greener face than Sammy's very pale pinkish one. And this other guy was leering at her.

What was happening today?

"You okay?" Sammy had aborted the turn toward his cubicle. His worried scowl was like so many Sophie had seen from sane friends and family in her life.

"Uh, yeah. I didn't get enough sleep this weekend."

Again, Sammy seemed to abandon his exit, this time coordinated with that smarmy passenger whispering something in his ear. "You get lucky this weekend?" As soon as he said it, Sammy twisted his mouth into a grimace. "Don't know where that came from. Sorry."

Most guys wouldn't apologize for that kind of thing, of course. But Sophie and Sammy had been friends with the benefit of no harassment for almost three years now. His suggestive comment shattered that record. Nevertheless, Sophie knew where it came from.

When Sammy finally did retreat to his cube, a distracted wave his only goodbye, Sophie sat down in her chair and considered the evidence. She must have done something to mess up the equilibrium of her place in the cosmos. Of course, she had intervened against one of the creatures she usually tried to ignore. And the universe was ticked off now. That might explain the grope she received on the train and the leering she had received from two imps and her best friend in the office. She was probably suffering payback. The sleepless nights had started earlier, of course. When did that floating head show up the first time?

The head. That's what she called him by default. She didn't want to say his name. That psychic master guy.

He spoke *her* name last time. Like they were friends. Or at least *had* been friends.

Was he right? Had she given him access to her life? Did her visit to his New Age training group give him permission to talk to her at night? Those virtual appearances drove her to see Detta in the first place.

What about these others? Charlie's parasite was acting up, and Sammy had a new slimy shadow. Were these creatures free to mess with her? Had something changed for them?

Detta had emphasized over and again that she would be praying for Sophie. She had hit that theme harder than her gratitude for the help with the serpent thing.

And what about that serpent? Sophie had been flipping back and forth on how it could be that Detta was suffering from a cough related to a serpent thing slithering into her chest. In the natural world, a reptile in the chest would make you cough—at least. But could these virtual projections have physical impact? Medical impact? She paused to wonder if she had seen that before—a person carrying something that clearly made them sick.

If the snake could give Detta a bad cough, could that psychic master really harm her in the physical world? Besides driving her crazy with lack of sleep?

She was clicking through email as she explored the conundrum of the glass wall between the natural world and the spooky world. The next problem to solve was how she could possibly get any work done today.

Something pulled her attention toward the window in Randy's office, her only clear line of sight to the outside world—if Randy left his door open. A large, dark blue face loomed outside that window. It was one of the office-building sized creatures she tried not to see when she came downtown. Some of them were as big as city blocks, and she only experienced them as colored air she stepped into when she crossed a street. From red to blue, from green to orange. Some of them bothered her with more than clashing colors. Nausea or a headache sometimes came or went, depending on which block she was on. There were a few blocks she avoided all together. The county courthouse was on that list.

Were those headaches like the cough Detta got from that beast on her chest?

Right now, that blue giant was leering at Sophie. Or was it just leering in the window in general? It appeared to be both human and beastly. And big, of course. It might have been standing on the street and still peering in the twelfth-floor window. Then Randy entered his office and closed his door behind him.

How much of this was always there? Had she lost some of her ability to shut it out? She huffed and tightened her shoulders, leaning toward her computer monitors. The purple baseball cap next to the right monitor invited her to take advantage of its low, curved bill. She pulled it down over her straight black hair, down to her eyebrows.

A tentacle reached around the left-hand monitor, obscuring the list of files she was supposed to be converting. This was getting serious. Focusing on work had never been this hard. Sophie sighed, considering going home. She didn't have much paid time off left. On the other hand, there were only a few weeks till the end of the year.

Then, as unexpectedly as everything else on this weird day, a rising sun seemed to brighten her cubicle. The tentacle gripping her monitor slipped away. The lumpy imp from Charlie's cube sank back into his usual place. And Sophie felt the air around her cleansed, like smoke being drawn out by an exhaust fan.

"Whoa. What was that?" She managed not to say that aloud.

Janice stopping by her cube just then made Sophie doubly grateful for her restraint.

"I want you to come with me to meet with the hotdog people tomorrow. You know the app better than anybody. You'll look more competent demoing it than me and Kyle."

The hotdog people were a big food manufacturer headquartered downtown. It would be a half-mile walk to the meeting the next morning. Sophie could handle that. And she was the mother of the new app. She knew her baby well.

"Okay. Sure thing."

More competent was a good affirmation coming from Janice. Janice was certainly competent, though not so much with a new web app. She was on top of the concepts of the campaigns and familiar with the client's business, but Sophie could troubleshoot the app on site if necessary.

"I'll load it on a laptop today and double test it."

"Excellent. Thanks, Sophie."

No high five, but warm feelings nonetheless.

Did something just change? Something real and not just imaginary? How? Why?

She was back to asking that unfamiliar question. Not *whether* she was seeing things, but *why* she was seeing this or that. Why did her virtual world change all of a sudden?

A liquid warmth soaked her chest, then rose to her head, coursing from there down to her fingertips and then her toes. Sophie stayed snapshot still. She wasn't doing anything. But something had shifted ... palpably.

She realized then that she wasn't alone. Just over her left shoulder, in the corner of her cube, stood a shining golden figure. It was like the ones at Detta's house. Like the one at her mother's house. Was it even the same one? Did they travel? What was this thing doing in her cube?

Turning her head slowly to her left in case she might scare it away, she looked squarely at the golden figure. Its attention seemed to be aimed over her head. No eye contact.

"What?" Her voice came low and breathy. She checked for observers to this unintended vocalization. She hadn't tried talking with one of the golden beings since she was a little girl. She had learned the dangers of doing it back then.

But the distant attention of the guardian implied that he or it wouldn't respond to her words. As she focused on its eyes, they grew brighter, as if being fed by light beamed from beyond that room. She felt certain that the shining person was there for her. It had chased away some flocking fears and confusing creatures circling her, but it seemed to be focused elsewhere.

Sophie looked for the usual cluster of lurkers that she generally tried not to see behind her. They were still there, but dim. Their beady eyes were locked onto the new arrival. Cowering came naturally to that little crowd, but Sophie had never seen them this subservient. Were there only five now? Didn't there used to be six?

Though she got distracted from thoughts of leaving, Sophie still wondered whether she could get any work done. This time that question seemed to come with an answer. She was okay. She would be protected. She could work if she wanted to.

Was that message coming from that golden figure? That guard in the corner?

Wherever it came from, she accepted the encouragement—no need for PTO today.

Throughout the day, she yielded to the temptation to sneak a peek at the golden person posted in her cube. Every silent query returned the same answer. She was safe. The situation was under control.

Whose control? Certainly not hers.

Test Results

Detta couldn't wait for the doctor to call her. She called the office twice on Monday afternoon.

Doctor Gandhi finally got back to her Tuesday afternoon. "I've been reviewing your CT report, Detta, and I'm having a hard time understanding it. We may have to schedule another. I'm waiting for a call back from a pulmonary specialist to see if he can help me make sense of this."

"What's the problem?" Detta was glad it was a phone conversation. Her girlish grin probably couldn't squeeze across the cell connection.

"Well, it's just the difference between the X-ray and the CT. They generally don't disagree so much. According to the CT, there's only the slightest hint of scarring, whereas the X-ray showed quite a bit."

She couldn't help herself. "Ha! Yes!"

"Detta?" Doctor Gandhi had been seeing her for several years. She was familiar enough to use Detta's nickname but unfamiliar with that sort of outburst.

"Sorry, Doctor. It's just that I know something you don't for a change." She chuckled some more. "Do you believe in miracles?" Over the years, Detta had promised many times to pray for the doctor, a commitment that usually evoked a mediocre thanks.

"Miracles? Oh. I don't know. Is that what you think I'm seeing on the CT scan?"

"I got some healing prayer from a friend after the X-ray, and my cough disappeared. It was before the CT scan."

Silence. Detta couldn't even hear breathing.

"Doctor?"

"Yes. Well. Of course my inclination is to get another scan to confirm ... uh ... that things are okay."

Detta wondered how Medicare would treat the doctor's inclination. And she wondered whether she should agree to a rescan anyway, as a way to testify to Doctor Gandhi. Would it make a difference to her?

"How often is the CT scan wrong so that taking it again is worth doing?"

"Hmm. Actually, I don't see any sign that the CT scan was corrupted or anything. And the radiologist was completely satisfied with it. It's just ... that ..."

"Isn't sayin' it's a miracle the simplest way to explain it?"

"Uh." Doctor Gandhi laughed. "Well, medically speaking, it's not the simplest, really. But logistically it would make your life simpler ... and maybe mine too. If we redid the scan, I would have to justify it even though there's no sign that the first CT was faulty." Another silence.

"I think I'll pass on getting it retaken, then."

"Of course. I'm willing to accept the results we have. And ... well, it's good news." She seemed to recalibrate. "You have no more cough, you say?"

"All gone."

"Well, that was the reason for the scan. So if the symptoms are gone, then we can let it stand. We can revisit it if the cough recurs."

"Good. That sounds good."

"And Detta, congratulations then, if that's the right thing to say."

"Congratulations on my miracle?"

"Yes. I guess so."

"Thanks. Thank you, Doctor."

Later that afternoon, Anthony called. "How are you, Mama? Did the doctor call?"

"Yes, finally." She laid down her novel and sat up straighter in her recliner.

"What did she say?"

"Congratulations on my miracle."

"She said that?"

"In her uncomfortable way, eventually, she said that." Detta leaned forward and let the recliner rise to upright.

"Wait. So she says you're okay?"

"I am okay. No more cough. She was thinking their scanner was broken, but then she changed her mind about that 'cause there really was nothin' wrong with the scan. It was just different from the X-ray."

"Hmm. So she confirms that you were ... ah ... *are* ... okay?"

"I'm healed, Anthony. You saw it happen yourself. And Doctor Gandhi can't explain it otherwise. She was saying we should get another scan, but couldn't really explain why that would be necessary."

"Okay. You're better. That's what matters. That cough was worrying me."

"Thanks for worrying about me, Anthony. But you shouldn't, of course."

"Right. Have you heard anything from ... uh ... Sophie?"

Detta flexed her ankles, first left and then right, in preparation for standing up. They sounded their usual snap, crackle, and pop. "No. I'll try calling her tonight. I've been praying for her as often as I remember. Thanks for another reminder."

"Oh. Sure. Well, glad to hear you're all cleared."

"All cleared and all cured. Love you, Son."

"Love you too, Mama."

That evening before going to prayer meeting, Detta tried Sophie. She got voice mail. But as she was headed out to her car, her cell rang with the old-fashioned phone jingle Anthony had set as her default.

"Hello?"

"Detta?"

"How are you, Sophie?"

"Uh, well, pretty good, really. How are *you*, though?"

"I'm wonderful. Just heading out to a prayer meeting." As soon as she said that, Detta regretted the implication that she wasn't available to talk. She could be late. No pressure on that score.

"Oh. Okay. I was just returning your call. I was on the phone to my mom."

"Oh, that's good. Glad you stay in touch with her. Anthony just called to check on me." She was off track. "I really called to give you the good news that the doctor confirmed my fibrosis is healed. No problem. And my cough is still gone."

"That's good. So, was that a surprise for the doctor, or does it just happen sometimes?"

"It's an incurable disease according to the medical experts. And my doctor was having a real hard time trying to explain what happened between the X-ray and the CT scan."

"Oh, really? Incurable? Wow …" Her voice faded. Then her breathing elevated. "You know, you told me that I have a gift I could use to help people. Is this the kind of thing you were talking about?"

"It is, in fact. And other things as well. God gives gifts so we can serve him and help each other."

"God gave me this ... gift? Huh. I always wished I could give it back ..." Again, her reply came with a fade.

"I'll keep prayin' for you. You can decide for yourself what you wanna do about your gift. It's always gonna be up to you to decide."

"Oh. And Detta? Something happened. I ... uh ... I'm being followed. I mean there's a new one of those shining beings with me almost all the time now. A good one."

"Good? A good angel? A holy ..." She stopped the religious translation. "You feel like he's protecting you?"

"Or *it*. I can't tell if it's any kinda gender or anything, but it seems to be keeping the creepy ones back."

"Oh. That's good. Has this ever happened before?"

"I don't know. Maybe when I was little. But not lately. Not so ... so permanent."

Detta could picture Sophie joggling her head as she chased her own thoughts in a game of duck-duck-goose. Detta would definitely keep praying. And she would get some of the folks at the Tuesday prayer gathering to join her. Prayers seemed to be working so far.

A halting back-and-forth goodbye ended the conversation, and Detta hustled out to her car. She wasn't so worried about being late to the meeting as she was anxious to get the saints fighting the fight for Sophie and her gifts.

Keeping Company

Thursday afternoon toward the end of the workday, Peter Jamison meandered into the doorway of Sophie's cubicle. He had no work reason to be on that floor as far as she knew. His meander was an act, a clumsy ruse. He was on the prowl. He was prowling for her.

"Hello, Sophie. How's it goin'?" He raised his head as if to point his chin at her work displayed on the two large monitors. As if he knew anything about writing code or about the projects she was working on.

Peter was a sales associate, not a technical person. He was one of those salespeople who promised things he would never promise if he understood the technical hurdles required to fulfill those commitments. But Sophie had spent time with Peter outside the office. He was looking for company, obviously. He had found what he was looking for with Sophie before.

"I'm doing okay. How's the sales gig?" She regarded him with just her left eye, not willing to encourage him yet. Peter was standing next to that golden being, dwarfed by the shining giant. That comparison distracted Sophie.

"We're good. Doing good on monthly quotas. Nice break on that new restaurant account—Georgie's. Should be good." He ran his artificially tanned hand along the side of his expertly crafted hair.

Sophie knew she could torture Peter with endless small talk, ignoring the question implied by his presence in her cube. He would never ask her outright. The invitation was only ever implied. This covert approach was certainly influenced by the open office layout. No privacy.

At first Sophie had thought Peter's undercover operation indicated he was married or living with someone. But now she was sure that had never been the case. His invitation by implication likely came from fear of being accused of some impropriety at work. There were no rules against employees dating each other, but maybe there was some unwritten rule about a successful salesman dating a sketchy software developer.

She corrected the punctuation in the last line of code she had written before Peter filled the door to her cube. "Good. That's good to hear. Sounds like a good account. It'll keep us all employed." As it turned out, Sophie *was* in the mood for torturing Peter.

"So ..." He traced some shape on the blue carpet with the toe of one shiny brown shoe.

She suspected this was an escalation, a risky advance toward actually *hinting* that he wanted to hook up. Sophie looked squarely at Peter and saw the familiar red flame that flared from his shoulders whenever something didn't go his way. She pictured his office furniture all scorched from days when sales fell through. His couch at home must be crispy from times his team failed to pull out a win. She was fanning that flame right now.

The big golden guy was blended into the corner of the cube, just allowing room for Peter to stand there. The guard kept his eyes raised toward the invisible horizon, but his eyes had turned red just now, similar in color to the flames magically not consuming Peter's expensive button-down shirt.

Regarding plans that night, Sophie was still undecided about dropping in on Detta. Anthony was coming over for supper, and Detta had extended the invitation. Sophie still hadn't given a firm answer. Now she regretted that. She looked at the clock in the corner of the computer screen, clicking on it with her mouse to cause the calendar to pop up. That was a signal to Peter. She deciphered the signal for him. "I should be wrapping up here. I have dinner plans tonight."

"Oh, Yeah? Well, it is getting late." He kept the disappointment out of his voice, mostly. But those flames flared orange and even yellow, reaching nearly to the ceiling. "Okay then. See ya around. Uh ... have a good dinner."

"You too. See ya around." Sophie started typing again—a line she had to backspace through as soon as Peter got out of range.

What was that flame behind Peter? Was it like the fat imp lurking in Charlie's cube or the huddled mass cowering behind Sophie's chair? Why a flame and not a critter with eyes and hands and such? She assumed these *whys* were like all the others. Even Detta would have no definite answers for her.

Sophie pulled out her phone and dialed Detta's cell number. Maybe she should get Anthony's number. He would probably respond to texts. Detta didn't seem to monitor her texts.

"Hello, Sophie. You coming to dinner?"

"Yes. I'd like that. I need to ask you some more questions."

"Of course. Good. I'll see you at six thirty."

"Yeah. Six thirty." When she hung up and sat staring at her screen, Sophie recognized some guilt over dinner at Detta's house when she hadn't arranged to see her own mother this week. She would call her mother on the way to the train.

She checked the golden being posted behind her and noted his eyes were no longer red. She had decided he was male, or at least *she* identified him as male, even if *he* didn't identify that way. He wasn't talking, so she would have to settle it for herself.

What was he looking at? His gaze was rock steady, his face never disturbed or concerned. Even when his eyes had burned with that red flame, he seemed unmoved. But not like he didn't care, or like he had no feelings. He just seemed anchored.

"You really have plans, or you just ducking Peter Piper these days?" Charlie was leaning over the wall of the cube, his pale forearms resting along the metal frame. This was a rare intrusion.

"I really have plans. What about you? Getting together with your gamer friends?"

"Online tonight. A big tournament for amateurs. Should be a blast. Probably up past midnight."

"That's a plan. Well, good luck."

"Thanks, yeah. I should get going. Gotta eat first. Won't get much chance for that once the slaying begins." Charlie clucked a little laugh.

Sophie didn't look at him. She didn't like the grumpy stalker that stayed with Charlie. He was depressing—gray and fat and dirty, his eyes always downcast, and his mouth forced into an unnatural frown. Of course it was unnatural. *He* was unnatural.

She started closing files and uploading code to the development server. She would get going not long after five. Her mom would probably be reachable by then and would be able to talk. Grabbing her coat off the back of her chair, Sophie wondered why she hadn't bothered to hang it on the hook that morning. Maybe she had been distracted by the golden man poised behind her—like an academy award with more personality. A *bit* more, anyway.

A murmuring and muttering caught her attention. She craned her neck out of her cube and saw Charlie and his slumpy shadow walking toward the elevator. The spirit—if that's what it was—was even shorter and fatter than Charlie, and much darker. Like he had been left in the toaster too long. *He* was muttering.

But that was against protocol. Sophie generally didn't hear anything from the apparitions she saw following other people. Had something else changed? She didn't want to hear them any more than she wanted to see them.

Glancing at the golden guardian, she aimed a nonverbal apology at him with her eyes. She didn't really mind seeing *him*. She hesitated after her first step into the aisle, waiting for confirmation the big guy was coming with her.

He nodded and followed.

He nodded. It wasn't much, but it was something. Communication of a sort.

She nodded back and turned her boots toward the elevators.

Round Two

It probably wasn't appropriate for Anthony to think of this dinner as *round two*. That was just a hangover from the previous time Sophie visited his mom. Two spiritual heavyweights facing off. But it wouldn't be a fight. He knew that now. He hadn't, however, changed his mind about it being two heavy hitters he was having dinner with.

Maybe every boy thinks his mom is a superhero. Anthony knew it from the start, as soon as he could collect his thoughts and think of his mom as something other than his entire universe. With no father, she was pretty much that for him.

She was his guiding force all along, of course. But she wasn't always so confident and capable as she was now. That was hindsight projected back through his teen years when his expectations of superheroes were expanding and his mother's command of her world was too. Anthony's world had grown more secure as a result.

He remembered her crying in her bedroom when he was very small—one of his clearest early memories. There hadn't been any of that since. She hadn't turned hard or unemotional over the years, just less vulnerable. His best measure of his mother's mighty faith had always been what he saw in the eyes of the other people around them, and not just people in her church.

His mom knew who she was. That was the key. She was comfortable in her custom-made tights and cape. She knew they were hers to keep. Not just a Halloween costume.

Wiping the slush and rain from the bottom of his feet on the bristle brush mat outside the back door, Anthony turned the storm door handle. Sophie was already in there. She was early. Good thing it wasn't really a fight. The referee was the last to arrive.

"Hello, my dear." His mother grinned, carefully setting a ladle down before coming to hug him. He could smell the ham and bean soup on the stove. Homemade cornbread sat on the counter. Sophie was sipping tea or hot water and sitting at the kitchen table.

"Hi, Mama. Hi, Sophie. How ya doin?"

Sophie blinked at him. "I'm good. I'm still a freak, but I'm not so pissed off about it."

He laughed from deep in his belly. "Okay. I guess that's an improvement."

She smiled at him.

Had she done that smile before? It was like seeing her for the first time. A stranger pleasantly grinning where Sophie had been sitting a second ago. Nice.

He was staring. Then he realized that he was staring. And he was still staring.

Sophie looked away, maybe even blushed.

Anthony let his hunger draw him away from Sophie's rosy reaction. "Need any help, Mama?" He suspected his mother knew this was code for "How can we get this on the table sooner?"

"No. Almost there. You just take a seat. How was work?"

"Good. Just got word from the marketing people that we have to switch the office application suite within the next six months." He sank into the chair, having kicked his shoes toward the back door. "That's quicker than we thought. My boss was … pretty upset." Around the church ladies he watched his language, though his mama was usually forgiving. He didn't know how to think about Sophie in that regard. He didn't expect she had church standards for words allowed, but the question of her cultural gap with Anthony's mother nudged him toward caution—the default setting around the church ladies.

"Marketing people." Sophie said it with mock disgust. He had forgotten that she worked for a marketing firm.

"Yeah. You know how hard they are to please." He nodded at her.

"And totally nontechnical. Hardly know what they're asking for most of the time."

Yes. They were comrades in arms. Anthony and this code warrior, if not Anthony and the spiritual warrior. Low blood sugar was loosening his lips. "You see angels and demons while you're at work?"

The raise of her eyebrows and quirk at the corner of her mouth might have been grateful. Not the spite he feared as soon as he blurted his curiosity.

She nodded. "The guy next to me has this fat little gray thing that sits in his cube all day, stinking up the air with depression and stuff."

"You can *smell* them?" Anthony recoiled.

"Not literally. No, fortunately. I bet they stink like ..." Time for Sophie to edit her vocabulary, apparently.

"So, do you say anything to the people at work? The ones with those things hanging around them?"

"They pretty much all have something that shows up at some point. And no, I would never say anything about it." She turned toward Detta and leaned on her right fist, her elbow finding a spot between placemats.

Anthony could see the bud of a rose tattoo on that forearm, her sleeve hitched up a bit.

"I've been seeing that new visitor at work this week." Sophie was looking at his mom. "And really almost everywhere, but especially at work and on trains and buses. He's a big shiny guy. He seems kinda like my bodyguard or something."

His mother was carrying two heavy ceramic soup bowls, the ones with the thick white glaze dripped over brown. "Sounds like a guardian angel to me. Didn't you ever see a guardian angel with you before?"

Sophie sat up, pulling her elbow out of the way of her soup. "Uh, I have seen different shiny ones in the past. And once in a while I've seen ones that kinda follow me around. Good ones, I mean, if that's what they are."

Was she more certain about this than she was letting on? It was like she was pulling back, afraid to say what she was really thinking.

"Well, I don't think there's any way to prove this, but I have been praying for you lots since last week. I felt the prompt on Monday especially. And I even had folks at church praying for you, though I didn't tell 'em your name or any personal information."

"How do you do that?"

"What? Make a prayer request without giving personal information? We do it all the time. Best to respect the privacy of the folks who aren't there to share their own concerns."

Sophie's head tilt might have expressed her appreciation for the privacy as much as for the prayers.

"Did your prayers send a guardian angel to Sophie's office?" Anthony was still waiting for the cornbread to land on the table. His mother was being distracted by the conversation, stalled between the table and the counter.

"I can't send angels anywhere. I'm not in charge of any angels. But the One I pray to *is* in charge of lots of angels. He can send any number wherever he wants. Our prayin' might get answered by an angel or two, I expect." She picked up her pace and brought the cornbread and margarine to the table with her.

That was a cool idea, God sending lots of angels. Cool enough to delay grabbing hands with the others to pray for the meal.

When they did link hands, Sophie bowed her head without hesitation. Was she starting to believe? At least starting to tolerate the religious stuff?

When his mother said *amen*, she hung onto his hand as if she forgot she was holding it. She was looking at Sophie. "Can you see that guardian angel now?" Her voice was hushed one notch.

Anthony's spine lit, neurons slapping each other awake.

Sophie glanced around the room. "No. I don't see him—if it is a him. I guess I lost track of him about the time I got to your house. Or maybe when I got in my car. Though he might have been riding on the roof or flying above the car."

Snorting laughter delayed Anthony's supper a bit longer.

Sophie scowled. She wasn't joking.

Oh. "Sorry."

His mother shook her head. "I can't say I ever put much thought into how all this works, but I have a pretty clear sense when there's some activity of dark spirits or holy angels in a room. I just don't get anything so specific and visual as what you get."

The deference with which his mother handled Sophie's wild claims was impressive. She was a conservative person in lots of ways. Not one to tolerate a lot of speculating and exaggerating. Maybe she was using some of her superpowers to tell that Sophie was for real.

Cornbread and ham soup steaming in his face pulled Anthony away from his silent speculations. He generally kept them to himself, especially after he passed age twenty. Sophie's scowl was intimidating, but nothing compared to his mother's cloudy face. She didn't respond well to his more fanciful sci-fi ideas. *Fanciful* was her word, of course.

"So, do you think that shining one is my guardian angel?" Sophie lifted a spoonful of soup, blew briefly through her thin red lips, and slurped.

Anthony winced. His mother was no fan of slurping.

But she seemed captivated by the question. "Oh, I don't really know. Does everyone have a particular guardian angel? Is God making more angels 'cause so many more people are being born? Anything is possible. Any way God wants to do it is just fine by me." She took a nibble of cornbread and lifted her face a bit, as if she just remembered something. "But that doesn't mean you can't ask questions. Just 'cause I don't know the answer doesn't mean it's a bad question."

Sophie seemed captivated by the cornbread now, one small bite stimulating a bigger one right away. Anthony recognized the symptoms.

"One thing I think we can't really know is whether you see all angelic activity around you at a given time. What if that guardian was always there, and you just started seeing it 'cause something changed for you?" His mother was doing pretty well at speculating for someone who claimed enmity with flights of fancy.

Anthony didn't say any of that. The ham and bean soup was almost as preoccupying as the cornbread. And he wasn't confident enough in his comprehension of that other dimension to say anything aloud. Probably only his friend Brice would tolerate his ideas about the fifth dimension and alternate realities without any eye-rolling.

"I never thought about whether I'm seeing everything. There are people who seem to have ... *spirits* with them only sometimes. Like this one guy who's always trying to ask me out. He usually just looks normal, but when he gets upset, there's this red flame that comes off him."

"Like an aura?" Anthony said that with his mouth full, and with little forethought.

His mother's clenched eyebrows confirmed the need for continued restraint.

Sophie didn't hesitate. "Aura? I don't know. My friend Crystal is into all that. Maybe I should have her with me sometime when I'm telling Peter I don't wanna go out with him."

Anthony had just assumed this girl was either not going out with anyone because she was so weird, or maybe because she wasn't interested in men. Her tough girl voice and punky clothes could mean anything. Was she ticking off that guy at work because she wasn't interested in men, or because she was just not interested in him? So much room for speculation on so many matters. He probably wasn't enjoying this sweet and savory meal as much as usual.

"I don't know anything about auras." His mother swallowed a bite of Waldorf salad. "But I expect these spirits don't have to look like people lots of times. They're really not human. And who knows if they can change shape at different times?"

"So, because they're spirits, they can change shape, or they don't have to look like a set shape?" Sophie swallowed and wiped her mouth with a paper napkin. "Some look like monsters or bugs, not people."

Anthony was staring, but hopefully not staring right at Sophie. This was all so weird.

Sophie seemed distracted by something and turned her head toward the door to the living room.

His mother followed that quick turn, but she kept quiet. That was definitely one of her superpowers. If she wore a vest, her cards would be held close to it when the stakes were big.

Anthony hadn't inherited that superpower. "What do you see? You see something there?" He couldn't stop geeking out. But so far no one had told him to stop.

Sophie lowered her brow. She looked right at him. Or maybe she was looking right through him. Was she seeing something on him? She wasn't telling.

He got another one of those shivers. His shoulders got away from him and did a little breakdance without his permission. He let loose an expletive.

"Sorry, Mama."

What Does Priscilla Know?

Priscilla Maynard was one of Sophie's closest friends. But Priscilla wasn't the best person to confide in. She generally lacked the verbal discretion Sophie would like. Right now, however, Sophie needed Priscilla to translate things for her, even at the risk of a few boundary violations.

"Why are you not working tonight?" Sophie sipped her rum and Coke and arched her eyebrows at Priscilla.

"Day off. Worked too many hours during the week." Priscilla leaned back a bit. "It's okay. I need the break. And I can live without the Saturday night tips this week."

Priscilla and Sophie had met at the city college where Sophie got her degree in computer science, Priscilla in history. Her friend had planned to be a lawyer, but it turned out Priscilla didn't really like studying.

Tonight she was wearing her big hair in little ringlets that covered both shoulders. Sophie could never live with that much hair. She liked the way her recent cut just covered her neck above a T-shirt collar.

"I've been visiting that church lady, Bernadetta."

"You have? Good. Is she helping? I know I can't help you with all that stuff you say you see."

Even though Priscilla still talked about Sophie's sightings as if she were reserving judgement, Sophie was confident Priscilla believed her as much as she needed her to. Who could really be absolutely sure of something invisible?

"She has been really helpful, but now I'm stuck trying to figure out where this is gonna go if I don't convert to her religion. I mean, your religion. Or religion in general."

"Did she say you gotta repent and be baptized, thus saith ...?"

"No 'thus saiths' so far. She's pretty cool."

"And her son, Anthony? You met him?"

"Yeah. He's okay. I think he just hangs around to make it less awkward. Maybe he's not even necessary anymore. I'm probably more comfortable with *her* now than with him. He stares at me."

"He thinks you're cute."

"He thinks I'm a lunatic."

"A cute lunatic." Priscilla flashed her eyes wide. She might say just about anything. No worries. Only occasional apologies.

Sophie allowed a little grin. No need for Priscilla to apologize for that one. The rum was taking effect. The rum was willing to spill more to Priscilla. "I don't mind it when he stares at me." Her voice came out dim, about three-quarters strength.

Priscilla snickered. She rolled her eyes toward two guys playing pool beyond the dining section where she and Sophie were seated. Priscilla could ignore boring unattractive people the way Sophie could ignore the flocking, floating, and flatulating hordes filling the spaces between visible humans, attractive or otherwise. But hot guys like that received some serious scrutiny from Priscilla.

"Those guys will want you to go to bed with them." Sophie's lips were loose.

"Both of them?" Priscilla was either intrigued or disgusted. Probably both. She was still saving herself for marriage. Or at least for a compelling romance.

"I need you to get serious, 'Cilla." That came out more forcefully than Sophie intended. She tried to screw down her face to match the intensity of her words, but her face wasn't cooperating. They were waiting for their food to be delivered. Slow service.

"Serious about what? What's up?" Priscilla was drinking white wine. Sipping. Tippling. She was probably still sober.

"I have to decide. I don't wanna keep goin' to see Detta if this isn't gonna go anywhere. If I have to have faith for it to go anywhere, and if I just can't do that."

"Wait. Are you saying you've decided you can't believe in Jesus and all that?"

Shaking her head made the room rock a bit too far left and right. Sophie stopped. "No. No, I haven't decided. That's what I mean. Help me decide. Can I just get some advice about my visions from Detta and not really commit?"

"You call her Detta?"

"Bernadetta. Right. That's her. Anthony's mom. That hot weird *Star Trek* guy's mom."

Priscilla seemed to fake once toward that bait about Anthony, but she drove toward the real question instead. She had been a high school basketball player. "I think you should try believing. Try going to church some, or to one of her prayer meetings. Or you don't have to go to her holy roller church. You could come to my church. We're friendly people. Hardly ever rolling around on the floor." She snickered and lowered her head, flicking a cluster of hair over her right shoulder.

The little circling buzzards above those two guys at the pool table turned and flocked toward Priscilla, perhaps beckoned by that hair toss. Did one of those guys send them? The Middle-Eastern-looking one was glancing at Priscilla about every five seconds. She attracted a lot of attention. Priscilla had disappointed countless buzzards over the years.

Their food finally arrived. Sophie ate with intensity and drank little except water. She really did want to have a serious conversation with Priscilla, as rare as that might be. "What does it take to go to your church? Like, paying dues or something?"

"Dues? It's not Brownies."

"Oh. But I know a guy who's Jewish."

Priscilla shrugged. "I don't know anything about that. Sara never talks about her synagogue. But no, you don't have to pay anything. Even the donuts are free. My church has a thing for donuts, even setting 'em out next to the healthy fresh fruit you get at the big meetings."

"You get free food? Do people go there for the free food?"

"Some do, I suppose." Priscilla had a shard of coleslaw clinging to her ample lower lip. "Really the food's just to get you to the church so you can see how great it is."

"Why is it great? How is it great?"

Priscilla bobbled her head side to side. "I just think it's great to be part of a community. And it's great to get to know God more."

"You get to know God? Do you, like, see God or something?"

Squinting one eye intensely, that bit of coleslaw disappearing into her lap, Priscilla shook her head. "I don't think anyone says they actually see God. That's why you have to have faith. Faith is for things you can't see. It says that in the Bible."

"Oh. The Bible. I'm not gonna have to read that if I go there, am I?"

"You don't *have* to read it, but it's a good idea. You might like it more than you think. You could get a modern translation—one that doesn't use words like *saith*." She sat up straight suddenly. "Hey. And there's lots of people in the Bible who saw angels."

"Really?" Sophie knew about the Christmas story. There were little kids with cardboard wings involved somehow. Not that they resembled the beings she had been seeing since she was a kid. Right then there was a boney thing, kind of a flying skeleton, over the bar. That apparition was about the size of an elementary school kid.

Priscilla watched Sophie monitor the action in the air above the bar patrons. "Are you, like, scoping everyone's angels and demons right now, even while you're chomping on a burger?"

Sophie was. She was chomping on a veggie burger and watching critters and random lights play above the people. She wasn't ignoring. She wasn't tunneling her vision to avoid the oddity and the confusion. Maybe she was feeling less confused. "Is that really what they are? Have I been seeing angels and demons all my life?"

The waitress pulled to a stop at the side of the table, probably more abruptly than usual. How much had she heard?

Sophie smiled sheepishly at her.

"Huh. How's the food?" The server didn't sound fully invested in getting an answer. Maybe she wanted to ask a different question.

Sophie watched a squirrelly thing crawl around the waitress's shoulders like it was bring-your-pet-to-work day.

The waitress leaned forward a tad and studied Sophie as if she were checking for something.

Did she want help? Help taking care of that squirrel? It wasn't exactly a squirrel. It had fangs and wings. But still. The girl might need animal control for that thing.

The food had dulled the effects of the rum, but not entirely.

Priscilla and Sophie both assured the waitress the food was good, and Sophie continued to monitor that little critter. It seemed to be threatening to jump over to her. That was the sort of thing that had started her religiously ignoring all these illusions.

That thought brought back something to which she hadn't paid much attention. Where were her usual stalkers? She watched the waitress turn toward the next table before she checked for the ugly entourage.

"Was she having something, or ... I mean, *carrying* something?" Priscilla dropped a sweet potato fry and glanced over her shoulder at the waitress.

Here was another reason to try *not* to see things. It really distracted the people Sophie was with. She should probably just get back to that.

Sophie eventually finished eating, leaving a fragment of burger and half her fries. She hadn't finished her second drink either. The Saturday night crowd made her claustrophobic with no filter to block the affiliated beings patrons brought in.

Where was her guardian angel, by the way? As soon as she formed that question and set down her water glass, the golden guy was standing next to the table. Had she summoned him, like calling the waitress to bring the check? Detta said no one could tell them to come or go, but how much did she really know?

The brief hug outside the restaurant, before Priscilla climbed into a cab and Sophie turned to walk toward her apartment, reminded Sophie that she had wanted more from this evening, more from Priscilla. But she wasn't going to clutch onto her friend until she was satisfied.

A powdery snow was forming ropes of white along the edges of the sidewalk. Sophie paid attention to her footing, seeking clear gray pavement for her Doc Martens. Those boots were good for stomping punks and tromping snow, but not so good for skating on ice. Not that she had ever stomped any punks.

She thought she heard a chuckle at that last thought. Maybe it was just her laughing at herself. Maybe she'd drunk more rum and Coke than she realized.

Sophie picked up her stride. Time to get home. Time to get to bed.

And What About Crystal?

"Nodes on my vocal cords. That's all. No more heavy metal career." She smiled with one side of her mouth. "No great loss."

"Yeah. That probably had a short lifespan for lots of reasons." Sophie was standing behind the black faux-granite counter between her kitchen and her dinette. She looked away, trying to talk to Crystal without looking at her—without seeing the floating fairies spinning above her head.

"I went to that healer woman I told you about. Just wanted to see if there were any organic medicinals I could use to smooth my voice a bit."

"But your voice is sexy." This was from an old conversation replayed frequently in years past. Sophie wasn't trying to convince Crystal this time, or even compliment her, really. Distractions diverted her to default replies. Those fairies were detouring her brain away from rational interaction.

Crystal was still on topic. "Well, that only goes so far. I only get the guys with a thing for Janis Joplin."

"Who?"

"Janis Joplin. Raspy singer from the hippie days. My mom loves her. Or loved her. Dead a long time now." One of those fairies seemed to collapse into tears at the news of the singer's demise. Crystal faded a bit as well.

Sophie tried to keep it light. "Oh, well *there's* your problem. You don't wanna go out with guys *that* old."

"Clearly that's the issue." Crystal's feeble retort implied she was forcing the effort too.

The maypole dance of fairies was too much for Sophie to ignore. She slipped around the counter and hauled out the chair across from Crystal. She set her big mug of coffee on the gray Melamine surface. "You went to a healer? I thought you said you weren't going back to that shaman?"

"Not 'that shaman.' A natural healer. She does homeopathic remedies and such."

"And such?"

"What are you looking at? What's up with you?" Crystal's blonde eyebrows crowded toward each other, the line between them cleaving deep. Her light blue eyes squinted. This was as close to mad as Sophie had seen Crystal for a long time.

Sophie cleared her throat to buy some time. "Uh, well, I'm seeing four or five or more little flying things around you. I don't think I've seen even one of those with you recently."

"Only recently? You saw them before?"

"I don't know. I used to be pretty good at not seeing. Or at least trying not to."

"So what's different now?"

"You went to that healer woman, I think?"

"No, I mean what's different for *you* now? Why are you looking right at whatever it is you see there?" Crystal rotated her head side to side and up and down like she was checking a chiropractic adjustment to her neck. Did she see something? Her nose tracked roughly with at least one of those little flying folk.

"What changed for me? Well, I helped that church lady get healed of her chronic cough, which turned out to be from some fibrosis thing that was really serious. Only I saw this snake burrowing into her chest and she told me how to get it off her. And that made me think that maybe there *was* possibly a purpose to what I see, and maybe I *could* help other people with my ... gifts. And that head that comes at night and hovers over my bed is making bigger threats now, so I might ..." She was babbling.

Crystal was shuddering, shaking, nodding, and shrugging all at once. Those contortions stopped Sophie. Crystal had been the first one to try convincing Sophie there could be some use for her visions. Now she seemed affirmative and negative all at once. But maybe none of her gyrations were even about Sophie.

Focusing on the six little fairies circling Crystal's head, Sophie could see their faces turning more and more ferocious. One by one they transformed from cute little flying maidens to fanged monsters.

And Crystal roared. Literally. She roared like a big cat of some kind.

Sophie froze. Then she started to vibrate, her nerves hitting a breaking point, circuits popping. "Crys—Crystal?"

Crystal hooted and shook her head hard, snapping out of whatever that was. "Sophie? What's happening to me?"

"I think ... I think it's those little things flying around your head." That wasn't all she meant to say, but the foam on top of the truth was all she could get into her mouth at the moment.

"Flying things? How do I stop them?"

A flash of revelation. Sophie pulled out her phone. Her hands shook so badly she nearly dropped it on the table. She forced a slow breath. Then she tried again.

Unlock phone. Contacts. Detta. Call.

Ring. Ring. Ring. Ring. Too many rings. Detta wasn't answering.

Then— "Sophie? What's going on?" An urgent answer. Did Detta know this call was urgent? How?

"I need help, Detta. My friend Crystal went to a healer and got these little angel things—they're the bad kind, I think—

flying around her with these fangs and making her totally freak out."

Crystal, at that very moment, was starting to growl. Both hands were pressed to the table like she was about to stand up, but she just sat there turning purple.

"Oh, Lord Jesus! Tell the interfering spirits to be quiet and stop ... interfering with your friend ... Crystal."

Struggling to reconstruct what Detta had said while concentrating on keeping her voice from screeching, Sophie stopped stuttering when that guardian guy showed up next to Crystal. A wave of warmth, like tropical sunlight, swept up Sophie's arms to her neck and face.

Settled a bit, she tried again. "You stop interfering with Crystal now ... in the name of Jesus." Was that allowed? Probably not from *her*. But maybe that angel brought something with him. And Detta was on the other end of the phone call.

"Sophie? How's it going?"

She pressed the phone against the side of her face again. "Uh, Crystal just stopped growling. Now she looks like she's gonna cry."

Crystal's face was red instead of purple, and it crumpled into a hard sob. "Sophie, Sophie, help me. What's happening to me?"

"Let me talk to her, Sophie."

Sophie was happy to get out of the middle. She held her phone out toward Crystal, but Crystal just stared at it like she expected something to ooze out of it.

The guardian next to them glowed brighter, and the little monsters around Crystal dulled, dark around the edges. And maybe there were fewer of them. Was it six before?

"Take the phone, Crystal. She can help you." Sophie jabbed the phone at her more forcefully.

Crystal raised one hand from the tabletop. Sophie could see a small puddle of sweat where that hand had been planted. Shaking like she had a severe fever, Crystal took the phone. Still, she just stared at it.

"Talk to her. It's my friend, Detta." That spontaneous promotion to "friend" was something Sophie could think about later.

Crystal put the phone to her ear. Perspiration beaded on her forehead and wisps of golden curls clung to her even paler skin. The flush of tears had faded along with the purple of blood vessels bulging. "Huh?" That was Crystal's response to whatever Detta was saying over the phone.

Sophie couldn't hear what followed, but she saw the impact. Two more of those monster fairies vanished. And the golden guardian slipped an arm around Crystal. Was that allowed? Could she feel his touch?

Crystal's breathing calmed visibly.

Then there was another of those golden figures. This one looked like a woman. A serious queen of a woman, glowing almost white compared to Sophie's golden bodyguard.

"Holy sh—" She whispered the only thing she could think to say.

But then she thought of something better. "Thank you, Jesus."

Helping the Needy

"Maybe you could bring her to church tomorrow." Detta noted the dullness in her own voice. Lack of hope. Sophie probably wasn't ready to stick her nose into a church building. But Crystal needed something more, and maybe that would get Sophie over the threshold—into the church building if not into the church as part of it.

"I don't know. You think that's what she needs?"

"She needs Jesus. That's what I think. But you know that's what I believe. I don't know what *she* believes."

"Isn't it just enough for her to stay away from that organic healer woman? I didn't used to see those flying things around her before. Not like that, anyway."

"Oh, I'm sure that would help." It was late on Saturday. This was about the fifth phone call between her and Sophie and Sophie's friend.

"I'll talk to her. I can bring her to church if she's willing." Sophie's words were dragging too. "What if we went to Priscilla's church?"

"Uh-huh. That could be helpful. Sure. Just get in the atmosphere of God's presence." Detta's response wasn't as enthusiastic as she'd intended. Sleep was calling, her bed inviting.

"I'll talk to her." An abbreviated response, absent the excuses they both could recite.

Finally, the battle for Sophie's friend stilled for the night, Detta was free to go to bed. Crystal seemed to be stable from what she could tell over the phone—and from what she felt in her spirit. The whole experience reminded her of when Anthony got a new car with all those electronic things on it—

remote door locks, connection to his phone, even seat warmers. It was like Crystal got a new ride that day. Upgraded. Unfamiliar and troublesome, but with some promise.

"Mm-hmm."

Her bedroom was dark—unusually dark—when Detta woke in the middle of the night. It could have been early morning. Maybe she was still asleep.

She wasn't alone.

"Jesus?" She said it aloud, and the air changed.

Some space had opened in the darkness, but something was still there. Something she had not invited.

"Come, Lord Jesus."

The air around her rippled. She expected a crack like lightning. At least a crackle like static.

"Oh, Lord. Help." Her voice rasped.

A pain in her chest. Something moving down there. "Stop it. I ain't takin' you back. You get outta here!"

A pause. Her chest stilled. Breathless. Detta was breathless, and so was her room.

"Lord Jesus!"

A lift, like flying over a dip in the road. And a launch, like a flock of doves all taking flight around her.

The room was hers again. The room was full of Detta and her Lord. No one else. Except maybe a few angels. Did she sense the angels? Did she need to?

She felt the Spirit. That was enough.

The next morning, Detta didn't see Sophie and her friend at church. No pale girls cowering in the corner. That was no surprise. It would have been a risk for those young women. Her church wasn't for everyone. That's why Priscilla no longer accompanied her mother to the services.

"Sister Maynard."

"Sister Washington." They met near the back of the sanctuary, shuffling with the crowd toward the fellowship hall. The two friends followed gravy-flavored air toward the buffet lunch. "I heard Priscilla's friends are going to church with her today."

"You did? Sophie and Crystal?" Detta stopped her slow progress to face the slightly stooped and slender woman who had been her friend for decades.

"I believe so." Sister Maynard—Candace—stretched her mouth wide. A wait-and-see expression. Not a smile.

"Well, I bless that. I trust the Spirit will get ahold of 'em."

"All three of 'em. Mm-hmm." Candace bowed a deep nod.

Detta let her eyebrows ride high but kept her eyes just above Candace's newly styled hair. She offered a sort of "no comment" comment. No need to say more. She knew what a mother wanted for her children. Priscilla was probably only a little more devoted than Anthony. When was the last time *he* was in church?

Familiar themes accompanied them on the slow walk through the lobby and down the stairs to the buffet line. People catching up. Detta and her friend recalling and consoling.

Candace's husband had been in the military at the same time as Detta's. Her man had died of a heart attack just two years ago. That loss had cemented the bond between the two women. No longer was she just a consoler for Detta's grief, she was a sister in widowhood. And they both carried the burden of their adult children. Candace had three.

"How's Timothy doing?" Detta picked up a stiff paper plate from the end of the buffet table, the greenish florescence in the fellowship hall dimming the festive design on the plate.

"His law practice is keeping him busy twenty-four seven. But I fear for his soul. He's not takin' care of eternal things."

Detta could only respond to her friend's words and obvious mood. She wouldn't try to judge Timothy or his faith. A muffled tweeting interrupted her reply.

Candace set down her paper plate and foraged in her purse. Lifting her phone, she answered. "Priscilla. How are you, dear?"

She listened for a few seconds. "Oh. That's too bad. Well, we'll keep prayin' for both of 'em. And you just keep bein' their friend. You can be a lifeline to those girls." She listened again and then said goodbye.

Detta knew the news. She was glad to hear Candace's encouragement for her youngest child. Priscilla had been strategic for Sophie already. Who knew what the future would hold? Detta was glad to not be the only godly contact Sophie had in the visible world.

Running with Angels

Sophie had not tried very hard to convince Crystal to go to church that morning. What would happen if they went? Sophie didn't know what to do in a church, though Priscilla had offered to be her guide in that foreign territory, a life-long resident of those holy lands.

Checking her texts for the latest from Crystal, she brushed off a distraction from one of her familiar followers. He was curling into himself in the corner of her living room. Another of the shadowy band was scolding him like a nagging mother. She was even waving a clawed finger at him. Shaming the sulking lump.

As soon as the word shame crossed her screen, that golden guardian appeared at the end of the sofa. He stood at attention. Had she summoned him? *"Report for duty, Angel Numero Uno."*

He was an angel, wasn't he? That was real. And he was good. Whenever she saw him, she could tell something good was happening, or about to happen. Or maybe was just on offer.

She hadn't been awakened at 3:33 a.m. to threats from that gruesome visitor the last couple nights. Was the angel responsible for that?

Crystal sent a text just then. **"Feeling mch btr. Thx fr keeping in touch."**

She was better. Even if not following the full prescription Detta had offered, Crystal seemed to be recovering.

Sophie liked the angel that had showed up for Crystal. The shining guardian that left with her friend was at least as impressive as Sophie's watchman. And more beautiful. But that fit for Crystal. She was delicate—translucent skin and pale eyes—more beautiful than Sophie.

That thought seemed to dull the glow of her guardian. Was he losing interest? Withdrawing his stoic offer of some unspecified assistance?

She checked the weather on her phone. A bit warmer and dry today, the pavement should be clear. She would go for a run.

Surging off the couch, releasing a dose of adrenaline, she thumped across the hardwood floor to her hot pink bedroom, through the clutter, and to the closet. The closet looked a bit like a tunnel with the majority of the clothes in there being black. The drawers in her dresser were like that too, just a few more colors among the T-shirts and underwear. She found a gray sports bra and black yoga pants and started to dress for the cold.

Her phone in her hoodie pocket and wireless earbuds in, she got a call on the way to the elevator.

"Hello, Sophie."

"Hi, Detta." Striding down the hall kept her slightly ahead of the guilty cringe this call provoked.

"How are you? And how is Crystal?"

"She's good. She seems stabilized, if that's what you call it." Sophie wondered if that shiny angel was still with Crystal. Was Crystal's guardian responsible for her stability? Sophie's guardian seemed to go invisible about half the time. She glanced over her shoulder. No golden boy, but no scruffy rag men either. Was she running unaccompanied? She got on the elevator.

"You two didn't go to church?"

"No. Couldn't talk her into it." She inhaled some courage. "I didn't really try too hard, to tell the truth. What am I gonna do at church?"

"Well, maybe you would see a lot of shiny angels. That might be encouraging."

"Uh-huh." Sophie had thought of that, of course, but an instant fear that she would also see mangy monsters erased the appeal. Would church people really be so clean of critters? She was afraid it wasn't so and that she would have to report that to Sister Washington or the good brothers and sisters at Priscilla's church. She didn't want to play that role.

The elevator door opened to the little white-tiled lobby. A man was pulling mail out of a stuffed metal box two columns down from hers. She didn't recognize him. Maybe he wasn't around much. He obviously didn't check mail very often.

A small lizard thing was clinging to the mail in that guy's hand, mail that included magazines in discreet black plastic wrappers. Whatever.

"You at church?" Sophie was idling in the conversation, but Detta didn't seem to be pushing hard at any agenda.

"I just got home. It's past two." A hint of correction deepened Detta's voice.

"Oh, I didn't realize. Late night yesterday. More reason not to crawl out to church."

Two young men in baggy pants and black hoodies—like the one she was wearing—were striding down the sidewalk in the opposite direction. One glossy ghoul was riding them both with an insect-like knee on the inside shoulder of each. It was like a giant cockroach riding two carriage horses.

Sophie and that hard-shelled critter made brief eye contact. She shook off his gaze and returned her attention to what Detta was saying.

Detta sounded slightly weary. "That's okay, dear. I understand. I'm fully aware that this is all new for you. It could really be life-changing. That doesn't come fast, and it doesn't come easy. I'll just keep praying for grace to go with you."

That reminded Sophie of a question. "I wanted to ask you about your prayers." She was stretching her quads on the front stoop, standing on one leg, grabbing the top of her other foot, and pulling it up to her butt. "When I first put Crystal on the phone with you, you were praying for her, right?"

"I was. I was prayin' in the Spirit. It's what I do when I don't know what to pray."

"Ah. Yeah. Okay. Well, the reason I was asking was about whether your prayers send angels. I mean, it was right then that this beautiful shining woman showed up next to Crystal." Sophie shivered at the memory even as she finished her stretch. She started to jog, running through that chill.

"Oh, Lord. Thank you, Jesus."

The shivers were running right along with Sophie. She laughed. "Yeah. That's what I said once I figured it out."

Detta let out a surprised chuckle. "Oh. That's fine. Good to hear." She sighed a long, high note. "Yes, sir. But I'm not gonna get caught up in trying to figure it all out. I especially don't plan on gettin' too fascinated with my powers or anything. Ha. Makes me think of stuff Anthony likes to talk about."

Snickering through her elevated breathing, Sophie could feel someone running up beside her. A big, strong runner. And there was that golden guy. Her Secret Service agent would be joining her for this jog. She chuckled some more.

"What are you laughing at now?"

"I'm jogging. Just started. And I was wondering where my guardian was. But when you and I started talking about that guardian for Crystal, and laughing about it, that big golden guy showed up to join me for my run."

"Ha! Oh, thank you, Lord. Oh, praise you, Jesus. Yes. That is a blessing."

Detta was certainly excited. Sophie was feeling it too. And her guard was glowing brighter, though still focused on the way ahead.

Sophie wasn't so focused. She was distracted. And so was the guy coming toward her. She got a glimpse of him from the corner of her eye as she turned to see the way ahead. He was staring down at his phone.

Just as she was about to collide with him, a hand gripped her arm. She swung past the distracted guy. It was a perfect spin move, worthy of an NFL running back.

The stranger tottered and twisted his head to see her before resuming his distracted stroll. She heard him laugh instead of swearing at her, as she would have expected if they crashed.

"Oh. Okay. I gotta focus on my running here. Thanks for calling, Detta."

"Sure. And thank you. You've encouraged me probably more than you know. Thanks for telling me what you're seeing, Sophie. It's a real blessing to me."

"Good. Well, happy Sunday, then."

"Ha. Okay. Goodbye, Sophie."

The warmth of Detta's responses to Sophie's odd experiences fueled her heart and energized her run. She was jogging and smiling and wondering at how she got hooked up with this old black woman who said things like "Praise you, Jesus" all the time.

Her angel stayed on her right side, close but not bumping her. And that reminded her that she had felt a hand on her

The Girl Who Sees Angels

arm when she almost crashed into that guy looking at his phone. Her guard had actually touched her.

Had she been ... touched by an angel?

She laughed and ran and laughed some more.

A Safe Home

Her mother's house was still Sophie's home even though she had moved out for the last time five years ago. She had lived with her mother longer than lots of her friends because her mother was alone. But also because Sophie needed to find a lasting sanity and figure out how to cope with the curse that was her gift.

This Sunday she was looking for signs of angels when she arrived home for supper. Her mother's house seemed a safe place to pay attention to the things she used to try to ignore. Even holy angels, as Detta called them, had been of no interest to Sophie before. But her mother surely liked them, and maybe even knew something about them.

"I almost went to church this morning, mostly to help a friend who's having a tough time." She wasn't planning to tell her mother everything. How much would her madrecita even understand?

"Really? What church?" Her mother set the pan of enchiladas on the table next to the rice and the beans.

"Oh, my friend's church. Priscilla's. We talked about it. We didn't wanna go to Detta's church—that would just be too strange."

"Why? Because it's a black church?"

"Oh, no. Not that. Actually I have no idea who goes to Priscilla's church. I think it's mixed. No, Mama. You know that wouldn't stop me. No. It's just kind of a wild service, I hear, with people rebuking things and stuff like that. I don't even know what all." Sophie resisted the distraction of the food, one of her father's favorites. "Whatever it is, Priscilla dropped out of there to go somewhere more modern. At least I think that's why she left."

"I just want to understand. Why wouldn't you come to church with me? Your friend can come too."

"Yeah, I know. But I got frustrated at your church. I couldn't go there. It got too complicated."

Her mother sat down and pushed the enchiladas closer to Sophie, seated across the table. "But that was when you were twelve. Maybe you won't feel so confused now that you're a woman."

They hadn't talked about this for years. Her mother knew how deeply disturbed Sophie had been in their Catholic church. At the time, neither of them knew what to think about what Sophie saw—especially what she saw on one of the priests. Her mother had thought Sophie might be suffering from some kind of curse, and that the priest might help. But that priest had been the most complex aspect of what Sophie saw in those days. She still hesitated to think back on it.

"If I go to church, it will be for a fresh start. I'm not judging your church, Mama. I just think I need something different." She shook her head. This was a hard castle to defend. She didn't know her way around. She couldn't justify her actions or even articulate her motivations.

Sophie dished enchiladas and pushed the glass baking dish back toward her mother. Scooping rice and beans next to the chicken enchilada, she wondered at how quiet and peaceful her mother's house was. This recalled the little gaggle of ghouls that usually followed her. Her instinct was to look to the corners of the room. But if those things were really spirits, did she need to turn her eyes toward them? They weren't physical beings. Did she need physical eyes to see them?

Instead of turning, she zoned out for a second, staring at her water glass and trying to sense those sloppy stalkers. An image of a pile of rags formed in her mind—gray, dirty, and rotting. That was them. They were here somewhere.

"Are you okay, *mija*?"

"What? Oh. Sure. I was just thinking. So many new things happening to me these days. I was just wondering what it all means."

"Perhaps it means that you are finding your way in the world, even if it is a way that not many others have found."

"You think others see spirits like I do, Mama?"

"You believe now that they are spirits?"

Had she not brought her mother into that much of her new experience? The numerous conversations with Detta may have intruded where her mother used to hold exclusive rights.

"I guess it just makes sense to me now. Angels and the others."

"The others? Evil spirits?"

"Evil spirits?" Had Detta called them that?

Her mother finished dishing her food. "Those are fallen angels. Michael and the other angels fought against them when Satan tried to take the throne away from God."

"What? How could he do that? I mean, God is God, right? How could anyone take that away? Is Satan really that strong?"

"*Claro*. Those are good questions. But we know that Satan was thrown down. He was defeated in heaven. And he was thrown down to the earth. God is always stronger than the devil. But the devil was given freedom to work on the earth. It is the angels, like Michael and Raphael, who fight on our behalf. That is why we sometimes pray to them."

"Wait. I don't think Detta has said anything like that. Is that 'cause she's not Catholic?" Her beans and rice were cooling on her plate, the cumin and chili steam diminishing. She picked up her fork.

"I think it is one of the Psalms that says, 'Praise the Lord, you his angels, you mighty ones who do his work.' That is talking to angels, saying for them to do what they are supposed to do. Others believe angels can carry their prayers to God." She cut into her enchilada with her fork. "You don't have to believe all that. It's not so important. You don't have to argue with Christians if they don't think you should pray to angels. But maybe it is okay to talk to them and encourage them to do their work."

"Why would you do that? Don't they know what they're supposed to do?"

"Sure, they know. But we pray lots of prayers that are not a new idea. Maybe we are just cooperating with the holy angels if we encourage their work. That makes us part of their holy mission."

Sophie slowly chewed a bite of enchilada, the chicken savory and tender, melting in her mouth. The physical world was easier. Much less complicated. That brought back their earlier conversation. "When I was a girl, there was one priest who had lots of dark things swirling around him whenever I saw him outside the mass. You told me not to blaspheme when I told you about them."

Her mother stopped chewing. She swallowed hard, slowly releasing her fork. It clicked against the edge of her plate. She furrowed her brow, as if trying to remember. Then she lifted her hand to her mouth. "Oh, *Mio Dios*." Now her mother was the one catching her breath. "Oh, Sophie. I remember. I remember which priest it was. Oh, mija." Her eyebrows were high, her eyes wide.

"What? What is it, Mama?"

"Oh, dear. I remember telling you not to say those things. Oh, Lord, forgive me. 'Out of the mouths of babes'." She was staring past Sophie.

"What is it? What are you talking about?"

"He was a bad priest. He was knocked ... uh, kicked ... he was removed from the church. He was a ... he did ... bad things to children." Her face was red, her hand shaking slightly where she held it over her mouth.

"He was a pedophile?" Sophie's voice blared out of control. Her chest tightened.

Her mother just nodded, staring at Sophie now. Then she started shaking her head slowly in a swaying motion. "I am so sorry, Sophia. I owe you a big apology. What you saw was true. You told the truth, and I rebuked you for that. Forgive me, mija." Tears filled her eyes, and she reached for Sophie's hand.

Sophie grasped that offered hand. "Oh, Mama. I forgive you. You didn't know." She sniffed a sigh. "I was just a girl. I wasn't making sense most of the time."

Her mother locked her eyes on Sophie and tightened her brows. "Maybe you were making a lot more sense than I admitted. Maybe what you said was right, and I didn't know what to do about it. And others too—the priests. We went to them just like we went to the counselors. And they didn't believe. They didn't understand." Her lower lip twitched. She gripped Sophie's hand desperately. "And I believed you more than I let you know back then, more than I told those people. I should have defended you more, my Sophie." She sobbed twice audibly and then clapped a hand over her eyes.

Sophie's eyes stung. Her nose itched. She sniffled hard. "Oh, Mama. You did your best. I wasn't an easy child to raise."

The golden guardian was next to Sophie. And there was another behind her mother. He was shorter. His attentive gaze toward her mother was wise and compassionate. His eyes glowed white. The smallest hint of a sympathetic smile shaped his cheeks.

Over Sophie's shoulder hovered four of those raggedy urchins that followed her. She turned to watch as one of them walked right through the wall.

"Oh." She couldn't help herself.

"What? What did you see?"

Sophie turned away from the three remaining rascals and smiled with half her mouth. "One of them left."

"One of who? Who left?"

"The dirty little ones that follow me around all the time. There are only three left. There used to be more."

"What are they?"

"I never knew. But maybe they're bad spirits. They don't seem very scary, really. Just disgusting." The two glowing angels drew her attention now. "But the guardian that has been following me around lately is right here. And over there is the one I always see at your house."

"Where?" Her mother glanced to her right and started praying in rapid Spanish, too fast for Sophie to translate. But she knew those old prayers, and they seemed to make her mother's guardian glow even brighter. Now he was definitely smiling.

Her mother apparently had a happy guardian angel.

A Possible Sighting

Anthony didn't get much out of his mother when he asked how things were going for Sophie, but it seemed like she was encouraged and only a little worried. It had been a relief to have his mother worry about someone besides him. No siblings, he got the full weight of her concern. It was probably good, really, assuming her prayers were powerful. Which he did assume.

Slipping his phone into his pocket, he decided to walk to the train. Eleven blocks. It was a bit warmer today, maybe the last day like this before winter. And he needed the exercise. He was feeling flabby. He hitched his backpack over one shoulder and headed north.

Three blocks into his hike, an old man caught his attention. Maybe he wasn't so old, just worn. His jacket was rumpled and dull, his shoes down at the heels, his khaki pants black on the backside.

When Anthony slowed, he realized the old guy was trying to help a younger man to stand. The young guy was out of his head, uttering noises that were probably supposed to be words.

"Hey, young brother. Could you give us a hand? I gotta get this kid to the emergency room. He's done OD'd."

Anthony stood speechless. But he had already stopped. It would be hard to refuse now. Generally he buzzed right past the panhandlers and con men. Why had he stopped for this man?

Looking at the old man's eyes, Anthony saw life, as opposed to the glassy stare he usually saw in the men and women begging for quarters and scamming for bucks. "Uh, sure. Where is the emergency room from here?" That was something a person living on the street would know, whereas a network tech working in a tall office building wouldn't.

"Just up there a few blocks." The old guy pointed toward a corner ahead of them and thrust his finger toward the west, around that corner.

Was this a scam? Were these two guys working together? Anthony was carrying a company laptop in his backpack. Were they gonna rob him and stuff him in a dumpster? Why stuff him in a dumpster? He forced himself out of his stunned pose. "Sure. Okay. Let's get him to the emergency room."

It was that old guy's eyes. They seemed true. Real. He seemed sober, if down on his luck. And the other guy couldn't be in on any scam. He was too far gone. No one was that good an actor. Anthony slid his arm around the young guy's shoulder. He was skinny and light, even more so than Anthony.

The doped-up guy lurched forward, leaned down, and retched.

Anthony winced and looked away. "*Dang. This could get bad.*" He kept that to himself.

The drugged guy hung onto his lunch, or whatever the last meal he ate was.

"Okay. Okay. You're gonna be okay. We got you. Let's just keep it moving." The old man had his arm around the young guy just like Anthony. He looked across their patient. "I'm Raphael." He released the drugged guy's hand and offered his for a shake.

Anthony ventured a quick opposite-hand grab and release, recapturing the left hand of the young guy again and keeping his backpack from sliding down his arm. "I'm Anthony. Who's this guy?"

"They call him Capper, but that's not his proper name. Most folks don't know his proper name."

"*He* doesn't seem to know *anything* right now."

"Yeah, I'll give you that. He's one of the ones who's in danger the most out here. If he doesn't die of the overdose, he might freeze to death tonight even before the real cold sets in."

"Uh-huh." Anthony could imagine that. "What's he on?"

"Oh, some prescription pills he bought on the street. Pain killers." Raphael huffed. "Just plain *killers*, if you ask me."

"Right. You say you don't really know him?"

"Oh, I know plenty about *him*. He just doesn't know *me*. No relation, ya know."

"Yeah. Okay. Uh, you live around here?"

"Staying at an SRO back that way." He nodded his head backward. "Been there a while. What about you?"

"Oh. I'm on the north side. Was headed to the train."

"Good thing about trains this time of day is there's always another one. And maybe the one you catch won't be so crowded as the one you were aimin' at. You never know."

Was that supposed to make Anthony feel better about interrupting his commute to do this four-legged race with these two strangers? It was starting to feel like a long-distance race. He really did need to exercise more.

"You got folks in the city?" Raphael was still getting acquainted.

"Close. My mama lives just north, in the 'burbs. Easy little drive."

"You have a car, but you take the train to work? That's good. Smart. Better for the air." He raised his salt-and-pepper beard in approval.

"Yeah. I think so too. What about you? You have folks in the city?" They had to wait at a light to cross a major street on their way west. Folks were taking a passing interest in their little mission, but no one said anything. It was pretty obvious what was happening.

"Oh, my people are far from here."

"They moved on, but you stayed?"

"You could say that."

"Uh-huh." While the old man seemed entirely believable, he was evasive, not volunteering his whole story. "What's, uh … Capper's story? He from around here?"

"Naw. He came from back east, thinking the grass was greener around here. Then he moved on from grass to harder stuff, you know." Raphael grinned painfully. "Been downhill all the way. And he's not a guy who takes help when it's offered."

"Ah. Yeah. You sound like a social worker. You still working?"

"You mean am I retired and living a life of ease in a pay-by-the-week hotel downtown?" He laughed a genuinely merry laugh.

"Well, I don't know. It just seems like you know plenty, and you take the time to help a guy like this."

"Sure. I understand. But helping is more than my job, it's my purpose in the world. Most people think of me as a messenger. Raphael the messenger. That's me."

"Oh. Okay." The stranger had upgraded his evasive answers to riddles.

Anthony lifted his head to measure the distance to the sign for the emergency room and the hospital general admissions desk. Capper needed the emergency room, of course. He was quivering, maybe shivering. It wasn't very cold, and the skinny guy was wearing a puffy blue winter coat. A warm coat that smelled like garbage. But Capper clearly had other things going on.

"I wanna thank you, young man, for stopping and helping two brothers in need. You done good. I really appreciate it." They were approaching the sliding doors, which opened almost silently. But those doors released a cacophony from the bustling hospital department inside. The three men aimed for an abandoned wheelchair.

"Glad I could help. This guy is lucky you were around. I would've just walked right past him if you hadn't been there." Anthony and Raphael were mostly dragging Capper by now, but the smooth floor made that easy.

"Glad to pull you into a real good thing. You might've helped save a life today. That's worth goin' outta your way for, ain't it?" Capper deposited in that wheelchair, Raphael stood up straight—impressively straight. He looked strong and young now. But maybe that was a trick of the hospital lighting.

Nodding, Anthony took Raphael's hand for a proper shake. "Well, good to meet you." He turned slowly back toward the doors as Raphael grabbed the attention of a guy in hospital scrubs.

When he exited the sliding doors, Anthony glanced back again and couldn't see either "the messenger" or the guy passed out in the wheelchair. But it was crowded in there.

That Thursday during dinner at his mother's house, Anthony arrested his mother with that story.

She stood holding a pan of baked beans, lowering it toward the floor before she caught herself. "He said his name was

Raphael? And he said he was called 'the messenger'?" She shuffled to the table and rested the pan on a hot pad.

"Something like that." It had seemed strange at the time. Now it sounded even weirder the way his mother said it. "What are you thinking?"

"I don't know. I guess all this stuff with Sophie has me thinking ..." She shook her head and pushed a fluff of white hair off her forehead with the back of her hand.

"What? Thinking what?"

His mama looked at him and did that duck-lip look. "Well, it says in the Scriptures that some folks have helped out angels without knowin' it. That's what I was thinking. Ya see, Raphael is the name of an angel in some stories that've been in the church for ages. I'm not real familiar with those stories myself, but I know it's supposed to be the name of an angel."

"You think that guy was an angel?" His voice cracked like he was thirteen again. "You think I saw an angel?"

"Makes you feel like Sophie, don't it?" She chuckled and turned to hoist the plate of ribs from the counter.

"Well, maybe not that. But ... the part about being the messenger, or a messenger. What was that about?"

"*Angel* is just a Bible word for messenger. I can't recall whether it's Greek or Hebrew, but I'm sure that angel means messenger. Raphael the messenger. Raphael the angel." She slipped into her chair with more of those jolly chuckles. She seemed pretty satisfied with herself, like she had just won the lottery by some clever trick.

"But how come I could see him? All those spirits Sophie sees are invisible to the rest of us."

"Not invisible to everyone. You remember Sister Frasier, don't you? She had the sight." His mother let her eyes wander toward the corner of the room.

Anthony expected she was looking at a memory, not an angel in the kitchen. "But still, angels aren't just like people. They don't look just like people."

"Lots of times in the Bible the angels are described as looking like a man. Sometimes real shiny. But sometimes folks didn't know they were talking to an angel at all. So they must just look normal, at least sometimes."

"Okay. Wow. Yeah. There's more to this than I realized."

"You thought you knew all the rules. You thought you'd figured out about the dimensions and the elements and such. But some of it is beyond human figuring. Even for my brilliant son."

Anthony shook his head and snickered. Then he forked some steaming, tender ribs onto his plate.

A Weird Week

On a Friday morning, Sophie lay in bed calculating whether she could take the day off. Her projects were up to date and she had some PTO available. She had planned to use some of it around the holidays. Thanksgiving was almost a week away. But the first four days of the week had been increasingly weird. Home felt safer, at least during the daytime.

Monday included her glowing guardian accompanying her. She was getting used to being escorted by that big guy and was still chuckling about the other guardian she had seen at her mom's house. Did that one go with her mom when she left home?

Those sulking sad sacks that still followed her around were looking timid around the golden guy. What would it take to get them to go away entirely?

That morning at her desk, Sophie had been getting ready for her next project. She was supposed to be fixing Jennifer's code—Jennifer with the cubicle over by Janice's office. She was Janice's favorite.

Jennifer came with a sassy, sexy little flying escort. That red demon was generally mad, and she was all about spreading the madness. But Sophie's golden guardian seemed to keep her from inciting the three little pigs that cowered in the corner of Sophie's cube. Somehow that made it easier for her to tolerate Jennifer.

"I don't think there's much for you to do on this. I've been over it a hundred times. But we gotta follow protocol, right?"

"Of course. I'll just look it over. No problem." As little said as possible. More words led to more arguments, defensiveness, and blame throwing.

Jennifer looked like she was about to respond, her lipsticked mouth like a bud ready to blossom. But the guardian cast one glance at the imp hanging over Jennifer's head, and the little red demon turned away, rebuffed.

Pivoting on her high heels, Jennifer left Sophie to do her work.

Sophie spoke to the guardian without thinking about whether that was a good idea. "Thanks for that."

Jennifer stopped and looked back at Sophie. "What did you say? Did you say something to me?" A strident challenge.

What had she said? "Uh, I just said thanks. But wasn't really talking to you."

"Who were you talking to, then?" Jennifer was drifting back toward Sophie's cube, bringing regret and that little devil with her.

"Sorry. Pretty much talking to myself. Bad habit." Sophie glanced at the guardian, thinking she might be in trouble for bending the truth. She certainly wasn't going to tell Jennifer who she was really talking to. Jenn would be in Janice's office telling her all about it in two seconds.

Puckered and squinted, Jennifer advertised her disbelief.

Sophie couldn't blame her. Her explanation was unbelievable. But the truth was even more so.

Nobody lost their job, or any blood, that day. The incident cautioned Sophie, however, to keep her head down and to keep her angel talk to herself.

Tuesday wasn't too bad. The chubby imp from Charlie's cube kept trying to distract her. He seemed to know she could see him. Distraction was his game. The guardian repelled him a few times with a laser look from his diamond eyes.

Why did her mom get a smiling angel, by the way?

Wednesday was the day of the cash demon. That's what she called the thing with the bulging pockets that hung on Patricia's back. Patricia was from accounting. She did auditing for various departments, including the software development group. When Sophie saw that guy with the bulging pockets—really it was more of a troll than a guy—the word *embezzling* came to mind. Not something she normally thought about. She probably couldn't even spell it. But that's what popped into her head when Patricia came out of Frank's office. The bulging-pockets thing was with *her*, so Patricia was probably the one skimming cash.

Staring at the lady from accounting was understandably frowned upon. Patricia aimed curvy eyebrows and haunted eyes back at Sophie, but she didn't say anything. She just lowered her head and averted her gaze before scuttling back to the elevator. It looked like a clean getaway.

No way was Sophie going to say anything to anyone. Even if she was a hundred percent sure she knew someone was robbing the company, she wouldn't report it. What could she say about *how* she knew it?

In general, she figured she should stop staring suspiciously at people walking by her cube if she wanted to keep her job.

Keeping the angel sightings under wraps had long been about maintaining her reputation. Holding onto her job was part of that. And she was far from ready to let her visions bend her real world, not in a way that threatened anyone's employment.

What did it really mean that Patricia was carrying that cash bag demon? It didn't necessarily mean she was stealing. But there was that word that flashed through Sophie's head. She shook it off and managed to get back to work on the convoluted code from Jennifer.

Next came Thursday. What were those things running up and down the aisle? It was like someone had brought their kids *and* their pets to work and let them run wild.

Sophie was used to seeing spirits attached to people. There were also some that seemed attached to particular places. Maybe there were even combo spirits, connected to places and people both. But where were these little monsters from? It was like a zoo train of barking, squawking, and cursing invaders. From where? Why now? Were they invited by someone? Sent by someone?

That last thought seemed to ring true. She looked at the guardian and thought she detected assent from him. He didn't say anything, but she felt she knew his moods. Or maybe just read his face.

The fact that she could hear this little party of poopers raised other issues. She was usually spared the audio to go with the video of other people's spiritual shadows. The language of the gross critters that she did hear was often gross. If not that, it was threatening. If not that, it was depressing. Today's visitors were distracting. Who would send distracting spirits to this floor of the company? An enemy of the company?

It would be nice if her guardian did speak. "Bingo," he could say, when she figured something out. That would be helpful. At least it would lift her out of her mental spin cycle so she could get back to work.

Sophie stretched her neck and tried to monitor the other folks in the office. That's when she noticed that midday Thursday sounded a lot like end-of-day Friday. There was usually an elevated disruption in the office as the weekend approached. Holidays were the worst. Perhaps the other staff didn't see or hear the rioting swarm, but they seemed to echo them, in a way.

For Sophie, the distraction was complete. She couldn't work like this. So maybe the rowdy riot was just there to mess with *her*. She hunkered and stayed as late as she could. Only four o'clock, as it turned out.

Now, in bed on Friday morning, burrowing in seemed attractive. But her guardian pulled her out of that duck-and-cover by crossing her room and passing through her bedroom door. Leaving the door closed was an old defense from childhood, a level of protection which rarely kept the specters out.

Under the closed door, Sophie could see an intensifying light. Unnatural light. She scooted closer to the edge of the bed to get a fuller view. Gold to yellow to white, the sun seemed to be rising in her living room.

She swore quietly. More angels? Was she really dealing with angels? Were they gathering for choir practice in her living room? The urge to see who was out there dragged her from under the covers on a cold November morning. Fascination pushed her. Curiosity had been drawing her past more of her fears in recent days.

Sophie untwisted her sweatpants and T-shirt and grabbed her plush fleece robe from the hook on her door. She wrapped it around her before touching the doorknob. Would it be hot? No. That was in house fires. But ... maybe.

Sophie took a chance and tugged the door open. It didn't latch properly, the door not quite fitting into the frame, so she opened it without turning the knob. The knob wasn't hot. Cold, actually.

The expanding wedge of light cutting into her bedroom reminded her of a science-fiction movie she saw as a child.

Which one? Maybe more than one. She squinted against that light and raised one hand to create a shelter for her eyes.

Her guardian turned toward her from where he stood at the end of the couch, next to the kitchenette. Or was that another shining visitor?

Her jelly legs slowed her. Her heart thumped. Her lungs begged for help.

Another shining figure stood in the far corner. It looked more like a woman than a man. Clearly it was another angel. Angels in her living room. Had she ever seen more than one hanging out in her place? These were not just zipping through her walls on the way to something more urgent, somewhere more important.

She reached the kitchenette and counted five of the tall, sun-shining guests in the living room. They all looked toward the ceiling, and three had their hands raised above their heads.

As Sophie gawked at the scene, something shot into her belly like a fast-moving subway train slamming into her gut.

Light.

She was filled with light. Eyes closed, her own hands drifting toward the ceiling, she could see light inside. Her mind was filled. Her heart accelerated, beating double time. The fear she felt seemed pure, clean, and true. Not fear of the unknown. More like a sudden realization—a revelation of stunning truth.

Her eyes were pried open by insistent hands. In the middle of the five shining figures an even brighter light appeared. Then that light coalesced into the shape of a person. A man. He shone with light beamed from the guardians around him, but he seemed human. He smiled at her and beckoned for her to come to him.

That was the last thing she remembered.
The overwhelming light blinked off.
Blackness.
Unconsciousness.

What Was That?

"I think I must have passed … I must have just, just … black … blacked out on the floor."

Detta listened to the shivering stutters stilting Sophie's voice. At least now the girl was speaking in sentences. "Where are you now?"

"Hiding. Behind … uh … my couch." She gulped air. "Detta, what was that? Who was that?"

Chills layered over the ones Detta was already huddling against, her bathrobe pulled close around her neck. What could she say? What if she said the wrong thing? "I can't tell you for sure, Sophie." She breathed through her nose and closed her eyes. *Help me, Lord.* "I think you and I can guess. I mean, we have an idea what … *who* that was. But I—I just can't say for sure." Detta held her breath for a few seconds. "I do believe that God is taking care of you. Jesus is sending holy angels to protect you. And maybe … maybe even showing you other things. Since you see *them*—the angels, I mean—maybe he wants to use them to show you more. And the most important thing … well, the most important one is Jesus." There. She said it.

Panting like she was struggling to rise to her feet, Sophie said nothing for several seconds. "I … what if … what if I can't handle it? What if I'm not up to this?" Just as her voice leveled, she barked one quick vowel.

"Sophie?"

"Detta." She was whispering. "He's sitting in the chair. The man is sitting in the chair. The chair across the room. And my guardian is here, but not the others." Her voice broke off suddenly.

The Girl Who Sees Angels

Pulling her phone away from her ear, Detta checked. The call had terminated. What had happened? Should she rush over to Sophie's place to make sure she was okay? Did she even know where Sophie lived? Priscilla would know. Detta started to calculate whether it was worth calling Candace Maynard to get Priscilla's number so Detta could call Priscilla and get Sophie's address …

That was a lot of trouble. And what would she say? "*I think Sophie is meeting with Jesus now, and I wanna go help her out*"? She groaned there in her kitchen chair. "Oh, Lord, help that girl. But then, you probably are helping her already. Is that why she can't come to the phone right now?"

She chuckled nervously as she shuffled toward the sink. Breakfast dishes awaited a wash and dry. She needed to do something with her hands.

Standing at her sink rinsing a small plate, Detta heard the tone of an incoming call above the sing of the faucet. She dropped the heavy plate into the plastic wash tub, shut off the water, and fumbled for her phone with wet hands. "Sophie?"

"Sorry. I guess I hung up on you." She took a deep breath. "I thought I saw him. That man. But then he was gone." Her voice was riding a long slope downward. "Maybe it was just my imagination. Maybe it was *all* just my imagination."

"Huh. Okay. But can you tell me … can you tell me how you felt when you saw Him?"

"Saw *Him*?" Was Sophie capitalizing over the phone? "Uh, I felt scared. Excited. Afraid. Glad. Maybe. Maybe all of that."

Detta was nodding. "Yes. Sure. That makes sense to me." But she wasn't going to pretend she knew everything about it. "Is that angel still there? Your guardian?"

"Yes. He seems to be, like, stationed here or something. He comes to work with me too." She snorted or sniffled. "But yesterday at work was really strange. So many strange, uh … appearances and, well, even sounds. Why would a bunch of new creepy things come to my office all the sudden?"

That was one of those questions Detta answered easily in her own mind. But she slowed herself to wait for an answer appropriate for Sophie. "Hmm. I guess there are all kinds o' reasons that could happen. Could be that someone else there caused it, and it has nothing to do with you." She wiped her hands on the dish towel next to the sink. Probably too late. Her bathrobe was damp in several spots. "Uh, but I think I probably mentioned that there might be some of the dark angels that get after you when you start to … to get more involved with the holy angels and with God."

"Did you tell me that?"

"I thought I did. I should have, if I didn't. Hmm. You're at home?"

"Yeah. But I should go to work. I'll be late, but I think I'd rather be there than here."

Detta was thinking the opposite. She wouldn't leave that space where Jesus himself had probably showed up. She might never leave. But that wasn't right either. He was always with her wherever she went, right?

And Sophie had other visitors at her place. At least one that would make Detta want to leave. When were she and Sophie going to address that? "Okay, I'll let you go then. But call me if you need anything. I'll keep praying for you."

"Huh. Okay. But maybe that's what started this new trouble."

"What? Praying started trouble?"

"Oh, I don't know. Maybe not. Maybe I'm just confused. Or afraid."

"That's okay. I understand. You didn't really sign up for any of this. We never do. God gives us gifts on his own design and in his own way. We just have to deal with it."

"Yeah, I suppose. Okay, I gotta rush to get to work. Thanks, Detta."

"You are quite welcome, Sophie." She touched the red circle on her phone.

What had just happened? If the angel sightings were real, did that mean that Sophie had also really seen the Lord Jesus in her apartment? That probably wasn't the same gift. But what did Detta know?

She knew lots of things that Sophie didn't know—mostly Scriptures. But so much of what was happening to Sophie was outside that box, as Anthony would say.

Sophie sounded like she might be thinking of giving up. Wasn't that implied in what she said about Detta's prayers? And she wanted to leave the place where all those holy angels, and even Jesus, had appeared.

Had Detta's prayers really caused Sophie trouble? Sophie already had serious trouble when she came to see her.

"Well, Lord, what else can I do? I could be silent and just hope for the best. But maybe even those hopes are prayers. Is it right that prayers send angels? Is it right that prayers start trouble? I guess it's all fighting for your kingdom. I guess it's like pickin' a fight, isn't it? I mean, the devil has his forces in place, and you want us to contend with those forces. So, Lord, help Sophie in the fight. Help her to know her place in the fight. And mostly help her to accept you into her life—even into her living room."

Detta chuckled as she folded her dishtowel and shuffled out of the kitchen. Time to get dressed for the day. Dressed for battle.

The Craziest Kind of Crazy

Sophie allowed the train to rock her. She was fully awake. It wouldn't rock her back to sleep. It was more like shaking her to keep alert. She had been resting on Detta's interpretation of her visions. It was time to get serious and think for herself.

Things had gotten crazier since she started believing Detta. Crazier than …? Crazier than a crazy big building with bars on the windows and meds dispensed twice a day.

The last time Sophie was in the hospital, she had admitted herself. In her mid-twenties, she was back where she had last been at sixteen. Back inside, she soon regretted that choice. She regretted it most when her meds wore off. Her mother's visit one Sunday had finally convinced her to get out.

Her mother loved Sophie no matter what. That was solid. That was sound. That was the opposite of crazy. But it was also irrational. How could her mom love such a messed-up person? But maybe irrational wasn't always crazy. A rational twenty-four-year-old could almost convince herself that was true.

At sixteen or fifteen or thirteen, the crazy house had been the enemy. And her loving mother had signed the papers to get her in there. Still, Sophie didn't blame her mother. Sophie was out of control. She wasn't just beyond her mother's reason, she was beyond all reason. Hospitalization had seemed a necessary evil. Becoming a drugged zombie was the best solution they could come up with—the doctors, her mother, and even herself.

But the visions didn't stop. Oh, no. Even if some were dulled by meds, they were still there. And in the hospital, there were new visitors. The creatures crawling and crowing and catapulting from one person to another in the hospital were the worst kind. At least in her mind they were. Her sometimes-rational mind.

What level of desperation had erased the horrible memories of the hospital when she committed herself at twenty-four?

Suicide. That's what.

She was done with college, ready to be a grown-up in the world, ready to break free from everyone's control. But a big smothering creature had filled her apartment that year. An ape-like presence. A she-ape. An oppressive female animal. That big beast hated Sophie. She wanted Sophie dead. And she shadowed her every thought.

"You have tried all your life to be normal. You will never succeed. You can't do it. Now is the time to surrender and just end it. You killed your father with all your craziness. You're killing your mother. Go ahead. Put her out of her misery. End your miserable life."

Classic suicidal messages. That was a reason to commit herself to the hospital. It was a rational choice. A choice influenced by a swollen female thing oozing depression into her apartment. Not all reasons are reasonable.

For the first two days in the hospital that last time, it seemed that the she-ape had divided herself into three. A council of doom surrounded Sophie, their faces clear and their voices sawtooth sharp. "Failure. Crazy. Deceiver." She recognized their accusations. She saw some truth in all of them. Three days of meds dulled the blade of those accusations.

And then a little pack of crustaceans took over. They were like an infestation she picked up from the linens, but worse than bedbugs. They didn't speak to her. They just crawled.

Their spiny appendages pricked her and hooked her. And they overwhelmed her with their numbers. One night, she struggled against wrist restraints after trying to scratch her eyes to get the spiny bugs from under her lids.

That was the craziest depth of crazy. That was the deepest darkness. Alone with those creatures nipping at her like she was carrion lying on the side of the road. She was alone with them because no one would believe her. No one else could see them, so they didn't exist in the real world—only in her head. Her head wasn't part of the real world.

In the midst of that dive into insanity, she allowed the love of her mother to slow her descent, to wipe away some of the infestation. A look in her mother's eyes during a Sunday visit had reached the living part of Sophie. Sitting in that chair in the rec room, clutching her brown purse with both hands, her mother brought just enough clarity for Sophie to demand that she be released. She had admitted herself. She wanted to be released. The crazy outside the hospital, the insanity without the heavy meds, was preferable.

A day program, moving back in with her mother, and ongoing therapy taught her new ways to cope. How to keep her head down. How to fill her mind with compelling occupations and purposes. How to drive right past those hovering and clinging creatures. The visions. The images of insanity.

Or insights into reality.

Of course, she had suspected it most of her life. What she saw was real. Others were blind. Those creatures she saw existed in the real world. Everyone else was just refusing to see.

The movie *The Matrix* had helped. She saw it for the first time years after it was released. And she watched it again when she got out of the hospital. She watched the original movie in the trilogy several times. In it, she found affirmation.

Most people live a false existence, one based on refusal to see the obvious. That was Sophie's world.

But she still had to survive in a world full of blind people. So she kept her head down, ignored the distractions, and pushed past occasional intimidations.

Until she met Maxwell Hartman.

Even more than other spiritual seers, he seemed to understand her. He sympathized. And he was excited about her potential. Instead of a life in and out of mental institutions, he offered promise.

Sophie had seen an article in a local paper about a man who believed in supernatural sightings. When she met him, he convinced her that he saw the things she saw. And he convinced her that she had potential for good. She had a powerful gift. He believed in her gift. Hartman offered an apprenticeship with him, and to join his group of gifted seers. She thought about his proposal night and day, even as she was settling into her current job. Hartman was offering more than a living. He was offering meaning. A purpose.

Again, the movie *The Matrix* influenced her thinking. She could be like Neo, the hero who could see beyond the veil that blinded the people around him. She could be a sort of superhero like Neo.

But that grandiose ambition pinched and dug into her. Had Hartman planted it in her? There was an element of revenge to those fantasies. She could show the world. She could prove they had all been wrong about her. She wasn't crazy. She wasn't a liar. She was gifted. She was powerful.

Sophie went to a meeting in the library of that old converted mansion. The tall, yellowed columns on the broad front porch of the gothic building almost prevented her from entering. It was cartoonish. A joke. A secret meeting in a creepy old mansion?

Ultimately, that was what stopped her. The creep factor. Every wall of that mansion seemed to be crawling with spirits. Most were small and merely grotesque. And they kept their distance from Sophie at first, unlike the insects in the hospital. Her instinct to turn and run rose and fell. Fear that she would alert the predatory DNA in those creatures restrained her urge to flee.

The biggest beast in the place sat in the chair with Maxwell Hartman. The other people in the circle—people sapped of spirit and drive, pale followers subjugated to the will of their master—evoked pity and not fear.

Except for the fear that Sophie would become like them.

But Hartman spoke directly into her head, assuring her. "You will be like *me*, Sophie. Not like them." He could read her internal assessment of the sycophants with whom he had surrounded himself. "You can be even more powerful than me. You have a unique gift."

What more did she want to hear? What more could anyone offer?

There was one thing.

Love.

Her mother offered her love. And the path Hartman offered would take her away from love. Her mother and her friends didn't fit in that transformed identity. Even Crystal wouldn't support Sophie becoming like that mental dictator.

She knew Hartman could detect her deception even as she withdrew from him. "I'll get back to you. It's a big commitment."

She loped toward the front door with strained strides. That biggest ghost-like presence followed her, though Hartman remained in the library. His giant spirit guide accompanied her, but it didn't pass out the door when she did. It didn't go with her to her apartment.

One of those dark little things did add itself to her entourage. And she was sick for three weeks after that meeting. A strange viral infection that doctors couldn't identify.

Her mother had prayed for her. She lit candles at church.

Sophie committed herself to staying away from Maxwell Hartman.

The sickness eventually lifted, and she forgot about him.

Until he began to interrupt her sleep at exactly 3:33 a.m. every day. Those nighttime terrors had been what finally drove her to seek help. That was why she agreed to meet with Detta. And then to go back to see her again.

The train lunged to a stop and the doors slid open. She recognized her stop just in time, launching out of her seat and through the doors, evading their attempt to bite her in two.

She stumbled on the way down the steep stairs, grabbing the paint-chipped railing more tightly to save herself. Where was her guardian? Was he close enough to catch her if she fell? Was that question evidence of an even deeper insanity?

Coping skills. That's what she'd learned in therapy over the years. The last round, in her twenties, had dug a tunnel through her life that she could follow. A sustainable solution. Was it safe to climb out of that tunnel now? Into the light? Safer than the darkness haunted by the spirit guide of Maxwell Hartman?

Today—at least for today—she was going to keep her head down and make it through. One foot in front of the other.

She glanced down at her feet as she strode toward work, her feet clad in Converse All-Stars.

One was gray. The other was green.

"*Dang.*"

Out with Kimmy

Until Kimmy texted her around lunchtime, Sophie had forgotten she promised to go out that night. In head-down mode, she couldn't fulfill that promise. But before she started tapping a reply on her phone, she thought about Kimmy. She was the friend who demanded the least and offered an escape from the demands of others. Despite the fact they had met in the psych ward, Kimmy was a good remedy for craziness. Usually.

As she finished accepting Kimmy's invite, she lifted her head and idly regarded the golden guy standing in the corner of her cube. As usual, he was really *in* the corner, embedded in the structure of the cubicle. At least that's how it appeared to her.

As she regarded him, a sort of 3D copy of the golden man separated. A pair of guards? An upgrade? But as soon as she flipped that flippant explanation over, an even stranger thought plunked into her head.

The second guy is for Kimmy.

Really? Was she supposed to be some kind of angel delivery service?

Whatever.

The bit of code she was supposed to compose from scratch that day surely took her twice as long as it should, and the result was a mess. She was still debugging when five o'clock hit. The usual Friday freneticism further muddled her head as critters clattered and pounced back and forth between cubes and up and down the aisles.

When she escaped after five fifty, late to meet Kimmy, the two guardians seemed to be hustling her out like a public figure ushered through a crowd of reporters.

Into a corner bar four blocks from her work, the two golden giants escorted her. One effect of this accompaniment was to distract Sophie from other entities flying overhead or riding on passersby. The outline of several beings registered, but it was easy to ignore them against the glow of her two companions.

And it felt like some people—actual human beings—gave her a wider path, stepping around the guards whom they presumably couldn't see. Three chatting women at the end of the bar fell silent when Sophie slipped by. She didn't try to answer the questions this raised. She was arrowing toward Kimmy.

Kimmy beamed her squinty smile at Sophie. Despite the juvenile name, Kimmy was older than Sophie's other friends. Pushing forty at least. But she would always be Kimmy, never Kimberly or just plain Kim.

Sophie landed on the stool next to her. At the same time, a flock was settling at the other end of the bar. With conscious effort, she pulled her attention away from those little demons. "Sorry I'm so late."

Kimmy swirled her drink. "Oh, don't worry about it. I've just been debating politics with the bartender. Didn't even notice you were late, dear." Her hair was cut a bit shorter, just off her collar and pulled behind her ears. Long golden earrings dangled there, swaying to emphasize Kimmy's words.

"Really? Debating politics?"

"Sure. He says …" A squawking from the beasts on the other side of Kimmy broke her explanation into fragments. "… whenever they can … the best way to recover … and that's why they're so expensive." Kimmy shook her head and finished her martini. "I totally disagree."

Sophie nodded at Kimmy and tugged her eyes away from the scuffle beyond her. She could imagine what her friend had said. She knew Kimmy's political concerns mostly centered on retail pricing and the availability of fashions from whatever country manufactured her latest obsession.

Puffing some of the tension off, Sophie rested her eyes on Kimmy in the way she wished she could rest her head. It might come to that—her head on Kimmy's shoulder—before the evening was over. Sophie was anticipating a regrettably large liquor bill by the end of the night.

"You look stressed. You need to go shopping." Kimmy chuckled, the last note of her laugh like a tiny accordion winding down.

"Shopping? Yeah, I suppose." Sophie didn't want to delve into her troubles—at least not so soon. "How are *you* doing? She signaled the bartender, who had just settled a pair of beer glasses on the bar to her left.

"Oh, I'm hanging in there."

Again, Sophie lost track of what Kimmy was saying. Her answer was obscured by the appearance of a bat-like creature above her head, dangling upside down from an invisible perch.

After the bartender took their orders, Kimmy talked about her work and some pressures there.

"You still going to therapy?" Sophie hoped Kimmy had finished what she was saying before being hit with that inquisition.

"Huh? Therapy?" She giggled and shrugged. "I just go to the NA meetings. Those work for me. I'm a regular with the druggies." Kimmy's self-serve pharmaceuticals had landed her in the hospital at the same time twenty-four-year-old Sophie admitted herself. Kimmy hadn't dragged herself to the emergency room like Sophie had. An ambulance crew had saved her life.

"Oh. That sounds good." Something dripped from that bat thing. Sophie had to force herself not to wince. She didn't want whatever that was to land on her. Actually, she didn't want it to land on Kimmy either.

And here it was, the mall of new possibilities to which Detta had brought Sophie. In the past, Sophie had simply been an observer. A spectator. An *unwilling* spectator. She couldn't do anything about what she saw. It was enough to try to ignore it. Even pausing to wish a friend wasn't carrying a semi-transparent parasite had hardly ever happened before. "You're not using again, are you?" Okay, that was pushy and nosey.

Kimmy looked away and then back. She giggled much less comfortably. "Why would you ask that?"

Sophie checked for her guardian. He was to her left behind the bar. He had been obscured by Kimmy and another patron. When she focused on him, he shone through, his light penetrating everyone and everything. And then there was his clone. That other one was seated on the stool just past Kimmy. Glancing at him seemed to turn up his dimmer switch too.

"You know that I see things, right?" She couldn't remember how much of this she had explained to Kimmy and at what stage in her life. It had been a while, probably.

"See things? You mean, like, those visions? Wait! Did you have a vision of me ... doing something?"

The bat thing spread its wings.

The guardian behind Kimmy stood from his stool and eased right next to her. He was looking at the bat thing too.

"Sophia! You're freaking me out. What are you seeing?" Kimmy drew Sophie from the supernatural drama by using her formal name, but that only diverted Sophie's gaze for a second.

"I'm seeing things happening around you that make me worry you might ... be having some kind of trouble."

"Huh." Kimmy bowed over her fresh drink. She slid a small napkin back and forth on the smooth bar. "Uh, well, I'm not using ... this week, anyway. But it's been hard lately." She pushed her golden-brown hair away from her face, avoiding Sophie's eyes.

Sophie suspected Kimmy would be some combination of brunette and gray if she stopped coloring.

Kimmy angled her large brown eyes toward Sophie and scowled gently. "You think I'm in trouble?"

"Well, I don't know anything you don't know, but I just wonder if you could use some help. I sorta found this thing that seems to help me, though I'm really just trying to get used to it." Wow, that was so half-baked.

"What? You found a new therapy?"

"No, more of a spiritual thing." She wondered if she could call Detta for instructions. But maybe even Detta didn't know how this worked. She seemed to operate without a complete explanation much of the time.

The pleading look from Kimmy and the wrinkles around her eyes between the clumps of eye makeup decided it for Sophie. She told Kimmy as much as she could in a crowded bar.

They moved to a table when one freed up in the corner near the bathrooms. And they ate bar snacks and drank martinis, though not as many as Sophie had planned.

Kimmy's watery eyes expanded and expanded until Sophie thought they might pop. Of course they didn't literally pop. Neither did they splash tears into her drink. But the end of Sophie's story sank both women into a staring silence.

"I always knew you had something special, even if I didn't really get it." Kimmy stirred what was left of her third martini with a stubby finger that belied her slim figure.

"*Special* can go both ways." Sophie did air quotes. "But I'm thinking maybe I've found a use for it, after that church lady got free of her cough." Sophie was getting cold next to the brick wall. Slinking back into her jacket, she tried not to look like she was anxious to leave. "Just cold."

"So what do you think you can do for me?"

Sophie glanced toward the two guardians who stood like bathroom bouncers behind Kimmy. "Well, I think I'm supposed to leave you with a guardian … uh … an angel, like the one that follows me." She glanced up at the bat thing still hanging magically above Kimmy, not even pretending to use the coat rack a few feet away. "I think it'll help you with your … problems."

"Problems?"

"I've been seeing this …" What good would it do to tell Kimmy what was hovering over her? It would probably give her nightmares. "I mean, I've been appreciating my guardian's help when I come upon some of those nastier creatures."

Kimmy shook her head. She was no more inclined to fake understanding than any of Sophie's other friends, Detta included. "So what do you have to do?" She chuckled airily. "Is there some kinda ceremony or something?"

Sophie shrugged. "I have no idea. Maybe you just have to say you accept him accompanying you—accept him as your guardian."

"Him? Is it a guy angel?"

"Well, he looks pretty masculine, but what do I know about angel gender identity?"

Snickering in the back of her nose, Kimmy peered furtively left and right.

"He's right behind you." Sophie raised her head toward the serious golden man that probably identified as an angel, at least.

Kimmy shivered visibly. "Uh, okay. I accept my guardian angel." She was grinning when she started that simple statement, but her eyes rounded and the corners of her mouth started to turn down before she was done.

"Well, he looks happy about it. At least as happy as I've ever seen my guy look. My mom's angel is much jollier."

Kimmy wavered in her seat, as if she had downed twice as many cocktails and no snacks. The empty appetizer baskets and nearly empty plate of bruschetta weighed against that interpretation. At least half sober, she still tottered forward so far that Sophie feared she would catch her hair on fire in the little centerpiece candle.

"Hang on." She reached across the table and propped one of Kimmy's shoulders.

Giggling again, Kimmy sat up straighter. "Angel drunk, I guess."

Hovering a Bit

Detta left a voice message. "Well, Sophie, I don't wanna be one of those controlling-mother types, but I would really be glad for you to call me. I could even figure out the texting thing if that's what works for you. I just wanna make sure you're okay after this week."

What was she really worried about? That Sophie had come to some harm, preventing her from taking Detta's calls? It was Friday night. A girl would be out with friends or with a man. Did Sophie have a man? A boyfriend?

"None o' my business." Detta shuffled toward her living room, cup of tea in hand. The first flurry of an early season snowstorm was ticking against the front window. This one was supposed to pile a load of white stuff on the city. Detta lived north of the city. They were supposed to get hit even harder.

Her phone buzzed. Just once. *Oh, a text message.* Her ceramic mug settled safely on the little table next to her chair—atop the *Guideposts* and the newspaper—she pulled her phone from her sweater pocket. It took two tries. That homemade sweater, from her late sister, had pockets too small to warm her hands but just perfect to stow a phone. An alert said she had a message from Sophie.

"**Thanks for asking, Detta. Just saying goodbye to my friend Kimmy. She just accepted her guardian angel. I'll tell you about it.**"

"What? You *better* tell me about that, girl. And don't leave me hangin' for long. Just accepted her guardian angel? How does that work?" Interesting that Sophie hadn't called Detta before doing this angel-accepting ministry.

It didn't sound like Sophie was giving up on seeing angels. But could she really help someone accept their guardian angel? Shaking her head at herself, Detta carefully lifted her mug to her lips. "Well, I accept my angel, and any other messengers God wants to send my way." She sipped her tea and remembered something her mother used to say. "*When you go astray, your angels go away.*"

That rule seemed a serious threat to a little girl. Who would want their angels to go away? The holy ones protected her from nightmares. They watched her when crossing the street in front of their slumping old house in Mississippi. They kept the Klan away from the door—most of the time. Of course the implication was that some man who was dragged behind a car or hung from a tree outside of town had gone astray. That's why his angels didn't protect him.

To grown-up Detta, that all sounded like a world without God.

She had watched, at least for a little while, a TV program about people who saw angels. One woman talked about it as if it was just people and angels in the world. Nothing about the devil and not even much about God. Jesus? No mention.

"Lord, I need your wisdom in this. Help me to be wise for Sophie's sake." Hmm. Wisdom. That was in Sophie's name, wasn't it? Maybe that was a good thing to pray for *her*. Maybe Sophie was supposed to have extra wisdom about things like angels and demons and even Jesus. "Let it happen for her, Lord."

Her phone buzzed again. Sophie again. That was when Detta realized she should have responded to that first text message.

"Are you there?"

Detta had seen Anthony do this lots of times. How did it go? He had tried to show her again recently. Could she just start typing on that little keyboard? It took her a few minutes to compose the broken message, accidentally sent in two parts.

"Yes sophie I am here sorry I forgive forgot to answer before sounds like good news and very interes … sorry sent that by accident not sure exactly how to work this thing call me if you want to talk about it"

A few minutes later, Detta's phone jingled with an incoming call. "Hello, girl. Thanks for calling me. Sorry if I was buggin' you with my phone message."

"Oh, I don't mind. I know I must have worried you this morning."

"Yes. You sounded like you were ready to give up—at least give up on something." It occurred to Detta now that she might just be afraid Sophie was about to give up on *her*. Was she getting too invested in hearing her stories about angels?

"I really was thinking it was getting to be more trouble than it's worth. But then I saw Kimmy for drinks after work, and I could see this bat thing hanging over her and dripping this stuff. And I thought maybe she was using drugs again, so I got really worried. Sort of intervention-mode, I guess."

"And you intervened with an angel?" Detta's voice jumped an octave or two.

Sophie giggled sharply, a surprising response from her. "Actually, it really felt like that—like I was supposed to deliver an angel to her." She slowed down, perhaps walking as she spoke. "And that golden guy went with her when we left the bar. My guy is still with me, of course."

"Well, I was wondering if you have a boyfriend. Sounds like you *do* have a man in your life."

"Ha. Yeah. I like this big handsome guy. But he seems kinda reserved. Not talkative at all."

"That can be a blessing." Detta chuckled.

Sophie hummed a bit. "I was wondering, with Kimmy, if it was really me delivering that angel, or if I was just being the messenger, sent to tell her he's available."

Sophie's more thoughtful tone sobered Detta. "I always had the impression that everyone already has a guardian angel, but I can't quote a verse that proves it. Some of what we know about angels, or think we know, comes out of the culture around us, really. And how reliable could that be?"

"Yeah. And what about ... well, Jesus? It's not just angels and bat things. I thought I actually saw Jesus sitting in my living room."

That raised a big grin on Detta's face. "I don't doubt you did. You have a very unusual gift. You're a seer. And a discerner of spirits. There's no greater spirit than the Spirit of Jesus." She held her breath, sure she had pushed into a corner where Sophie would feel trapped.

"Yeah. Something to think about."

It was getting late for Detta. A bit of reading before bed was all she had planned for the night. She suspected this wasn't so late for Sophie, but her young friend was sounding tired too. "You going home now?"

"I am. I'm walking in the snow and watching these lights mixed in with the big flakes. It's almost like candles falling from the sky. My guardian—my *angel*—is watching them and almost smiling."

Detta clung to her tea, fighting those chills that often got stirred during a conversation with Sophie. "Oh, my. Well, praise Jesus for that."

"Yeah. It's really something."

"Goodnight, Sophie."

"Goodnight, Detta. And thanks."

"Oh. You're quite welcome, of course. You've given me lots to think about. And I really care what happens to you."

"Thanks."

"Goodbye."

The air in Detta's house was mostly warm, though a little draft was sneaking in at the window. Her shivers weren't all about angel sightings. "Like candles from the sky? Are you doing that just for Sophie's entertainment? Hmm. It might be a way to get her into the fold." She breathed a long airy laugh. Here she was offering God advice on how to reach Sophie. Suddenly Detta was the expert on converting a young Hispanic woman with a pierced nose, black nail polish, and tattoos?

Detta shook her head at herself.

Glory in the Kitchen

It was originally supposed to be just Anthony at his mother's house for Sunday supper. His mama called him that afternoon to make sure it was okay if Sophie was there. He was pretty sure his mom wasn't trying to fix him up with that weird angel chick. The girl wasn't even a Christian, and his mom was strict about things like that.

At first he had just been there as translator, or cultural liaison, or something. Trying to relate to Sophie in ways his mother couldn't. But his mama didn't need that anymore. Anthony felt like *he* was the oddball when those two started talking about angels.

But what about that guy he helped on the way home from work? His mom thought that guy was an angel.

He pulled his car up in front of her house, icy snow crunching under his tires. If it wasn't for his mother, he wouldn't need a car most weeks. And there was Sophie's car in the drive. It was probably the same for her. She probably only had that car for visiting her mother.

Was Sophie's mom crazy like her? Or maybe crazy like *his* mom? Crazy wasn't the right way to think about it, of course. Not politically correct. At least he wouldn't say stuff like that out loud.

"Hello, dear." His mama turned toward the back door and spread her arms for a hug.

Sophie gave him a sideways smile from the doorway to the living room. She said it too. "Hello, dear."

He smiled at the joke. "Hello, Sophie. Mama." He kissed his mother on the cheek.

"You gonna tell Sophie about the angel you saw this week?" His mother turned toward the sink.

"You didn't tell her already?"

"We got more important things to talk about than you, my boy." His mother grinned at him over her shoulder.

He shook his head at his mother's feistiness.

Sophie was staring at him. She had purple highlights in her hair, framing her face. Her otherwise-black hair just reached her tight leather jacket. Was that purple there before?

"Uh, well, I didn't say he was an angel. That was your idea."

Dropping off his shoes next to Sophie's by the door, he craned his neck to see what was cooking. He caught sight of pork chops in a big frying pan. His nose had found them already, savory and peppery. His mother was spooning green beans into a serving dish. Sophie seemed poised to take the dish off the small square of counter next to the stove. She had also tipped her head toward him, as if poised for his story.

He told her about his encounter with the guy named Raphael, trying not to pad the evidence that the guy was anything other than a helpful old man.

"You really think an angel could look just like a regular person?" Sophie wasn't asking Anthony, of course. She was setting the green beans on a hot pad on the table and looking at his mother.

"It says in Scripture that some folks have hosted angels unaware of doing it. That makes it seem pretty likely that angels look like people sometimes." His mother turned off the last stove burner.

"Can they do that, like, whenever they want to? Or are there different types? Some that look like people and some that look like flying things with all kinds of colors and lights?" Sophie let her eyes drift toward the back door.

Anthony turned to look behind him. If he spent more time with Sophie, maybe he could learn to resist that urge. He felt foolish for looking. He wasn't going to see anything.

His mother was still half focused on the meal. She forked thick pork chops onto a big serving plate. "I have no idea. There's so much that Scripture doesn't tell us about these things. And my way of thinking used to be that the silence meant we weren't supposed to think about them too much. Maybe that's true for most of us, but I don't know why God would give you sight to see spirits if he didn't want you to know anything about 'em."

Anthony slipped into his usual chair at the table. "What if it's not from God? What if it's from ... something else?"

"Like what?" Despite the quick reply, Sophie sounded more curious than offended.

He twisted his mouth and shrugged. "I don't know. But don't some folks that aren't church people see things?" Now *he* was looking at his mother for answers.

But Sophie replied. "Sure. I've talked to a couple psychics who say they see things. I don't know for sure, but some of what they said seemed believable, sorta like what I've seen." Again, she glanced toward the back door.

He couldn't resist any longer. "What? What are you seeing over there?"

"Uh." Sophie shifted her dark chocolate eyes toward Anthony.

Of course she was measuring how much to tell him. He didn't blame her. He hadn't stopped being a skeptic. She certainly knew that. As she pondered, he tried to make his face friendlier, softer. More like his mother's. But that was a difficult makeover without a mirror. He ended his self-conscious contortions with a little grin.

Sophie finally answered. "Well, it's like a gathering of things over by the door. There's the golden guy that follows me around, a reduced version of the tough-looking guardians that come inside this house when I come in sometimes, and these two other sparkly ones. One of them is bluish, and one is reddish."

Anthony's empty stomach flipped, his head light and his palms suddenly sweaty. "Oh, weird." He caught his breath. "I just had this memory from somewhere. Maybe not a real memory. Maybe from a dream." He let it percolate to the surface. "This blue bird and this red bird. They were, like, flying with me. I guess I was flying." He stopped babbling. What was he saying?

His mama was staring at him. "You never told me anything about that."

"It was ... just a dream I had. Or maybe one I sometimes have. I feel like it's something I recognize when it comes to me—like I'm always in it or going back to it." He stopped himself from swearing. He was sounding as bizarre as the punky girl staring at him across the kitchen table.

Sophie looked above his shoulder and nodded. "Yeah. The blue one and red one look like birds, sorta. And they remind me of you." She stopped there. Everyone was taking turns staring at each other now.

"They look like Anthony?" His mama managed to land the plate of pork chops on the table.

"I know that was a weird thing to say." Then Sophie rocked back slightly in her chair. "Oh! This is so cool."

"What?" Anthony's skin was crawling with electricity. He had his hoodie on over two shirts, but shivers prickled up his arms.

"They're, like, whirling around together, like a dance. Gold and silver and red and blue, and, like, painting colors. And I think it's about something. They're doing something. Trying to communicate maybe."

His mama stared toward the back door. "The glory of God!" Her awestruck voice turned Anthony's shivers into a quick convulsion.

"Oh!" Sophie nearly screamed. "Lights. Big lights. More. More lights."

A serving fork clattered to the floor. "Glory to God!" His mother had her hands in the air. "Thank you, Jesus."

Anthony looked at her and laughed. But it wasn't mockery, not making fun of his mother's unhinged behavior. The laughs just popped out of him.

"God? Glory?" Sophie seemed to be trying Google searches with her voice, though her phone was nowhere in sight. She grabbed the table as if to keep from tipping over backward. The legs of her chair were tapping on the kitchen tiles.

"Oh, thank you, Jesus!" His mother had one hand on the table and was lowering herself to her knees.

"*Don't do that, Mama.*" Anthony could only think it. He couldn't speak. Maybe he wasn't allowed to say that. Rebuking his mother for worshipping God in the kitchen? How dare he?

The back of his head tickled, and there was a warmth from behind him. The back door and the kitchen window were there. They were no heat source, not on a freezing day. "What is goin' on?" He said it even though he didn't expect an answer. And he really knew what was going on. He didn't *need* an answer.

A bunch of angels and the glory of God had showed up in his mama's kitchen.

Of course.

Who Am I, Then?

Lots of things in Sophie's life were uncertain. Even her own identity was in flux. She was raised by a church-going mother who had rejected Sophie's visions, not recognizing them as angel sightings. Sophie had confounded the psychics and psychiatrists with the persistence with which she saw the impossible. She was a college-educated computer programmer. A woman in her thirties in the twenty-first century. She was half Puerto Rican, half Mexican. She was a lot of things. Including a pretty good dancer.

But she wasn't a church lady. She wasn't a holy roller. She wasn't a Bible thumper. She wasn't the kind of woman who kneels in her kitchen saying things like "Glory to God" and "Thank you, Jesus."

Of course Detta didn't tell Sophie she had to join her in doing that. Maybe she didn't think Sophie was that kind of person either.

And what did Anthony think? He hadn't said more than ten words after that explosion in the kitchen. At least not more than ten sentences. Maybe he was thinking *he* wasn't that kind of person. But he hadn't seen those sparkling beings twirling around the kitchen. He just had her word to go by—and his mother's reaction.

Detta's enthusiasm was pretty contagious. Maybe especially because she *didn't* push Sophie or Anthony to follow her example.

And why shouldn't Sophie have dropped to her knees and worshipped like Detta? Except that Detta was surely looking beyond the angels, worshipping something else. If Sophie raised her hands as she watched the dazzling display of lights, wouldn't she just be worshipping them? No one seemed to think that was the point.

These questions recalled a neighbor lady from when Sophie was small. Mrs. Gutierrez used to invite her and Hector over for fresh-baked cookies. The lonely old lady often clung to her as Sophie ate her cookies. Hector just stared with his large round eyes, watching their neighbor pet his sister and croon about angels and God's blessings on an innocent girl.

Sophie didn't feel innocent. She took things away from Hector when her mother wasn't watching. Her father probably left because Sophie was so hard to manage. Sophie felt anything but innocent. And the scary monsters that haunted her bedroom at night and threatened people around her by day were a wicked curse, not a blessing.

"Tell me, Sophie, what do you see now? Do you see my guardian angel?" Mrs. Gutierrez's house always smelled sharp, chilies of various kinds and various strengths. A string of red peppers hung drying in her kitchen most of the time.

Sophie could recall, all these years later, a metallic being with his hands behind his back. He looked like a statue, stuck in that position. He didn't look very powerful. But Sophie didn't want to insult Mrs. Gutierrez or her guardian angel. So she crafted a grand description of golden wings and shining white clothes, like the pictures she had seen at church. Mrs. Gutierrez sighed and wept at those stories, at those lies. And Sophie *knew* she wasn't an innocent little girl. She wasn't good. She would certainly burn in hell with those charred things that threatened her with their claws and teeth dripping with blood.

Sitting at her own kitchenette table, a cup of coffee cooling at her elbow, Sophie withdrew from those memories—memories of deception. She would never lie to Detta about what she saw. She didn't fear the truth now. She despised it at times, regretted it often, but she wasn't afraid of letting Detta know about any of it.

Still, she hesitated to update her new friend on what she had seen early this morning. The spectral appearance of Maxwell Hartman had woken her again. She had started to hope that her guardian was keeping him away, or maybe just keeping her asleep during the nightly haunting.

Not this time. She woke to an ethereal glow above her bed, like the moon reflecting the light of the distant sun. But it wasn't a celestial body. It was a head. A head without a body. And he was even angrier this time.

"You have betrayed me and betrayed your gift. Wasting time with these church people will dull your sight. Come back to me now before it's too late. Come back and find out what you've been missing, Sophie."

She answered him with spoken words this time. "No way. Never. I don't want anything to do with you. Go away!"

As if the boldness of her resistance was too much for him to bear, his eyes flashed furiously. "You cannot send me away. You don't have the authority. You belong to me." He glared his challenge. He seemed to be just barely restraining his spite.

She shook her head, then looked around the room. Where was her guardian? "Help. I need some help here."

As if in response to her plea, the detached head glowed red, and a stream of dark liquid began to drip from its gaping neck. "You will never receive the kind of authority you seek unless you come to me. Come back, so I can protect you."

"No. Never."

A stench filled the air, and then the head of Maxwell Hartman faded to invisibility.

At that moment, her guardian appeared next to her, standing by her bed. He held out a hand as if offering her a lift out of bed.

But she couldn't move. How could Hartman do this thing every night? Why did the guardian allow it? Would he also allow Hartman to harm her, to make her sick again—or worse?

She didn't take that offered hand, if that's what it was. She was mad at her guardian. Her guardian angel? Really?

Sitting at her kitchen table later that morning, still dark outside, her phone buzzed. The text was an alert of a pending delivery. It served as a reminder to stop staring toward the living room windows and get ready for work. It would be a short week, Thanksgiving just three days away. Her hair was still damp, and she hadn't decided on what to wear over her leggings and sports bra. The bathrobe probably wouldn't do, even in the software development department.

On the train, Sophie read the news on her phone. Keeping her eyes down was her default mode. But the critters clinging to and dangling over her fellow passengers still framed her awareness. If she tried, she could see them without looking. A sort of seeing without eyes. But generally she didn't try.

The news was the same stuff. Same accusations. Same lies. Boring. And the nighttime visit of Maxwell Hartman tugged her attention away again and again.

She had her headphones on, the big over-the-head wireless ones. But something lifted her gaze to the couple sitting across the aisle from her. Young, probably Hispanic. The girl was caramel brown with big eyes and a pout to her puffy lips. She was angry. Body language might have been enough to communicate that feeling, but Sophie was seeing her body language magnified and multiplied. More bodies. This was the point where she used to drop her eyes and find something else on her phone. But today the scene wouldn't let her go.

A sexy little imp was literally standing on the girl's shoulder. She had her hands on her hips and seemed to be feeding the girl some helpful hints on how to do a proper scolding. On top of the boy's head sat a sad little animal, like a beaten puppy, only with a more human face. Above the couple was a glowing red creature with wings. It was what Sophie had always thought of as a real devil, even before she met Detta.

But that wasn't all. Sophie could feel something pulling at her, as if it had hold of her collar, dragging her into the fight. People, both standing and seated, generally wore earphones or earbuds. But some of them seemed to be watching the couple as well. Many looked like something had hold of *their* collar, pulling *them* into the conflict too.

The more the girl scolded, the exact words concealed by Sophie's headphones, the sadder the puppy got and the hotter the devil seemed to grow, like a smoldering piece of charcoal. And the hands grasping the collars of the others on the train became more solid and insistent. Then that scolding little chick appeared on other shoulders. She hopped fast, so it seemed like she was in more than one place at a time. Bigger dogs stirred and began to bark, mostly perched on men who were sitting near the quarreling couple. Those angry dogs seemed to be trying to rouse the cowering puppy to fight back.

Sophie swiped at the hand on her collar and sat up straighter. She turned her eyes without rotating her head and collected a branching and interlinking diagram, like a flow chart for a software development project. No one but the young woman and her boyfriend were speaking, and the boy didn't say much. But Sophie saw at least a dozen people participating in the angry accusation-and-answer session via their spiritual accomplices. Many of the women carried little critters that obviously appreciated the girl's accusations. The boy's answers were weak. Creatures sitting with several men were upset about that.

Refocused on the visible humans instead of their critters, Sophie noted the scowls aimed at both the complaining girl and the cowering guy. Young men stared and then looked away. Older men scowled under heavy eyebrows. Women shook their heads and rolled their eyes. It was like seeing the puppets and the puppeteers at the same time. Sophie didn't like the show.

When the sign marking the platform for her train stop entered the corner of her eye, she stood, dropped her headphones to her neck, and grabbed the seat handle behind that couple. "Give it a break, sister. It's not helping." She spoke gently but firmly at the girl, then turned toward the guy. "You can do better than this. You don't deserve this sh—"

She stepped toward the doors as they slid open. She could feel the couple staring at her. Surely other eyes were also climbing up her back.

Sophie's knees quaked as she walked off the train platform. Her guardian was close at her side. Though she didn't feel him touch her or see him move to do so, his steps seemed to strengthen hers. She made it down to the street and turned the correct direction toward her office as the train resumed its path through downtown.

Like Maxwell Hartman, Detta seemed to think Sophie's gift could be useful. Her chronic cough was still gone, to prove that point. But Sophie was pretty sure any good that would come from her gift had to be better than harsh rebukes to fellow train passengers.

Maybe she could finally accept being the girl who sees angels, but she was still baffled about what she was supposed to do with that ability.

Lunch in the Library

On Tuesday, Sophie was still stewing about the Monday morning visit from Hartman's spirit and about that network of creatures on the train. Those disturbing events had kept her head down since. But inside that head, she was asking tons of questions.

She decided to take her questions to the city library, two blocks from her office. She picked up a Cuban sandwich on the way over and climbed the wedding cake of concrete stairs into the grand downtown library. She would keep her food in the paper bag until she found some books and a seat in the eating section on the second floor.

The thicker volumes might have contained the most information, but she avoided the most intimidating tomes. One of those seemed to have a snapping little reptile attached to it with a beak like a turtle and red eyes that pierced Sophie. No thanks. Only books without pets attached.

Her years of burying her mind under things to avoid the flying, flashing, or crawling creepies around her had honed her reading ability. She could skim and almost speed read. It was her own method.

With her sandwich carefully cupped in its paper wrapping to avoid dripping meaty juice, she flipped through the oldest volume she had found. A chapter titled "The Levels and Organization of Angels" drew her in. She read about archangels and commanders of angel armies. She scanned through biblical references, ancient philosophical arguments, and cultural legends. And she considered the possibility of a connected and hierarchical spiritual world.

A little gathering of creatures was lining up in front of her table as she read. They reminded her of a human wall for a soccer free kick. Some in that wall were defenders of something or other. Some were on her team, perhaps. Her guardian certainly was. Too bad she didn't have a ball handy. A hard shot into that wall would have felt good.

From a newer book by a Father somebody, she gleaned ideas about angels taken from cultures around the world. The most stunning evidence she found there was how widely angels were accepted, or at least beings like what Detta described as angels.

Sophie still couldn't think of a creature like the horned mantelope standing in front of her table as an angel—not even a dark angel. Creepy critters. That's what they were to her. But these books cataloged the broad acceptance of demons, devils, fallen angels, and evil spirits. Every culture seemed to include them. Even the modern technical cultures around the world maintained a fascination with supernatural beings through movies, literature, and thriving psychics and spiritual readers.

She had wondered, as a teen, whether she could make good money telling people about the fairies, beasts, and gods hanging around them. But where that would lead had always scared her, like a bottomless well. Maxwell Hartman had come along later to show her what was in the inky depths of that well—at least some of it.

Her sandwich was being neglected and was losing its appeal as it grew cold. She had to get back to work. As flexible as her work schedule was, people still complained if she was out to lunch too long. Not that that had happened more than once before.

Her longest previous lunch was also about angels and demons. It was soon after she took this job at the marketing firm. Her stomach seemed constantly to curdle and cramp. At first she had thought she was pregnant. A trip to the gynecologist kept her too late for even a long lunch hour.

Later that same week, alone in her new apartment, she had twisted and sobbed under the pressure mounting inside. She had tried to vomit, but nothing came. She tried to eat, but nothing satisfied. Not pregnant. No evidence of an ulcer or other serious stomach ailment. Still something built, something intensified. Until she screamed.

Deep in the night, she woke to the sensation of something trying to crawl out of her middle. When she saw the mammalian thing writhing half in and half out of her, she screamed. She yelled some version of "Get out of me!" And apparently it did. That ended the stomach ailment and canceled a couple more doctor's appointments. Without the nighttime revelation of that furry thing, she would have continued to assume she just needed to find the right doctor. A witch doctor, as it turned out.

That was a few months after she fled from Hartman and his little psychic club, a couple months after she recovered from that virus. Had that alien in her belly been related?

Back at work that afternoon, she was called into a meeting with Janice, Charlie, and Tammy—Janice's assistant. They were working on a website for a local construction company. Sophie positioned herself so she could stare out the window in case the other three brought a distracting array of cling-ons with them, which they usually did.

Tammy sat behind her laptop, her back to the tall windows, tapping out meeting notes. Sophie could see a flaming arrow piercing the display of the notebook computer. It still worked, even with that fiery projectile penetrating the display. Amazing. What was that about?

Cursing and backspacing, Tammy slumped lower in her seat. A black figure, like a cast iron robot, appeared. It was pressing down on her shoulders. A little guy with a small bow and arrows was sitting next to Janice, aiming one of those arrows at Tammy. It hit her chair, and she squirmed.

The close connection between that arrow and Tammy's squirm made Sophie squirm. Also squirmy was the way that arrow seemed to grow after hitting the chair. Then that archer turned its aim toward Charlie.

The same old dumpy imp that dragged around after Charlie was quaking in fear, like in an old Looney Tunes reel. The archer narrowly missed the whimpering lump.

Charlie was whining about the unreasonable requirements imposed by the client and appeared to be feeding his fat little friend as he did so.

Then Sophie heard her name.

"What do you think, Sophie? Is it really that hard?"

She wasn't ready to field questions. If she had been ready, she wouldn't have thrown Charlie out the twelfth-floor window like she did. "No. It's not that hard. Not so unreasonable." She winced in Charlie's direction as soon as she finished that betrayal. She wasn't really Charlie's friend, but she wasn't in the habit of roasting him in order to warm up a conference room.

"Really? See, Charlie? Sophie doesn't think it's unreasonable either." Janice glanced at Sophie, perhaps a bit surprised by what she was hearing.

The little guy with the arrows stood up and took aim at Sophie. She leaned back and looked for her guardian. After glancing over her shoulder, she turned back in time to witness the perfectly timed interception of a little arrow. And, instead of landing and expanding, it disappeared in the hand of her guardian.

That was when Sophie noticed a couple other guardians in the corners of the room. Did she have three guards for this meeting? That seemed excessive. Maybe it was a slow day elsewhere. But that clumsy speculation fell facedown before the thought that the other folks in the room might have guardians. Wasn't that what Detta had said? Didn't everyone have a guardian angel?

Checking first that Janice and Charlie were occupied with their "yes, it is—no, it isn't" argument, Sophie nodded her head at two of those guardians, small and dim in the corner. Her attention toward them seemed to work like hailing a cab. As if they were coming from a far greater distance than would fit in that conference room, they both grew considerably larger as they approached the table.

Sophie also noted that Tammy's typing had ceased. She turned and found the assistant staring at her. Tammy must have seen Sophie call for that cab. Was she thinking they should share it? She was probably thinking Sophie was nuts. Sophie might not contest that, but it didn't stop her now.

Instead of tipping her hand by tipping her head again, Sophie tried telepathic instructions to the guardians. "*Please help the people you're supposed to be guarding.*" Pretty generic, but suitably strange for the situation.

"Sophie?" Janice was pulling her in again. In fact, there was a red rope around Sophie's neck, and a sort of machine was attempting to haul her through the table to Janice's side. Or something like that.

She answered without hesitating. "Maybe we can take a breather here and just cool the air a bit." To Sophie, it wasn't

The Girl Who Sees Angels

enough to get the guardians to engage. She wanted the humans in the room to cooperate too.

Janice's expression didn't say, "What a great idea." It was more of the "What are you talking about?" variety. But she did pause. She did take a breath or two. And a pair of guardians passed over the table and landed next to Charlie and Janice.

Tammy was still staring at Sophie. She should be taking notes. Sophie wished someone was filming—filming what the humans were doing and including what she saw the angels doing.

There was no hugging or high-fiving between the angels, as Sophie might expect from Janice's guardian, but the proximity of the two guardians seemed to relax the combatants a bit. And the guy with the arrows plopped down and dropped his bow at his side. The red rope was gone, and Charlie's chubby friend was lying down for a nap.

Tammy sat up straighter. She smiled at Sophie—a rare astrological phenomenon—and began to type again. Maybe she knew how to make an angel emoticon with her word processor.

ξ (/⁻ ᵥ ⁻)/°°₀☆

Detta, I Need to Talk

Sophie had Detta to explain things for her now. That was why she could bear to look at some of the alien creatures amidst the people on the train and in the office. At least Detta would treat her as if she wasn't making up these things. Would she judge Sophie, though, if she told her that Hartman was still appearing to her at night?

"I really need to talk to you. Do you have some time tonight?"

"Oh. I'm headin' to prayer meeting. Might run until late, like ten o'clock."

"Are you driving there? Maybe we can talk while you drive."

"Hmm. I don't know how to do that. And it's not that long a drive, anyway." She made little popping noises with her lips. "I could just leave the meeting early. Okay if I call you at nine thirty?"

"Isn't that your bedtime?"

"Close, but I was gonna stay up for prayer meeting anyway."

"Doesn't it make you fall asleep, bowing your head and closing your eyes when it's past your bedtime?"

"Well, we don't just bow our heads at our prayer meetings, girl. More like jumping and shouting. Hard to fall asleep when you're standing with your hands in the air. Though I guess I know some folks who can do it."

Sophie did a quick shake of her head. "I've never heard of a prayer meeting like that."

"Well, you can come by and take a look. You could sit in the back and just watch. And then we can drive back to my place and talk. It might be easier for me to stay awake if we talk in person."

"Oh. I don't know. Maybe a short phone conversation will be enough. I would feel weird watching your prayer meeting."

"Nobody would mind. We're mostly old folks that are done carin' what other people think."

Sophie snorted a laugh. "I hope I can be like that someday."

Detta chuckled back at her. "Okay. Well, I'll call you when I get home."

And she did. It was just past nine thirty. Sophie didn't have to drive out to the suburbs to talk to Detta, and she was grateful for that. The temperature was well below freezing, record cold for November.

"What's goin' on with you Sophie? You sounded urgent but not discouraged. I count that as progress."

Sophie leaned back on her couch and pulled her new fur-like blanket up to the middle of her chest. "Yeah. I'm not nearly as discouraged as last week. But that doesn't mean I know what to do about things that are happening to me."

"What happened?"

"Remember when I first met with you, and I said I was having scary visitations in the night? Well, those are still happening."

"Oh. I was wondering about that. Is it the same as before? A man's head hanging in the air?"

"Yes. I know for sure now that it's Maxwell Hartman, a psychic trainer I met with a couple times. I'm not sure why it wasn't clear to me way back when I first told you."

"Well, these spirits specialize in deception and keepin' things hidden. He mighta blocked you from realizing at first."

"Yeah. I suppose so."

"So it's just the same thing?"

"No. He keeps changing what he says. At first he was just trying to get me to come back, but now he's more threatening, especially about … well, about you and me talking. I don't think he wants me to have anything to do with church."

Detta inhaled and released a long sigh. Maybe it was too late for such a heavy topic. "When was the last time he appeared to you?"

"Sunday night. Or really at 3:33 Monday morning. It's always the same time."

"Is it every night?"

"Maybe not. I don't know. Maybe I sleep through it sometimes. And I was thinking my guardian was keeping him away some nights."

"Maybe he is. I don't think we can really understand all the things that go on in that realm. Not even you, Sophie."

"Yeah. Maybe I need to keep that in mind. I was mad at my guardian for the last time the head appeared. But what do I know? It was probably me who did something."

"Well, you are doing something. You're welcoming holy angels and exploring what God might want for you. That's something that's gonna stir things up in the spirit realm, like I was telling you the other day."

"Uh-huh. I remember." Sophie paused to rerun the current conversation to see if she missed the part where Detta was judging her for allowing the nighttime visitor, or for not telling her about it all along. Nothing there that she could find.

"What if we say a prayer over the phone together and tell that evil spirit to stop coming to you?"

"We can do that?"

"I think we can. We have the authority, you and me agreeing together."

"He said I didn't have authority."

"But you are in charge of your own life. You can say what goes. On the other hand, you know what I think about following Jesus. That would sure help with something like this."

"Yeah. I ... I expect you're right. But can you pray for me now, even if I'm not ready to decide?"

"Of course I can. I pray for you all the time. But we can agree together here and have more power over this thing because we're together on it."

Sophie agreed to let Detta pray.

When she was done, Detta coached her. "You can just say 'amen' to show that you agree with what I prayed."

"Oh. Okay. Amen." Sophie leaned back on the couch and stared blankly at the ceiling. "Is that what *amen* means?"

"It is."

"There's so much for me to learn."

"Don't you worry yourself about getting it all right all at once. It's jist a growin' process." Detta's Mississippi accent seemed intensified by the late hour.

"Thanks, Detta. I should let you go to bed."

"You're welcome, dear. And I appreciate that. But tell me what you're doin' for Thanksgivin'."

"It's the time we get to see my grandma on my dad's side. She's getting really old now, so others host the meal, but Mama and me go to see her and sort of pay our respects."

"No bad feelings about your dad goin' missing?"

"She lost a son just like I lost a father and my mom lost a husband. There's no blame."

"Good. That sounds real healthy. Well, have a good week and a good holiday, Sophie. Let's talk this weekend."

"Yes. Happy Thanksgiving, Detta."

"Happy Thanksgiving, dear."

A Holiday Gathering

Sophie opened the car door for her mother and closed it when she was safely seated. Wind twirled her hair against her earmuffs. It was still in the twenties, though the promise of forty-degree weather waited behind the pale gray clouds. Brilliant and clear against the dull air were the two guardians—her mother's and Sophie's. Each stood on their respective side of the car. Would they run along beside like Secret Service agents in a parade?

Seated now and reaching back to grab her seatbelt, Sophie noted two backseat passengers. One of them was new or at least different. And where were the others? Her usual entourage? "Huh." She vocalized her curiosity without meaning to.

"What is it, dear?" Her mother wore a light gray knit hat loose over her hair, which was done up in a bun for the holiday gathering.

"Oh, sorry. I didn't mean to say anything."

"Sorry for what? I don't know what you were grunting about."

"I wasn't grunting, just *huh*-ing."

"It sounded like grunting to me." Her mother regarded her from a three-quarters angle.

Sophie laughed as she put the car in reverse and checked her mirrors. A glance over her shoulder confirmed her count. Two in the back seat. But which two were those? One was probably the same old raggedy grump that had long been part of her crew. The other looked like a little girl with tears streaming down her face, only the tears weren't normal—dirty, not transparent.

Looking at her mother only briefly, Sophie sighed. "Do you really wanna know this stuff, Madrecita?" Sharing her revelations with Detta had opened the envelope in which she usually kept her visions tucked. But her revelations generally remained concealed.

"You know the answer to that, mija. You can tell me anything you want to tell me."

Was it a good time for this conversation? They were driving into the city, to the west side where they would be greatly outnumbered by the in-laws. She still tended to think of them as the outlaws, but all her uncles were out of jail now as far as she knew.

Her mother might have been reading her mind. "What else should we talk about as we drive? It is a long enough journey."

Sophie sighed. Then she explained that her gray crowd of followers was getting smaller. Perhaps down to two now. "But one of them seems different. I don't know if an old stalker changed, or if a new one just showed up. I don't know how that works."

"You have long known about these followers? They are always with you?"

"I don't know about always. I'm used to checking on them when I get in the car. Just out of habit. Generally, I'm trying *not* to see them. They don't seem to ever do anything, just tag along."

Her mother crossed herself and muttered a prayer.

Sophie saw her mother's angel peering in the window. He seemed concerned, or at least serious. Sophie was driving, so she didn't have opportunity to reevaluate the two in the back seat. The new one seemed to be doing something, but she couldn't figure out what.

"What if they are evil spirits?" Her mother had stopped praying. She spoke while still staring out the front window, her concern turning her voice but not her head.

"They look more sad than evil, to me."

"But maybe they are spirits of sadness."

For nearly thirty years, Sophie had been dismissing her mother's fears about her visions. Mostly those fears had been unhelpful, often misdirected. But her mother seemed more settled, less afraid. Concerned, certainly, but not so panicked. Instead of brushing her speculation aside, Sophie considered what her mother was saying. She looked in the rearview mirror and studied that crying girl for two seconds. The girl looked more like her mother.

"What if the new one back there is related to you and not me? She looks a bit like the childhood pictures I've seen of you."

"Do you think I am sad?" As soon as she asked that question, her mother's angel seemed to relax. He appeared to be hanging onto the sideview mirror now, floating along with the car. Would he look more concerned if the answer to her mother's question was no?

"Aren't you sad, Mama? Aren't you still sad about Papa being gone? And here we are going to see his family. And then there's Hector too?"

"Your father is dead. I am sure of that in my heart. And I am sad about that. I feel that sadness more on Thanksgiving, since it is the day we go to see your grandmother and the rest of his family. I think I am feeling some of that sadness." She breathed hard through her nose. "And for Hector as well. He would be with us, of course."

Sophie allowed her mother's answer to slot into her racetrack of thoughts. After a minute of silence, she spoke while keeping her eyes on the tollway. "I wonder if I have to be a church lady like Detta to understand this stuff. Or like you."

"Your friend and I have the same God, I believe. And I pray for you always, that you will find faith in Him. It will help you to see many things better, I think."

That settled Sophie into a familiar nook, tucked away from her mother's faith and hoping to go unnoticed by whomever judged such things. She didn't want to reject everything, just the part that seemed to come with fanged and frightening phantoms.

Similar motivations had kept her from Maxwell Hartman. No repeat performance by him since Detta prayed. Clearly church ladies had something to offer.

When they finally arrived at the large wood-frame house on the west side, Sophie could tell the yellow paint was new. The white trim was like fresh snow. Her uncle Herman must be doing well these days. He had never been in the gangs like her other uncles. He was the responsible son, not a driven drinker like Sophie's father. Her *abuela*, her father's mother, lived with Herman, her eldest.

"Sophie!" Her aunt Esme greeted her at the door. "Isadora, dear." Esme hugged Sophie's mom as soon as she released Sophie.

That left Sophie face-to-face with her grandmother. Grandma Ramos was shuffling more slowly than the year before. She had fallen and injured her hip this past spring, but she was moving without a walker or cane now. "Sophie, *mi amor*." She wrapped her spindly arms around Sophie's waist.

At least this grandma still recognized her. When Sophie and her mother went to see her mother's mother after decades away, that abuela had to keep clarifying who the young woman was. That was a hard trip back to Mayaguez, Puerto Rico, for so many reasons.

Her father's family was Mexican, mostly. Aunt Esme came from Venezuela, one of the exceptions. Another was Sophie's Aunt Kate, a blonde woman who still looked like the cheerleader she had been twenty years ago when she married Uncle Javier. Even though Javier had died in a car accident ten years ago, Aunt Kate still attended many of these family gatherings despite her sparse Spanish.

Kate hovered behind the first wave of greetings, raising a hand at Sophie from over Grandma Ramos's shoulder.

Sophie smiled in reply and tried to block out the fiery trio of beings hovering near her aunt. The tangle of vines that enveloped her grandmother were easier to cope with, old and brittle and much less animated than Kate's blazing little flock.

Turning away to find her mother amid the hugging arms and cooing greetings, Sophie spotted that sad little girl that rode in the back of her car. Though her mother was clearly oblivious, occupied with explaining the Puerto Rican food she had brought in a paper grocery bag, that girl stood next to her with one arm outstretched. She seemed to be trying to hold hands with her mother. Sophie shivered at the thought.

"You cold, cousin?" Jeremy bumped shoulders with her as Sophie drifted toward the living room. He was just a year older than her. They had often drifted into each other on the rising and falling tides at these gatherings.

"Hi, Jeremy. Yeah. I'm not ready for winter to be here so soon." Her evasion came naturally. No one in this family knew about Sophie's spiritual sight.

"Yeah. It makes you wonder why these old folks ever left the tropical sunshine of their homelands." Jeremy's hair and beard were black, but his skin was paler than most of the relatives. His mother, Esme, had been a beauty with milky skin, born of a wealthy family in her home country. Her parents had come to the US to escape their political enemies in the 1960s.

"Venezuela is no picnic these days." Sophie avoided discussing politics with this family, but she trusted Jeremy wouldn't turn a greeting into a forum.

Jeremy's reply got lost in her distraction over his evil twin. That's how Sophie thought of his alter ego that frequently faded into and out of her view. That shadow's arrival was apparently related to Jeremy's moods. Like Sophie, Jeremy had survived some very dark moods when he was a teen. That was when Sophie first saw his doppelganger. She no longer met Jeremy outside these annual gatherings, but he seemed to have changed little.

Uncle Herman hugged Sophie stiffly and kissed her cheeks. His gaze down his nose had become less self-conscious over the years, growing into his role as family patriarch, perhaps. Over his shoulder, Sophie watched a sad little girl reaching a hand toward her grandmother. Then a similar girl appeared next to the old woman and took that specter's offered hand. It was her mother's sad girl holding hands with one attached to her grandmother.

Was the sad girl always with her mother, invisible to Sophie most of the time? Where was her mother's guardian?

Golden and silver guards lined the walls in the entryway and into the living room. Some were small and dim, others brighter and large. Sophie's guardian was staring at her, a reassuring confidence in his eyes. Those eyes illuminated as she absorbed comfort from his vigilant attention. Her mother's guardian was getting crowded aside. His gaze was downcast a bit, no grin on his face now.

Distraction over the crowd of nonhuman beings at these gatherings had often segmented her interactions. Sophie offered generic responses in English and Spanish, like copies of conversations from previous visits. Those template replies generally sufficed with people she didn't see more than once a year.

Seated in the living room before the meal, a mixture of ethnic foods adding calories to the air, Kate made the most concerted attempt to connect with Sophie. Part of that was probably the language barrier between Kate and the older family members. Part of it was also sympathy. She and Sophie were both joined to this clan by a person who was forever missing from these gatherings.

"How've you been doing these days, Sophie?" Kate twitched. Giving up smoking a few years ago seemed to double that penchant.

How much this side of the family knew about Sophie's psychiatric history was unclear. It wasn't polite holiday conversation. She had missed the Thanksgiving gathering one year, in her twenties, when she was enrolled in a therapeutic day program. The crowd at the Ramos Thanksgiving intimidated her and kept her away that time.

"I'm good. How are you doing? Still working at the department store?"

"I'm a shift manager for my department now."

"That's good. Do they have good benefits?"

The three incendiary creatures, draped around Kate like animated holiday decorations, seemed to be trying to draw Sophie's attention. One of them even waved a flaming claw at her as if to say, "Over here, look at me, over here." Maybe these family members spoke so delicately to Sophie not because she had lost her father at an early age or her brother as a teen. Maybe it was their natural reaction to her constant distraction while they tried to talk with her.

Kate described her benefits, raises, and promotions, and some of the liabilities of her supervisors. She seemed a bit distracted too, glancing left and right, checking over her shoulder. Perhaps she was keeping track of who was in the room. She hadn't always had a comfortable relationship with all the in-laws. Javier had been the most caustic in a family of rebels and had enemies even among the siblings. Sophie could see one of Kate's imps trying to pull her head back and forth, as if in charge of vigilance.

When Aunt Esme called everyone to the table, Sophie stood and located her mother. She looked different. Somehow out of focus. Then Sophie realized the sad little girl had become superimposed on her mother, as if they had integrated. That prompted her to look for her own little stalker. She found two of them sitting in the chair she had just risen from. Two? Wasn't there only one in the car?

Of course, it wasn't a question of how that second critter got to the Westside just because he wasn't visible in the car. Her confusion was more about why those things came and went, appeared and disappeared. Sophie was still wondering about that when the family stood around the table holding hands.

Uncle Herman inclined his head toward his wife, as if to concede her the floor for the prayer over the meal. Sophie glanced around the room and surveyed the gathered spirits hanging over the table. Many of them looked like sad children, such as her mother was carrying. Some looked like violent monsters, though small and almost tamed. But all of that disappeared when Sophie focused on her aunt.

Esme was a stout woman, no longer the slender beauty of her youth. She had been the spiritual leader of the family since her mother-in-law began to hunker into her aging shell. Now she lifted her face to offer the prayer of thanks—in English. "O gracious God, we give thanks for your overflowing generosity. Thank you for the blessing of the food and especially for this feast today. Thank you for our home, family, and friends—especially for the presence of those gathered here." It might have been memorized, perhaps from a prayer book. But to Sophie, it was real.

Plump beasts hovering over the family shriveled like rotten apples as Esme spoke the blessing. And the guardians drew closer. The guardian nearest Esme glowed at her like molten bronze, intent on her words. That angel seemed more feminine, and much more expressive, than Sophie's. That observation led her to glance at her own guardian. He was nodding in affirmation, his face raised toward heaven.

What had been a crowd of half strangers gathered under dark clouds briefly became a family basking in a sunny glow, though the day was still gray and sunless. Esme had powered a light with her prayer, and the guardians in the room had become incandescent. Large or small, masculine or feminine, they all raised their heads like cats warming themselves in the first rays of the morning.

Pronouncing the *amen*, Esme nodded toward her husband, her smile fading fast.

Sophie saw a metallic beast insert itself between Esme and Herman. The guardian with Esme stepped back and dimmed. The cloud was back. And Sophie retracted her sensors.

Early that evening on the way home, her mother allowed her head to rock on the headrest as Sophie aimed the car onto the tollway. The sad girl and the raggedy stalker were both in the back seat. Sophie could sense the guardians just above the car. She could see them through the roof if she concentrated on them. But she was driving. And she was concentrated on her mother's mood. Her madrecita's hands were tucked between her legs even though she wore brown leather gloves.

"You ever think we should stop going to Thanksgiving at their house?"

Her mother let her head turn in stages toward Sophie. "Oh, I don't know. I don't mind them. Your uncles are looking older now—not so much like your father anymore. Though Jeremy looks something like him from just before."

Sophie had forgotten about that. It had been years since her mother had mentioned the pain of seeing her lost husband in his brothers' faces. "I'm sorry, Mama. It must be hard." She inhaled deeply. "I'm not saying you shouldn't go, or that I won't go with you. Just wondering if it's worth it."

"Maybe when your abuela passes." Her mother was staring out the windshield again.

Sophie had hardly said a dozen words to her grandmother. Even the hugs were uncomfortable, the old woman so thin and almost lifeless. And then there were those tangling vines.

"Is abuela still sad?" Sophie knew the answer, she just wanted to hear what her mother would say.

"Sad and angry. She used to be much more talkative, more joyful before your father left and Javier died. Pablo's time in prison was hard for her too. And Angelina hasn't been speaking to her mother for years. Your abuela is bitter about all that, I think."

Bitter vines? Was that what Sophie had seen on her grandmother?

Her guardian appeared just over the windshield. He focused on her eyes as if he was about to say something, but he didn't speak. Perhaps he was communicating, and Sophie wasn't tuned in. That intense gaze seemed to say something.

But all Sophie could do just then was shake her head and concentrate on the cold gray road. Making her way home in the natural world.

Another Kind of Gathering

Alone in her apartment on Thanksgiving night, Sophie got a call from Detta.

"How was your holiday, Sophie?"

"The usual. Me trying to ignore the gang of spirits hanging around a crowd of people I don't know very well. And this time paying a bit more attention to the different kinds of things attached to different people."

"Ah. That doesn't sound very festive. Well, I was calling to see if you and your mother have any plans for tomorrow. Anthony has the day off, and he and I usually get together to eat leftovers and just hang out. I was wondering if you and your mother would like to join us."

"Me and my mother?"

"Of course. I'd love to meet her."

Sophie dragged a doubtful breath. But her doubts themselves seemed doubtable. What could go wrong? Her mother and Detta could exchange God stories, and Sophie and Anthony could find some nerdy movies on cable. Everyone would be happy. "Uh, I'll ask my mother. You want us to bring some food?"

"Sure, bring whatever you have—leftovers, something you eat at the holidays. We brought home some fixin's from my cousin's house today, and I got a fresh turkey breast I'm gonna roast. We'll have a little feast and just put puzzles together and watch holiday movies."

It sounded cozy. "I'll ask my mom and get back to you before you go to sleep."

That second holiday gathering would contrast with the first in every way. The best part for Sophie was the smaller crowd, both mortal and immortal. Though her mother had worked hard that morning to make the pasteles, including going to the market to get the banana leaves and green bananas, she too was more cheerful than the previous day.

"Is this the first time, uh, Detta has asked to meet me?" Her mother was sitting up straight in the passenger seat, checking the passing houses in the neighboring suburb.

"I think so. She's always been interested, but never said anything about hanging out together."

"Did she say it that way? 'Hanging out'?"

Sophie chuckled. "She did. I think sometimes the way she talks is from Anthony."

"He's a good son?"

"I do think he's a good son. At least as good as I am at being a daughter."

"You are a wonderful daughter to me."

They were near Detta's house, waiting at a stop light. Sophie checked the back seat again. Still no passengers. What did that mean? Were the critters taking the day off for some Black Friday shopping? They weren't in her face so much today. Sophie hoped that hanging out didn't mean she couldn't ask Detta a few questions about all this.

In her living room, Detta greeted Sophie's mother. "Hello, I'm Detta. I'm so glad you could come over."

"I'm Isadora. So glad to meet you. Sophie has told me so much about you."

To Sophie, her hands full with the pan of pasteles, her mother sounded like she was reciting an English lesson. She would get an A+ for this lesson, but Sophie would get a C- for her introduction skills. Her excuse, as usual, had to do with the others present.

Four guardians glowed golden-white in the middle of the room, a beam of light coming through the ceiling and casting a halo around the feet of the giants. Sophie stared at them until the heat of the glass pan penetrated the hot pads in each hand. She slipped between the guardians, ducking under their raised arms. She could feel Anthony watching her maneuver.

Breaking away from the awkward introductions at the door, he followed her to the kitchen. He cleared a spot on the counter. "Mmm. That smells good. What is it?"

"Pasteles. Sort of like Puerto Rican tamales with pork."

"Nice. What's that spice?" He inhaled deeply.

"Sweet chili peppers, I expect."

"Very nice. So your family does all, uh, Mex ... uh, Puerto Rican food on Thanksgiving?"

She stood up straight and faced Anthony. "Some of my family is Mexican, some are Puerto Rican. We have some traditional foods, but also turkey and stuffing for Thanksgiving. But my mama made these because Christmas is next. She's ready to get started, I guess."

Her mother and Detta were laughing about something, now squeezing into the kitchen behind the younger folks.

Anthony sidestepped and headed back toward the dining room. "You gonna do jigsaw puzzles or watch movies?"

Sophie was following. "Are those the only choices?"

"Family tradition in this house. But eating is top priority, of course. Wait till you try my aunt's sweet potato pie. Oh my." He rubbed his stomach like a little boy.

Sophie couldn't help smiling at the idea of Anthony as a little boy. With that thought, a dark green thing dashed over Anthony's head. The glimpse she caught reminded her of a military person—a helmet, some kind of weapon. Instead of puzzling over the meaning of that fleeting image, she grabbed an option from the limited ones on offer. "What kind of movies?"

"We get the Christmas season started with some classics. I like *Elf*, and Mama likes the Disney version of *A Christmas Carol*. Right now *A Christmas Story* is looping on one of the cable channels, so that's on."

"*A Christmas Story*? Is that the one with the dad who wins a lamp that looks like an exotic dancer's leg?"

"Ha. Yeah. Fishnet stockings and all." They stood in the living room now, the old movie from the '80s playing at low volume. "I usually watch the movies and make fun of 'em a bit, then come over and help Mama and whichever aunts are here with the puzzle."

"No aunts this year?" Sophie might have missed that part of the guest list.

"No aunts this year. There's only one of them left. It's just the four of us. That's what Mama wanted."

The two mothers were talking in the kitchen. A duet of laughter warmed Sophie and made her curious. "I had no idea how those two would get along." Relaxing her twist for looking at them, she turned back to Anthony.

He was checking out the action in the kitchen too, but he was still on the movies. "Hey, I bet your favorite Christmas movie is *It's a Wonderful Life*, what with the angels and all." His joker smile and wide eyes assured her that he wasn't serious. He wasn't wearing his glasses. Maybe he had contacts that didn't always last until supper—the only time of day she had seen him before.

She answered half seriously. "I've seen what your mother calls angels in all shapes and sizes. That chubby old white guy with a goofy grin may not be the usual profile, but it's not totally unbelievable to me. I just never see any of them that seem as confused and weak as him."

"Yes, but he hasn't got his wings yet, right?"

Sophie laughed. "Right." She followed Anthony toward the couch but diverted to Detta's recliner. "But don't you have problems with that movie, the way they portray the black maid and all?"

"Yeah. That's annoying, even offensive. But I told you I spend part of the day making fun of the Christmas classics."

"Ah. Yes. You did confess that."

The two women in the kitchen were deep in some discussion. Detta seemed to be interviewing Sophie's mom about her church.

"Speaking of confession ..." Anthony nodded toward the kitchen as Sophie's mother was saying something about Sophie going to Sunday services with her. "You still do that? Go to a priest to confess your sins?"

"I only went for a while when I was a kid. The priest told my mom not to bring me anymore."

"What? How's that possible?"

"Well, to me, the confessional was like this booth of truth. I just knew I had to tell exactly what I'd been up to. A lot of my sins had to do with having bad thoughts about people because of the evil creatures climbing on them or whatever. Or about people not believing me when I told them what I saw. I was usually hating somebody for that and wanting them dead."

"Ah. Yeah. You *would* have to confess that. So they said not to bring you back 'cause you were always talking about angels and demons?"

"I didn't call them that back then. My mom called them my visions. The priest didn't know what to think—until one time I told him about a vision I had of him."

"What was it?"

"I don't remember exactly. It was something bad though."

"Really? How could you not remember? You saw, like, some kinda devil hanging on your priest?"

"I've spent my whole life seeing these things. I can't remember all of them. I don't *want* to remember most of them."

The mothers were ambling into the room.

Anthony kept his focus on Sophie. "Do you have some of them you *do* want to remember?"

Sophie looked at her mother. "I do, actually. I remember this beautiful maiden that would stay with me after my mother said goodnight and led me in prayers. That glowing maiden gave me such peace and restfulness when I was little. It's the only way I could sleep at all, with all the other visions swirling in and out of the room. She didn't let any of them hurt me or even keep me awake."

"I remember you speaking about that." Her mother's voice was warm and low. "I hardly believed you when you told me in those days." She bowed and frowned contemplatively.

"Did you think that maiden was your guardian angel back then?" Detta was just behind Sophie's mother, a few inches taller but not really looming over her.

"I had heard of guardian angels, of course, but I was pretty doubtful about most of the things I heard in church. So many folks there were telling me that I didn't see what I clearly *did* see. They had very little credibility with me even early on."

Her mother nodded slow and silent.

"Well, praise God you came through all that and found some peace." Detta's glasses had slipped down her nose a bit.

She tipped her head back and looked at Sophie through the center of her lenses. Maybe she was examining the impact of her words.

"Yeah. Some peace. Thanks to you." She turned to her mom. "And you."

"I have not been much help." Her mother shook her head.

"You've been there for me even when you thought I was crazy. That's what moms do." Sophie tried to sweeten the air a bit, to replace the regrets smothering the aroma of roasting turkey and steaming pasteles.

More Reason for Thanks

Detta stood up from the jigsaw puzzle and listened to the soaring symphonic music accompanying her least favorite part of Disney's *A Christmas Carol*. She headed to the kitchen for a little more cleanup and to stretch her back.

Sophie followed her. "How are you feeling these days, Detta?"

"I am wonderfully healthy. Just stretchin' my back after hunching over that puzzle too long. I get caught up in it and forget to sit up straight."

"No more cough?"

"All gone, thanks to you."

"I had no idea what I was doing. I just told you what I saw. I see stuff all the time and never used to do anything about it."

"Used to? You been givin' it a try lately?"

"I did invite some guardians to get involved in a conference room meeting at work last week." She paused, as if checking where her mother was. "And I've been wondering about what I might have done about some things I saw yesterday. I noticed a sad girl hanging onto one of my relatives. You think that's something that should be cast out, or prayed against, or whatever?"

"Sadness is natural, but when it manifests as a spirit, it's out of control and has to be addressed some way."

"Addressed like we did with that snake in your chest?"

Mrs. Ramos now stood in the kitchen doorway—Isadora. She tilted her head to the side a bit and knit her brow at her daughter. "Who was that, dear?"

Sophie looked at her mother. She seemed to be deciding how to answer.

To Detta, it seemed obvious what made her hesitate. Something about Isadora struck Detta as sad, sort of chronically sad. She had lost a husband and a son, of course. She had reasons for deep sadness.

"A few people there were really sad. Grandma had this sad little girl with her."

"I'm not surprised." Isadora nodded sympathetically.

Sophie stood up a bit straighter. She was looking at the pantry door, but not in the way she did when she was watching some spirit. She was still avoiding something.

Isadora leaned toward her daughter. "What about me, Sophie? You said you might have seen something following me around."

After loading up a big breath, Sophie grinned quickly at her mother. "That other sad girl I saw yesterday. I don't see it today. A little girl with dirty tears running down her face. She tried to hold your hand at Uncle Herman's house. Then she held hands with abuela's sad girl."

Isadora was nodding slowly and puffing her lower lip. "I *was* incredibly sad yesterday. It felt like the darkest days after Hector died. I can think of your father going away without so much pain now, but not Hector." She clouded up. Then she caught her face in her hands and began to weep.

Detta stepped to Isadora's side, waiting for a few seconds. "Just let it out and let it go." She tentatively patted her guest on the shoulder. "I believe you can just let go of that sadness so it doesn't grab onto you so hard. Not that sadness is bad, just that you can have power over it instead of the other way around."

Isadora nodded as she wept, her head still bowed. But she stiffened as Sophie stepped closer. A wriggle twisted her shoulders.

Detta addressed that wriggle. "In the name of Jesus, I command that controlling sadness to get off my sister, Isadora." She waited to see if that took. A glance at Sophie confirmed her suspicion that the thing was hanging on. "Have you forgiven ... Hector, is it?" Detta got confirmation on that name from Sophie. "Have you forgiven Hector for dying?" She didn't know the exact circumstances of the boy's death, but just spoke what came to mind. She was trying to follow God's Spirit in this.

Isadora looked up, scowling, but that scowl softened when she looked at Sophie. She was nodding again, her eyes drifting toward the corner of the room. "I never thought of that, but it sounds right, I think. It sounds like I might need to do that. He rode his bicycle out into the street. I guess I have not forgiven him for doing that."

Sophie's eyebrows were high now. She seemed to be holding her breath.

"Get out of here now, you sad spirit." Detta stayed focused on Isadora.

Sophie arched her back and leaned away from her mother. She let out her breath.

"Well, what happened?" Detta raised her eyebrows at Sophie.

Isadora was looking at her daughter along with Detta, more curious than distressed now.

"That girl just flew up and pulled two small children with her. They were linked together and all going away." She monitored her mother as she answered.

Anthony was standing in the doorway to the dining room. "Cool."

Detta laughed. Anthony usually popped over to the dining room to set a couple puzzle pieces in place and then returned to his movie. Here he was poking his head in to see the results of the ministry in the kitchen.

He turned back to his movie again. All three of the women watched him go. Detta laughed a little harder, and Isadora and Sophie joined in.

They sat at the kitchen table during the rest of that movie. Detta talked with her guests about what had just happened. Isadora didn't seem shocked or anything, but she didn't seem familiar with such ministry either. Maybe it was time for her to get familiar, considering her daughter's gifts.

The Really Big Ones

Back to work on Monday, Sophie had to exit the train at a different station, having daydreamed right through her usual stop. This put her closer to the financial district and more of those huge things that stood like titanic statues honoring ancient kings. That's what they looked like from a distance, if Sophie bothered to look.

Closer up, when she walked through them, it was like passing from the green air of a thunderstorm to the red of a sunset. The atmosphere inside those giants was distinct, at least in color. She was glad if she was missing a difference in smell or sound. Some things she didn't want to know.

Most of this she didn't want to know. But maybe hanging around Detta was making her less cautious. She strained her neck like a tourist and assessed the blue giant looming over one of the oldest bank buildings in the city. Was he good? Was he evil? Should Detta come down here and cast this big bully out of town?

Sophie snickered. And she thought about what it meant that she relied on Detta to do the hands-on work. Detta named them and kicked them out. Was that something everyone at Detta's church did, or just the mothers? The warrior women.

A tug like an ocean current slowed her step off the curb next to another venerable financial institution. Only a slim strip along the center of the street separated that blue giant from the deep red monster in the next block. Too bad Anthony couldn't see this stuff. He could certainly tell her about a sci-fi movie these colossi called to mind.

The red one seemed heavier than the blue one—denser, harder for her to pass through. Was it aware of her? Was it holding her down, slowing her steps? She shook with sudden cold and pepped her pace. A harsh wind, cutting through her jacket, accused her of underdressing for the unseasonable weather.

Sophie had walked through downtown many times during the past seven years. But today, for a change, she allowed herself to look and wonder at these massive guardians, if that's what they were.

She was in that mode when she approached the office building in which her employer occupied four floors. The greenish being that stood tallest next to that building wasn't alone. Other lesser giants crowded against it. One of them, a slender figure over ten stories tall, bent toward her as she looked up. Did it meet her eye? Did it see her seeing it?

The monster teetered in her direction like the top half of a tall tree cut off by a chainsaw. But he wasn't falling. He was coming for her, eyes glaring like stop lights. She stumbled, suddenly worried that she couldn't run fast enough to get away. A talon-like hand reached for her. Pincers coming to grab her ...

"Sophie, what are you lookin' at? Somebody about to jump off a ledge?"

Startled and nearly tumbling over sideways, Sophie swore. She caught her balance and glowered at Sammy. "Don't sneak up on me like that."

"Sneak up? I was talking to you for, like, half a minute." Sammy was shoulder-to-shoulder now, his hand hooding his eyes as the clouds thinned and the sun brightened.

She shrugged hard against the cold and the momentary fright. "Oh. Sorry. I just never looked up at the building before—not really seeing it."

"You like the pink marble? I think it's pretty cool. Nice against all the black and gray around here. What style is it, do you think?"

"I don't know. I'm not an expert on architecture." She forced herself to stand up straight despite the sustained glare from that smoldering giant. He had faded slightly with the arrival of Sammy, but he was just as close and still intimidating.

"Yeah. I actually took a couple courses in college, but I can't remember what you call these buildings from the '80s with so much glass and those long lines of marble."

Sophie staggered forward and pushed through the revolving door to the lobby. She tried to think of something relevant to say in reply to Sammy, but her brain had turned to pudding during that staring contest with the black monster. Time to tune out and keep her head down again. Stick to her own business.

"Hey, you wanna see the augmented reality tour of that new building next to the train line?"

"Does it have pterodactyls in it?" She hit the button next to the elevator. She had enough giant monsters in her life already.

"Ha. No. Dick made me promise not to do that anymore. He was worried I'd forget to take 'em out and scare the sh— out of a client someday."

She snickered half-heartedly at Dick's reasonable concern and pulled up her sleeve to check her smart watch. "Huh. Okay. Sure. I can stop by for a minute." It wasn't like she had a meeting first thing, but she was still recovering and wasn't ready to make an important decision. Hopefully this wasn't a crucial choice.

Dropping her jacket and messenger bag in her cube, Sophie noticed her computer was powered off, no lights anywhere. Generally, everyone left their computers powered on overnight so employees could connect from home. Not that Sophie did that very often.

Sammy was whispering harshly and gesturing with one hand as if they were escaping a prison camp. She obeyed his coaxing, assuming the urgency was about his pride over what he had created for the architectural firm.

With the goggles on, Sophie took a tour with Sammy, walking beside an avatar of him. His avatar was a tall African-American guy with a large Afro and a basketball jersey. Maybe it was meant to look like a real-life basketball player, but Sophie wasn't up on sports. As he chatted about code branches and display resolution options, Sophie wondered about what had happened outside—before Sammy scared the pants off her. Was that tall thing threatening her personally? It didn't look happy. Was threatening people its thing? Clearly she wasn't supposed to look at it, or even notice it. Walking blindly past had never gotten that kind of response. She had apparently violated its rules, like it was a temperamental neighborhood bully.

When the virtual tour was over, at least as much as Sophie dared to stay for, she headed back to her cubicle. She hit the power button on her workstation. Nothing happened. She held the power button down longer. She checked the monitors, no lights indicating power was getting to them either. She crouched next to her desk and looked at the power strip tucked under it, testing the stretchiness of her tight pants. No light on at the switch. She glanced behind her, seeing only her guardian. Then she crawled under the counter. Flipping the power strip switch back and forth didn't do anything. She checked the plug at the outlet and flipped the switch a few more times. Nothing. No lights.

Then those talon-like fingers were reaching through the cubicle. Sophie recoiled and just avoided banging her head on the underside of her desk. She backed out as quickly as she could. As she caught her balance, fully upright, Janice slowed outside her cubicle.

"You okay, Sophie? Your face is all red."

"Oh. Uh … I just crawled out from under my desk. I … uh, don't seem to have any power. Electricity is out." She rubbed her hands down her black jeggings out of habit.

"Well, how can that be?" Janice craned her neck at Charlie and Debbie's cubes next door. They seemed engaged in work that required electricity. "How can it just be you?"

For Sophie, that triggered a lifetime of being the weird one. How could she see things reaching toward her under her desk when no one else could? She stuttered for an explanation.

But Janice stopped her. "I'm sure there's a switch or fuse or something someone can fix. I'll tell Tammy you have a problem."

That was better, except the last note. *Sophie has a problem*. A cauldron of angst bubbled in her. This was *her* problem. But it was, wasn't it? Hadn't she ticked off that evil giant? Why else would only her machine be affected by an electrical outage? Maybe he'd cut the power with his sharp claws.

She glanced at her guardian, who had planted himself in the corner of her cubicle when she first arrived. His eyes glowed red. Those red eyes reminded her of that tall black thing outside the building. Actually it had been *in* and *on* the building, not only outside. Her guardian glowed brighter, an edge of white intensifying his usual golden shine. And that red in his eyes was like someone was spotlighting him in red, not like an internal glow.

"You got electrical problems?"

Sophie swore. "Sammy! Stop doing that!"

"Doing what, talking to you?" He shook his head. "Call the IT guys to get an extension cord up here so you can grab power from Charlie or Debbie's cube."

That was a good idea. A rational idea. An idea that had nothing to do with giant spirits snipping her electrical connection. Besides, why would they do that? What did little Sophie mean to any of those titans?

When Deshawn had run the extension cord over the cubicle wall to Charlie's power outlet, and Sophie had collected a cup of coffee from the kitchen, she logged in to her computer. She took a deep breath. That breath caught short, however, when a message popped up on her screen.

"*Your computer has been infected by the Stormtrooper virus. Click here to clean up this infection.*" The title bar of the window included the name of a trusted software company. But Sophie didn't trust that message. She swore one more time.

"What now?" Charlie was holding his headphones poised above his head, interrupted from escaping into his music.

"Virus scam message. Some kind of infection."

"Don't touch anything." Charlie sounded like a guy warning people away from a poisonous snake.

"I know how this works." She shook her head, mad at herself for venting at Charlie.

"Deshawn!" Charlie called for help. Too loud. He spent most of the day wearing over-the-head earphones and generally got his vocal volume turned up too high. He also lacked the normal inhibitions that keep people from yelling across the top of cubicles.

Though Charlie was short, Deshawn was over six feet, and Sophie saw him acknowledge the alarm with a nod. When he found what was on Sophie's screen, he shooed her away from it and pulled out his cell phone. "I'll get Roger up here to go through the recovery steps. It'll take a while to restore your system to a clean version."

"A while?" Sophie had work to do. She wasn't paid for the number of widgets she produced, of course. She would be compensated the same for a day spent waiting for her computer to reboot several times as she would for debugging code. But she wanted today to get normal. Facing off with that dark giant had wobbled her off balance. She needed normal.

"Kiesha is out today. You can use her workstation until this gets fixed." Janice was part of the crowd of gawkers gathered at the door to Sophie's cube.

"Good." She took a deep breath. "Thanks, Janice."

"Of course. It sure helps that you're a hacker and know what to do when you see something like that." Janice probably meant that as a compliment.

Sophie sipped that affirmation. She was still struggling with a feeling that she had misbehaved. She wanted to wriggle free of that feeling, like extricating herself from a too-small jacket.

For whatever reason, this recalled a fight with her little brother. He was eleven, she was fifteen. She'd accidentally pulled his jacket from the closet and tried to shove her hands in the sleeves while storming out of the house. She was mad at her mother for something. Thus the mistaken coat selection.

Thus the hasty slam of fist in sleeve. Thus the rip in Hector's favorite jacket.

"Oh, grow up!" she had shouted at Hector like it was his fault somehow. That's what she did back then. Blame someone else. Blame anyone else.

She was to blame for far too much by then. Messing up their family with her bizarre visions was the worst. Wearing at her mother's frayed nerves. Chasing her father away. And costing the family so much money in doctor bills. At fifteen, her shoulders were narrower than today. She couldn't carry so much. But dumping on Hector never helped. How much had she piled onto his even narrower shoulders?

She ran a finger over the tattoo of Hector's name on the back of her hand. A dark specter in her peripheral vision startled her as she approached Kiesha's cubicle. She just managed to stop herself from swatting at the divebombing spirit. Then it aimed a dagger at her.

"Damn. I need help here." She muttered that too low for anyone to hear, even if they didn't have headphones on and music canceling her voice.

The specter soared away as her guardian pushed past her. The golden guy went airborne and stretched out his arms as if to provide her cover. Air cover.

She sent him a mental request. *Can you make sure nothing goes wrong in Kiesha's cube?*

He rushed ahead of her and planted himself next to Kiesha's Dayton University pennant.

"Okay. Go Flyers." Sophie nodded toward the pennant and honored the mascot of her coworker's school. Something fluttered near that pennant and vanished. She didn't investigate.

The computer was already powered up. Sophie set her coffee down and pulled out the chair. She remembered her headphones then but decided not to go back to her cube just yet. "Let's see if this works first."

Her login worked. She found her files on the network. And the chair didn't collapse under her 135 pounds. Some normality was being restored. Sophie glanced at her guardian.

"Thanks, buddy."

Dinner with Crystal

"It's been a totally freaky day. I'm still working at someone else's computer. My cubicle seems to have a poltergeist or something." Sophie hunched toward the wall of Kiesha's cubicle in the corner of the office. She cupped her hand around her mouth to isolate her voice to the cell phone.

"Really? I wonder what that's about."

Most people would assume it was about computer viruses, software bugs, and electrical fuses, but Crystal had a broader worldview for such things. She was especially suspicious of technology—in a spiritual way.

"I'll tell you about it sometime."

"What about tonight? Wanna get supper?" Crystal worked downtown as a graphic designer for a home décor company. She was a short bus ride away.

Sophie sighed. "Sure. That sounds good. I need someone to talk to." Then she brightened a bit. "And you gotta tell me how you've been doing since I saw you last."

"Yes, I will. It's been weird and cool."

"Your voice sounds different."

"Not so rough, right?"

"Yeah. What happened?"

"I'll tell you tonight. You wanna meet at Lacey's at six?"

"Lacey's? Okay. See you at six." Six was safe. They both usually finished work around five, though Sophie would have reason to stay a little late tonight to make up for the slow start. Even though Janice hadn't blamed her, Sophie felt responsible. Her confrontation with that tall guardian, or whatever it was, seemed too coincidental. The IT guys had told her that her cube turned out to be on its own power fuse, which was odd. And that fuse was the only one that went bad. Which, of course, had nothing to do with the fake virus phishing attempt—another issue entirely.

When the network directory she had been working in for the past month disappeared that afternoon, Sophie stopped to consider her guardian, stolid and vigilant. "Did I do something that even you can't defend?" She barely said it aloud.

The guardian raised his eyes toward the top corner of the room.

Sophie followed that gaze, expecting to find something hovering there. But, through the usual air traffic of ghouls passing, she saw nothing special in that corner. The guardian kept his eyes there nevertheless, so she tried to focus harder, maybe even penetrate the building to look beyond the concrete and steel. "X-ray vision," she muttered under her breath.

There, on the outside of the building, was that dark tower of a beast. She flinched and let him disappear from her sight. But her guardian was still focused there. She followed his lead again. And maybe what she saw was a different giant. His eyes were orange. She expanded her view to two other giants leaning against the building. There was a taller one that glowed along jagged lines in its skin, bubbling like magma. That giant was maybe struggling with the black figure she had stared down this morning. Then there was a deep blue monster, thicker and just as tall. He wrapped outrageously long arms around the others, as if to restrain their conflict. His face grimaced disgust, as if tired of it all. But the sort of choreographed struggle Sophie was seeing made it seem like an old conflict, like the giants were opposed but familiar with each other.

"Frenemies."

"What? What are you looking at?" Peter Jamison stood leaning on the doorpost to Kiesha's cubicle.

Sophie pulled off her headphones. She had heard what he said—her music was paused. But she pretended she didn't know the question, raising her eyebrows innocently.

"Who are you talking to?"

She grinned sheepishly. "Myself, of course. Always my best conversation partner."

Peter chuckled, but not with the easy laugh of someone who recognized the feeling. His chuckles sounded manufactured. "Ah, sure. Huh. Well, I see you're trying to hide from me." He forced more of that laughter.

"Yep. Lotta good it did me though." That sounded too much like flirting. She avoided eye contact. "Blown fuse and a phishing scam. Had to move to a working computer." Sophie was done with Peter. She had decided that since his last visit.

"Monday after a holiday. I guess weird stuff happens." He gave her his crooked grin and ran a hand over his hair.

Really? Was that a thing? Or was Mr. Nontechnical just pretending it was a thing?

She shrugged one shoulder. "Could happen any day." Any day she got caught spying on the colossal beings propping up the office building.

"Uh-huh."

This was probably the part where she was supposed to reveal that she was available tonight. But she had plans. "It's a good day to get together with my friend Crystal for supper, though." That was awkward. Appropriately so for her typically tangled interaction with Peter—part sign language, part telepathy, part rain dance.

"Ah. Crystal. You told me about her, right?"

"Sure. We've been friends since college. She was in a web design class I took. But she's totally nontechnical, really."

"Ah. One of us folks who see computers as a necessary evil."

"Exactly." Again, Sophie caught herself on the way to flirting. With Peter, some part of her hit flirt mode without consulting the rest of her brain. *Brakes on. We're getting out of this car.*

Charlie rescued her. "D' you have a moment to meet with me and Janice? I need an ally." Charlie knew plenty about Sophie and Peter, so he wouldn't be surprised to find the sales guy lurking by her alternate cubicle. And his social awkwardness certainly freed Charlie to interrupt whatever was going on just then.

Sophie was grateful. That gratitude spilled into her bouncy reply. "Oh, sure. Yeah, I'll be *glad* to help out."

Recoiling from the neck up, Charlie didn't say anything, just scrunched his face like he was trying to suppress a sudden bowel pain.

Sophie's most embarrassing pain right then was Peter. She glanced at him and saw a wolf-like muzzle emerging from his face. She had forgotten about that one. She hadn't seen the wolf face for a while. She hung onto the back of her chair for a second while Peter stood in her way. For the briefest moment, she wondered if that wolf would bite.

Then Peter backed up, and the wolf transformed into a boring sales guy. Those flames over his shoulders were flaring brightly, however.

Fire wolf. Huh.

"See ya." She squeezed past him without making physical contact.

The Girl Who Sees Angels

After work, sitting at a polished wooden block of a table at Lacey's bistro, Sophie watched Crystal wind her way over the main dining floor. Two guys turned hungrily to watch her backside as she approached Sophie. A tiny flight of fighter planes launched from that other table and flew in formation over Crystal. Well, maybe not actual planes, but that was what they reminded Sophie of.

"Bus was delayed. Sorry I'm late." Crystal offered her hands for a hug as she sloughed off her purple cloth coat.

Sophie stepped into the hug once the coat was settled. "I was early. You're not that late." She sat back down as they slid free from that brief embrace. "How have you been since … you know?"

Raising both hands, Crystal shrugged. "I feel great. My throat is better. At least it doesn't bug me and doesn't sound so bad. And I'm sleeping well. I even lost a few pounds since you saw me last."

"You didn't need to lose weight." Sophie wasn't just saying it. Crystal was lighter than her, less athletic, and smaller framed. She surely weighed less than Sophie.

"I was getting a tummy." Crystal patted herself below her wide red belt. Then she smoothed the cream sweater dress and sat down.

"Are we drinking tonight?" Sophie had a preference but wanted to consult Crystal.

"I wanna talk, so maybe just wine for me."

"Sounds good. I wanna try their Rosso Dolce again." Sophie tried to flag their server, but the girl was busy flirting with those two guys and their fighter squadron. The petite waitress was carrying an immense female specter, a monster woman blown up like a Thanksgiving parade balloon. That bulging beast made Sophie less anxious to have the girl visit their table. It reminded her of a haunting she had escaped a while back. She let her hand sink back to the table.

"What about you? You still hanging out with that church lady?" Crystal had finished scooting her chair. She rested the palms of her hands on the reflective surface between them.

"I had dinner with them and my mom on Friday after Thanksgiving, actually."

"You going to her church yet? Or Priscilla's church?"

Crystal and Priscilla had never been close, only both getting together with Sophie a few times. Priscilla always seemed suspicious of Crystal and sort of judgmental, though Sophie couldn't figure out exactly why. "No. They haven't roped me into that yet."

"Are you still determined to stay away?" Crystal raised her eyes toward that waitress, who was heading toward them.

"I'll probably give in sooner or later."

Their orders interrupted the conversation for a few minutes. Sophie had been to this restaurant several times. She ordered the tapas tray, a mix of moderately authentic Spanish nibblers. Crystal ordered a dinner salad.

"So, tell me what happened after you left with your angel lady." As soon as she said that, Sophie paused to kick herself under the table.

But Crystal stretched an amused smile. She laughed lightly. "You saw something?" Her voice dipped. "Of course you saw something. What did it look like? A lady?"

"Sorry, I forgot I didn't tell you about that. Yeah. It was this beautiful guardian angel. Though maybe I wouldn't have called her that at the time." Sophie caught a glance from a woman at the next table. What had she heard?

"She was with me when I left you?"

Sophie tuned her super senses to the space around Crystal. That beautiful guardian appeared just behind her, as if she was ready to pull out Crystal's chair for her. But Crystal wasn't going anywhere. "She's right there. Standing behind you."

Crystal started to turn her head but aborted. She wouldn't expect to see anything even if she believed what Sophie was saying.

The dark woman at the next table, with rich red lipstick and shiny black hair in a bun, furrowed her artfully crafted eyebrows toward Crystal.

When Sophie focused on that table, she realized there were only two regular people seated there, but she was seeing all four chairs occupied. Apparently that woman brought ghosts that needed to take a load off their feet. Or maybe they were just so comfortable with her that they felt welcomed at her table. Should Sophie invite her guardian to have a seat? She glanced at him and then looked at an empty chair. He didn't take the hint.

"What is it? You see something else?" Crystal's fascination with what Sophie could see had often sidetracked normal conversations.

Sophie raised a dismissive hand. "Nothing so unusual. I was just wondering why our guardians always stand. Can't they sit down and relax?"

"Not if they're really guarding us." Crystal stopped there, a smile frozen on her face, as the server delivered their wine glasses.

The spirit riding on that server tottered, threatening to slip off and land on their table, her unwieldly girth too much for the small woman to carry. But there was no slide, no crash. The female thing tipped and loomed but didn't fall. How much could a spirit weigh, after all?

Sophie sighed when the waitress left. "Let's talk about how your throat has improved." She wanted to bracket her attention onto Crystal and let all the spooks around them disappear. *If only.*

"Now that I know what you saw at your apartment, I think it's been one of those ... *guardians* taking care of me. I've felt it. I've felt it ever since I talked to that woman on the phone."

"Detta."

"Yeah, Detta. I feel better. I feel good. Like I'm getting some kind of therapy. Like I'm at peace with the world."

"That sounds great."

"What about you? You said something about a guardian. Is that your angel, then?" Crystal had always been fascinated by angels. A whole corner of her apartment was decorated with artsy portrayals of angels, only a few of them chubby cherubs.

"He's with me most of the time. Or I see him most of the time. Pretty much whenever I want to." As she said that, her guardian glowed more brightly where he stood to her right. But he still didn't look like he was ready to pull out a chair and order a glass of wine.

"You sound a bit hesitant about them—angels, I mean."

"I always tried to stay out of defining what they were. So many people seemed to have this heavy agenda attached to their ideas about spirits and angels. I just always tried to stay out of it."

"People like me and my gurus?"

"Not just you. But yeah, you in contrast to the church people like my mother and her priests. And whoever. I didn't wanna choose sides."

Crystal nodded and lifted her wine glass. "Right. You would really be caught in the middle if you had to agree with anyone's interpretation of what you're seeing. Especially since you see them so much more clearly than everyone else."

The woman with the shiny brown face and curious black eyes broke the barrier between tables, leaning as close to Sophie as she could while keeping her seat. "I'm sorry, but I couldn't help overhearing." She studied Sophie's startled face. "Can you see spirits?"

Sophie glanced at Crystal. She wasn't blaming her friend, but she was feeling hemmed in. She didn't want to lie in front of Crystal, but she didn't want to get sucked into a debate or something worse. When she landed her gaze back on that woman, however, the sincerity of her question seemed apparent in her pleading eyes. "I can."

"Well, it's just that I feel like there's something that follows me all the time. Can you see it?"

Sophie looked at the two inhuman figures seated with that woman and her friend. She ignored the other woman, of similar complexion but shorter and stouter than the one with the question. "There's this guy with a turban. A blue turban. He's reaching toward you. He looks strict and angry. He looks pissed at me right now, in fact."

Just then his face shifted, a monstrous mouth full of fangs replacing his mostly human appearance.

The curious woman sat up straight and followed Sophie's attention to the empty chair. "*Aiiyyeee.* That is like my uncle. He was a holy man. He died a few years ago." Her voice deepened. "That was around the time when I first felt it." She looked at her friend and shook visibly as she released a breath over a series of speedbumps.

Not knowing what to say next, Sophie hung halfway between eye contact with that woman and surveying the guy in the blue turban. Back to his human appearance, he seemed to be daring her. Still threatening. But threatening what?

"Okay. Thank you. Thank you for telling me." The stranger offered a weak grin.

"You're welcome." Sophie tweaked a slight grin back. She suspected the other woman at that table was about to ask for the same service. Hunkering toward her nearly full glass of wine, Sophie hoped to escape meddling more. That blue turban guy was pretty intimidating.

The waitress helped by delivering some of their food. And then they were all back to being restaurant patrons. Normal people.

Nothing to see here.

What About Kimmy?

Catching up with Crystal recalled what had happened when Sophie and Kimmy got together last. How was Kimmy doing with *her* angel friend? The texts between them hadn't been very clear. Kimmy often left Sophie wondering at the exact meaning of her cryptic text abbreviations.

Sophie was in the hallway near the elevators in her office. "You wanna get dinner tonight?" Her cubicle was functional again, and her computer had been restored and stabilized. But her desk was right in the middle of the floor, less conducive to a private phone conversation than Keshia's corner cube.

"Uh, I'm home today. Got a cold." That last bit of explanation was unnecessary. Kimmy's voice sounded like she had tried to swallow a sock and failed.

"Yeah, you sound beat. Maybe I can stop by and bring you some chicken soup from the deli."

"Oh, that would be awesome. But I don't wanna give you my germs."

Sophie wanted to see Kimmy and her apartment to assess whether her friend was doing okay with more than her cold. "I'll keep my distance. I don't wanna get sick either, but I know it's a bummer being stuck at home alone."

"Oh, I'm not alone, remember? I still have my angel." She snickered and then sniffled hard. That started a small coughing fit.

"Oh. Yeah. Okay. I'll let you go. I should be there before six. See you then."

The deli nearest Kimmy's apartment, where she and Sophie had bought soup and sandwiches a few times, was run by a guy named Rodrigo. He always spoke to Sophie in Spanish.

When he was busy, he talked fast. Her Spanish was too rusty for a high-speed conversation with a stranger. With her mother working hard on English, Sophie had little opportunity to practice Spanish these days.

"*Hola, señorita!*" The owner was friendly as ever, but he was bent over one of the machines behind the counter.

"Hola!" Sophie smiled at his tossed greeting.

The girl behind the register asked Sophie in Spanish what she could get her.

Sophie answered in English. "A large chicken soup and a large fruit cup. Do you have orange juice?"

"You got a cold?" The cashier pouted her lips sympathetically. It occurred to Sophie that the young woman might be related to the owner. Something in the chin and cheeks.

"No, it's my friend who has a cold."

The cashier asked Rodrigo if they had orange juice. He explained where she could find it without pulling his face out of the stainless steel appliance he was wrestling.

As Sophie witnessed that interaction, she also monitored something rolling from Rodrigo to the girl, bouncing off and rolling back. She squinted for a better look, even if her natural eyes weren't involved. The visions she saw were often clearly good or bad, threatening or helpful. The rattling ball didn't seem good, but it didn't seem scary either.

As the young woman scooped soup and then sped to the back room, Rodrigo waited on another customer. When the girl returned to the front, that rolling ball rattled off her and smacked into the owner.

"Are you his daughter?" Sophie nodded toward Rodrigo, who was describing one of their sandwiches to a gray-haired lady with thick glasses.

"Yes. You can tell?" The girl snuffled a self-conscious laugh. She was stocky, her face round with a little lump of a chin like a tiny kneecap.

Sophie snickered, though she didn't know exactly what the girl meant. "I can see the resemblance."

"Too much alike, Mama says." That metallic ball clattered off her and jingled back toward her father.

He cocked his head at Sophie and his daughter, and that ball turned back.

Sophie wanted to ask about the meaning of that rolling ball, but who would she ask? "Chip off the old block?" That was her automatic response.

"Mama says 'another car off the same assembly line.' She works in a factory."

Still trying to act normal, Sophie smiled and nodded. Was that ball a product from the mother's factory? Sophie shied from asking more questions and just paid for her cold remedies and said goodbye.

"*Buenos noches,* señorita!" Rodrigo raised his head from his sandwich making to see her off.

The front door to Kimmy's apartment was standing open when Sophie reached the second floor. Kimmy had apparently opened it after buzzing her in at the lobby door.

"Hola!" Sophie called. Then she grunted at herself. "I mean, hello!"

"In here." Kimmy's muffled voice came from the living room and from deep in her congested throat.

"Hey. You look so cute." Sophie set the paper bag on a sideboard and unzipped her leather jacket.

"Cute? I look like a corpse."

"No. I've seen some of those. You don't look nearly that bad."

"You have?"

Sophie shook that off, not wanting to explain the array of maimed and decapitated souls she had seen through her life, some zombie-walking, some dangling in the air. "I guess your angel doesn't protect from colds." She unrolled the top of the paper bag.

"No, but he sure is helping me stay straight." Kimmy shrugged her shoulders and held that pose. "A cold used to be the worst time for me to stay clean. Cold meds would lead to pain meds, and pain meds would lead to coke."

The conversation had gotten real serious real fast. "Oh." That medication spiral sounded familiar from Kimmy's confessions in previous years. "Wait. So, you think the angel is helping you keep off drugs?" She didn't stop to edit, too fascinated with this new bit of data.

"Well, I wasn't lying to you before. I have been staying clean, but it's been a struggle."

Sophie headed for the kitchen to get a bowl and spoon for Kimmy. She glanced over her shoulder to see if she could detect that bat thing hanging over her friend. Nothing there. But she did see something hunkered by the little phone table, which had no phone on it these days. It was similarly ghastly but much more subdued than the bat thing had been. Was there some significance to that little table? Even if she was curious, Sophie didn't want to grill Kimmy, especially while she was sick.

"It's great that ..." Sophie forgot what she had intended to say before she spotted that little creature with its folded wings. "Uh, bowls? Where do you keep soup bowls?" She found the cupboard as soon as she asked. "Here. I got 'em."

"You gonna eat with me?"

"Well, I think I'm less likely to catch anything here if I don't eat, right? Besides, it would be like me using up some of your medicine just to keep you company."

"Oh, okay. Thanks for getting this stuff, Sophie. Is that orange juice?"

"Yes, dear. And a fruit cup."

"Nice. Can you put some of the fruit in the orange juice?"

"Really?" Her voice squeaked. "Uh, okay. Sure."

Once she spooned the grapes, apple chunks, mandarin orange slices, and pineapple into a bowl of the O.J., it made sense. "Looks good."

"You could have some."

"No. Seriously. This stuff is meant to get you well."

"Thanks." Kimmy grinned pitifully as she received the bowl of juicy fruit, and Sophie set the soup bowl on top of a clothes catalog.

Kimmy was wearing pink flannel pajamas and a purple fleece robe. That was why Sophie had said she looked cute. Her nose and eye rims were a shade of red that fit nicely between that pink and purple.

"Tell me about how things have been better." Sophie settled into the chair at the far side of the living room.

Kimmy reached for the remote and muted the movie on her TV. She chewed and swallowed some fruit, her mouth open slightly, and her breathing noisy. "I sleep much better these days, for one thing."

"Someone else I know said something about that recently. Like angels are sleep aids."

"Better than drugs. No side effects." Kimmy tried to laugh but had to stop for a hard sniffle.

"I should let you eat in peace. It's hard to talk and eat at the same time when you can't even breathe."

Kimmy nodded. "But tell me what's been happening for *you*."

Sophie paused a few seconds while she drafted a selective report about her last several days. She omitted some of the more ominous elements. Speculating with Detta made sense, and Crystal had a sort of grid for this stuff, but Kimmy was the friend Sophie had relied on to *not* know or care about her spiritual visions.

Kimmy stopped slurping soup during a pause in Sophie's report. "You feel like you've finally figured out your purpose? Like, discovered your destiny? I mean, you can do so much with what you have, right? Like for that lady in the restaurant."

Sophie had included the story of the Indian woman in the restaurant mostly because it seemed harmless, but also because she was curious about it. "I'm not sure it really helped her."

"But why not? She seemed like she was grateful, didn't she?" Kimmy sniffled and reached for one of the paper napkins Sophie had left on the coffee table.

"She thanked me. But what good does it do for her to know what that spook looks like? Or even to know that he's related to her uncle?"

"I don't know, but it seems like you should figure that out. I think this really is something you could use to help people. Maybe you'll get better at it as you go along."

Sophie sucked a long breath through her teeth and immediately questioned the health ramifications of doing that in this apartment. "Yeah. It seems like being willing to look has made a difference."

"And what about that church lady's help?"

"Yeah. Detta has made a difference. I never saw the guardian with me before I met her." She left off the part about Detta praying for her, still not sure how that worked, and not wanting to complicate things in front of Kimmy.

"When are you gonna just start calling it your guardian angel like everyone else?"

Sophie rolled her eyes. In this realm, she had worked hard to *not* be like everyone else. Everyone else was blind compared to her. And they all seemed to have their own agenda attached to defining what she saw. But maybe having an agenda wasn't always bad. There was such a thing as a good agenda, wasn't there?

Sophie glanced toward where the two golden guardians were standing together near the end of the couch, the head of Kimmy's sick bed. For the first time, she spoke to a guardian in front of one of her friends. "Don't you angels do healing? Kimmy could use some of that."

Kimmy stopped scooping fruit and turned toward the two guardians. "Did they say anything?"

Chortling deep in her chest, Sophie shook her head. "No, they didn't say anything. I seem to see 'em a lot better than I hear 'em."

"Huh." Kimmy nodded and stared at Sophie. "I bet you can work on that."

"Yeah, but do I really want to?"

Worried about What?

Detta invited Sophie to dinner on Thursday. Anthony was busy with something—probably a date, though he didn't admit that to his mom.

She stirred the sauce, finding one bay leaf, the other one lost in the opaque red depths. Italian sausage, hints of onions, and green peppers, it would probably not impress a real Italian, but it was the spaghetti sauce Anthony had eaten all his life. The only one Detta knew how to make. She wasn't about to buy sauce in a jar.

"Hello." A knock at the back door and then Sophie's voice. This was becoming homey and familiar. Like a child coming to visit. And, like a child, Sophie worried Detta. She had been worrying her more and more lately.

"Hello, Sophie. Come on in. No need to even knock, as long as I'm expecting you." Detta waved her in and shuffled across the floor for a hug, interrupting Sophie pulling at her black leather jacket. That jacket worried Detta. And those tattoos. But why? She shooed away those thoughts. She was just being old.

Sophie seemed unusually hesitant in the gentleness of the hug, sending quick glances around the kitchen. "Is it just you and me tonight?"

"Yep. Anthony's busy. Probably got a girlfriend he's hiding from me." She grinned, hoping Sophie would know it was a joke.

"Oh. Okay." Her tone was as nervous as a mourning dove on a busy sidewalk.

"How have you been, Sophie? Tell me what's goin' on with you."

"With me? Uh, well, I told you about those giant things at work and the computer problems. That was the weirdest thing. But Crystal and Kimmy both told me good things about what happened after they each got, or became aware of, their guard— uh, their angels."

Detta nodded, trying to unravel some internal distractions. She stepped to the stove to turn off a burner, preventing the spaghetti from getting gummy. And she checked the flame under the sauce, but she had already turned that down. There was something else she was forgetting. Surveying the table, she found that the salads were next to the placemats, and the Italian bread was in the middle.

"How have *you* been, Detta? Is everything okay with you?" The way Sophie said that, like a bad actor in an amateur play, tripped an alarm.

"I'm *fiiiiinne*." She could play act as well as her guest. "I've been quite well. Doin' the usual stuff. I heard a story this week about a man in lots of spiritual trouble. I'm hopin' we're gonna get a chance to help him. But I'm doing real well myself." Her answer came from multiple directions, gluing bits of this to pieces of that.

Sophie was sneaking glances around the room.

"Now you gotta tell me what you're seeing." Detta shut off the last burner on the stove and squared up at Sophie with her hands on her hips.

"Well, it's hard to say. Things are different today. There's something here that isn't ... right." Sophie had her jacket off and hung over the back of Anthony's usual chair. She had stuffed her hands into the pockets of her black jeans so only her thumbs showed. Dark purple nail polish this time.

"What do you think it is?"

"Has something changed? I mean, did something happen?"

"No. Like I said, everything's just as usual. I've been worried about this young man with a severe spiritual oppression on him. You might even say possession. But that's him and not me. And, you know, the usual worries." She stopped herself before she blamed her worries on Anthony. Her concern about him wasn't different this week. Her anxieties about Sophie had been mounting, however. That was the truth of it.

"What are you *not* telling me?" Sophie shifted her weight from one foot to the other.

"I guess I need to confess something." Detta offered an apologetic smile. "I've been worried about *you*, really."

"What about me?" Sophie pulled her chair out and settled in, no sign of being spooked by Detta's motherly hovering. That was a change from when Sophie first sat in that chair.

"I want you to come to faith. You know that. I'm not telling you anything different about that. But I've been worried about you staying back, keepin' your distance from the Lord."

"Why now?"

"Well, I just think the longer you know you're seein' God's angels and his enemies, and you keep yourself on the outside, the more trouble might come your way. Like with those big spirits at your work messing with you." She took a big breath and let her shoulders slack a bit more. "And someone at prayer group was sayin' we should invite you to help with this oppressed young man if we can get him to prayer meetin' for some deliverance. That made me worried more for you."

"Deliverance?"

"Casting out evil spirits. This man has so much on him that it's gonna take a miracle to set him free. And you seein' spirits like you do is about the most miraculous thing any of us have heard about for quite a while."

Sophie shook her head. She shifted in her chair, then picked a piece out of her salad and slipped it between her lips. "Are you talking about an exorcism?"

"Oh, we don't use that word, what with the movies and such."

"*The Exorcist*?"

"That and other ones like it."

"I never watched any of those. Too much activity around people even talking about those kind of movies."

"Hmm." Detta had stayed away too, for about the same reason.

She was interrupted by Sophie reaching for another piece of her salad.

"Where are my manners? Here I am troubling you with my worries, and I'm not feedin' you." Detta turned back to the stove and pulled the lid off the sauce. She let her hands take over the familiar task of putting a meal on the table. "So, you're seein' something different here in the house?" She squeezed the words out between tension and distraction, her head down over the stove and the plates.

Sophie took a deep breath. "Well, I see this little crowd. It's like strangers crowded by the back door. It's hard to tell how many there are. They sort of have shadows, or copies. Sort of blurry. Maybe there's not so many, but it just feels like the room is getting filled up."

"Lord, have mercy."

"I think it has to do with you worrying." Sophie raised her face to Detta and offered half a grin, tipping her head to the side. A sort of challenge nested in an apology.

"Hmm. Yes. I guess I can believe that. I think I might have made an opening by all my worrying. Hmm." She turned her attention to the Spirit of God in her, trying to hear an *amen* to her suspicion.

"Both of your guardians are in the room with mine, and all three are starting to glow more as we talk about this." Sophie's voice was lower, more reverent.

Detta shrugged against the fingertips skittering up her back to her neck. "Thank you, Jesus. Lord, have mercy. Thank you, Jesus."

The food was on the plates. Her hands had done their work. She noticed those hands shaking after she set the plates on the table. "Oh, Lord, have mercy on me." She stood next to the table, her head raised. "I confess my worries and fears, and I submit my will to you, Lord. I renounce any spirits I have empowered with my fretting, in the name of the true Lord Jesus. Now be gone, you evil spirits." She managed to get all that out in about two breaths.

A feeling like wind rushing out of the room followed her command.

Sophie jumped in her seat, her chair rocking onto two legs. She swore and then gripped the edge of the table. She seemed to be watching a flight of fireflies rising toward the sky on a summer evening.

"Did you see 'em go?" Detta grabbed the other corner of the table and pulled her chair out with her left hand. Settling her behind into the chair wasn't as easy as it should have been, but she landed without knocking the chair over.

"I did. They left. I saw them leave all at once."

"Thank you, Jesus."

"They all bunched together till it was just three of them, and then they took off. The angels are all glowing bright now."

"Thank you, Lord. It's the glory of God. That glowing is the glory of God. Thank you, Jesus." The table was shaking, glasses clinking, silverware clanking. Detta let go of the table and chuckled. What relief! The room *had* felt crowded, full of her worries. She had filled up her own kitchen with a bunch of troublemakers. "*Whooweee*. Thank you, Lord."

Sophie was laughing. And she might not have just been laughing at Detta's nutty behavior. She seemed relieved at seeing that crowd leave the house.

By the time they stopped laughing and wiping tears, the spaghetti was lukewarm. "Feel free to heat it in the microwave. I'm not bein' the best host today. But you're family now, Sophie, so you better get used to it."

It was a silly thing to say, and it started Detta laughing all over again.

After another round of nose-blowing, taking turns putting their plates in and out of the microwave, and settling properly into their chairs, they were finally ready to eat. There were still chuckles and a few questions back and forth, but Sophie was obviously hungry, and Detta was feeling it too.

Halfway through her spaghetti, Sophie sipped some water and furrowed her brow. "What were you saying about a guy who was ... did you say, *possessed*?"

"Uh, yeah. Maybe that's not the best term. But when we started thinking about ministering to him, that's about the time I started worrying extra hard about you. He's a real serious case, as far as I understand. And some were sayin' we should invite you to come and see what's on him."

"Me?" She poked the tines of her fork into the remnants of sauce-stained pasta on her plate.

"Well, it sure helps if we know what's comin' and goin' when we're setting someone free of bad spirits. It's hard to tell what's happening sometimes."

"Why did that make you worry about me?"

"Oh. Well, it did seem like the sorta thing you could help with, but this guy is far gone, and the spirits in him must be powerful. I didn't want you to be exposed to that."

Sophie shook her head. "Can you at least tell me about him?"

Anthony's Speculations

Wesley Chalmers had been Anthony's friend since recreation-league basketball in sixth grade. Wesley was a pure outside shooter who could also pass pretty well at age eleven. Anthony was a ballhandler and liked to drive to the hoop, even back when he could barely hoist the ball high enough for a layup.

Wesley's brother was a therapist, the psychological kind. And his brother, Jonathan, had been assigned to help a guy who Wesley said was "totally outta his mind, like he was possessed or something."

"Possessed or something?" Anthony and Jasmine were driving to meet Wesley and his girlfriend, Carley, at a restaurant near downtown. Anthony was talking to himself about the story Wesley had told him.

"What are you mumbling about?" Jasmine put her phone down and gazed at Anthony.

He had to keep from staring back at her inquisitive posture. It was one of her best looks—those luscious lips parted, her eyes as big as plumbs, and her upper body leaning toward him like she wanted something from him. Though all she really wanted was an answer to her question.

"It's this story Wesley told me, and I looked it up on the internet. His brother has this guy as a client, so *he's* not telling any details, but the story in the paper was freaky enough. And Wesley knows another guy who just became a cop. He told him about some of the other parts of it."

"What did this freaky guy do?" She sounded about half interested. Clearly short of fascinated, which was more like where Anthony was, along with Wesley.

"He, like, beat up a dozen cops, or at least broke away from 'em. But I think if he really did beat 'em up, he'd be in maximum security. So at least he did some supernatural escape sh— and left the cops in the dust. They only captured him later 'cause he turned himself in. For no apparent reason."

"But *what* did he do? This is all confused." Her confused look was pretty cute too, but it was pivoting toward a look that might best be described as disgusted.

Anthony didn't want to see *that* look fully formed. He focused on the road. "It sounds like he was running around a graveyard howling and screaming. A bunch of cops came to round him up and take him in. Wesley said he heard the guy was totally naked in freezing weather when the cops got to him. And when they tried to taser him, he just busted through and ran away. That's the part where he mighta beat up some cops, or maybe just made a superhuman escape. That part's in dispute, at least in the stories I heard."

"So the guy is just crazy."

"Crazy is one thing, but being immune to a taser? That's some superhero or supervillain kinda stuff."

"Oh, so you think this guy's a superhero? Man of steel?" She lifted her phone, ready to move on.

"Like, can't be stopped by electric shock? That would make him more like a man of Teflon, or something nonconductive."

"What? What are you talking about?" Jasmine wasn't a science whiz. Her confused look was back, and that disgusted look was getting itself ready.

"Well, it really happened. This is a real guy. And Wesley's brother is his therapist. The guy's family wanted him to have a Christian counselor. That's all Wesley can say about his brother's part."

"Why do they want a Christian counselor? The guy's crazy. He just needs drugs or prison or something." This wasn't Jasmine's most charming side.

"I don't know what he needs. It was just a weird story, and someone I know knows something about it," he muttered. "Been hearing a lot of weird things lately."

"Like that chick who talks to angels?"

"I don't know if she talks to 'em so much as she sees 'em."

"And you believe her?"

This was the part that kept Anthony from bringing Jasmine home to meet his mama. They probably wouldn't understand each other at all.

He drew a long breath and turned his head away, fogging half of his side window with the release of that breath. When he turned back, Jasmine was on her phone again. She was a spectacular beauty, but there might not be any long-term future for them.

At the restaurant, Wesley waved them over to the square table he and Carley occupied. This would be another test for Anthony's relationship with Jasmine. How would she get along with his white friends?

"Hey, Anthony." Wesley grabbed him in a hug. He was as tall as Anthony and a bit more muscular. He hit the gym a lot more than Anthony did.

Anthony always wondered if Wesley did those public hugs to make a kind of statement about his openness and racial inclusion. But maybe Anthony was thinking too hard. Jasmine's presence tonight was probably encouraging his overthinking tendencies.

"Hey, Wesley. How ya doin', Carley?" Anthony gave her a one-armed side hug. "This is Jasmine." He reached for her where she was staying outside their little circle.

"Jasmine, so glad to meet you." Carley took one bold step into Jasmine's space, but she didn't land a hug. Maybe she changed her mind on the way in.

Jasmine just nodded and stiffly extended a hand. Not a good sign. She was sometimes a little shy, but not usually that awkward.

Wesley tried to bridge the gap. "Hello, Jasmine. Anthony can't stop talking about you. I feel like I already know you."

That probably didn't help Jasmine any, but Anthony just grinned gamely. It had to get better.

After a few minutes of meet and greet, they were talking about Wesley's brother and his new client. "Usually I don't know anything about any of Jonathan's clients. I mean, there's all this confidentiality. It's just that this guy was in the papers. And at least one TV station covered it. So it's, like, public knowledge." Wesley gently tipped his beer glass with the thumb and forefinger of one hand. He was looking at Anthony mostly, just bouncing his gaze to Jasmine for a second at a time. He was probably trying to figure out that look on her face.

Anthony suspected she was tuning up her disgusted look.

"You say public *knowledge*, but it's really more like an urban *legend*." Carley didn't have a disgusted look that Anthony had seen. Her round face generally looked jolly even when she was sounding skeptical.

"Yeah, well, you don't have to believe all of it. Like Anthony says, if he really beat up a bunch of cops, he wouldn't be in a psych ward with visiting privileges."

"We don't even know if the part about the psych ward is true." Anthony wasn't about to adopt Jasmine's disgusted outlook, but Carley's skepticism might be a safe middle ground.

"Do you think it could be true that he was tasered and just ran off with the thing stuck to his chest? That's what one of the cops said." Wesley's eyes gleamed like when he was a kid. He was worse than Anthony about comic book superhero stuff.

"Maybe the taser was defective. Electronics fail all the time." Anthony knew this from his work on computer networks. Wesley would know it from the cell phone store he managed.

"Why are you acting so hinky about this all of a sudden?" Wesley lifted his beer and glanced from Anthony to Jasmine, maybe answering his own question.

Anthony mirrored that turn toward Jasmine. "Well, like you say, we can't really know everything, with confidentiality and all. And the news always wants t' make a story more dramatic so they can sell more papers."

"You really think people bought newspapers just to read about a guy running naked through a graveyard?" Jasmine's first contribution on the topic was a doubtful question, of course.

Wesley and Carley joined Anthony in facing Jasmine. In near perfect unison, they all three answered. "Yes."

Jasmine smiled for the first time since they arrived at the restaurant.

That was when the waiter appeared with their appetizers.

The Ultimatum

In her dream, someone was calling Sophie. No, he was shouting at her. Not just inviting. Threatening.

"Huh?" She was awake.

And he was there. Or at least his head was there. Maxwell Hartman. It was him, only less alive. Less human. A gruesome imitation of Maxwell Hartman's severed head. It dripped dark red liquid that didn't seem to actually land on her covers. He glowered at her.

Sophie's hand shook where she clutched the blanket up to her chin. "Go away!" She wanted to say more. Something powerful. What would Detta say in this situation?

Detta would never *be* in this situation.

"I cannot go away. I am tied to you now. We are one."

"That's not true." Her protest felt unconvincing even to her. Not enough breath in her lungs to sound confident.

"You came to *me*. You *offered* yourself to me. And you came to benefit from what I have to offer you. Now you *owe* me."

"But …" Did it even make sense to argue with this hovering head?

"You were about to tell me that you didn't benefit. That you took nothing from me. But you know that's not true. You took confidence. You took affirmation. I believed in you. I respected you and your gifts. You gained that from me. You owe me now."

Could he read her thoughts? Or was this really just a dream?

It felt like Sophie was actually talking. "I don't need any of that from you now." Her voice was shrill but still weak.

"You can't give it back. And you can't take it back." He sounded certain, as if he knew those rules Sophie kept wishing she understood.

Detta understood the rules. What would she say to this? Sophie scrunched her eyes closed and tried to imagine Detta there with her. "Go away from me ... in the name of Jesus."

"Ha!"

That wasn't what he was supposed to say.

"You have no Savior. You don't have the authority to use that name with me."

Was that true? It seemed true. And regrettable.

"Come and see me, Sophie. Let's talk. We can work something out." His tone had suddenly gone low and consoling. It sounded more like the real Maxwell Hartman.

The projection above her bed had always seemed an imitation of Hartman. A spectral clone of him. Bigger and scarier. The head was actually much bigger than a natural human head.

When she didn't respond, he started to drip more stuff, even if there wouldn't be an actual stain to remove.

"I don't trust you. And I'm sorry I ever *did* trust you." She groped for some way to make that stick. To make her distrust the permanent status of their relationship. There had to be something.

A faint glow in the corner of the room drew her eyes. Then in another corner. And another. It felt like light leaking into darkness. Like an inky black page stained with gold at the edges.

For most of her life, Sophie had fought against labeling what she saw. Spiritual darkness wasn't a real thing to her. But maybe that had changed. She had seen Crystal and

Kimmy freed. And her mother. And Detta. Freed from evil. That was real.

Time to take sides.

The glow in the corners intensified after that thought coalesced.

The head of Maxwell Hartman began to grow even more monstrous. His eye sockets darkened, and his mouth stretched wide. Shark teeth had replaced human teeth in that cavernous mouth. A gargling noise emanated from the slashed throat of that hideous vision. And something inside his gaping mouth fluttered.

A horde of black bugs, flying critters, flushed from his mouth. The sound that came with that disgorging grew in volume and ferocity. And the tiny creatures seemed to each grow as soon as they buzzed into the air, swarming and whirling around the room. What started as bugs from Hartman's harsh breath became a thousand beastly attackers filling her room, each with evil in its eyes and with fangs bared.

"I will send these to your mother's house. And to your friends. I will kill and destroy everything you value." The bellowing entity that used to resemble Maxwell Hartman roared this threat and then coughed one last expulsion of little demons.

"You can't. You can't! No. I refuse to let you." Sophie threw the blankets off and tried to stand, but a hundred little demons pounced on her. Did they have weight? Could they hold her down? She couldn't rise. "Help me! Angels! Where are the angels?"

The eyes in that bodiless head glowed greenish yellow. From his nose, a yellow smoke oozed into the room. Sulfur. Rotten eggs.

As the hideous head opened its mouth again, she winced, anticipating more of those creatures swarming around her room. She hoped they were all still in her room. That none of them had left for her mother's house, or Kimmy's, or Crystal's.

"I need help. Protect my mother. Jesus, you have to protect my mother." All four corners of the room glowed more brightly now, like a giant candle had been lit behind each.

Why weren't angels appearing? Why just that distant light?

"I'm sorry I trusted Hartman. I renounce my ... my ... anything I did with him ... or got from him ... or gave him ... or anything. I don't want it!" She screamed that last declaration to penetrate the cloud of demons.

The intensity of that scream seemed to release something in her. And something let go of her, like shackles off her wrists.

"Go away, now! And never come back!" If certainty was required, she knew her words would make a difference. She definitely wanted nothing to do with Hartman ever again. And she wanted the light. She was ready to choose sides.

"Help me, Jesus."

Angels appeared in those four corners now.

Maxwell Hartman's head was shriveling. Not just getting smaller. Shriveling. Like air being sucked out of a beach ball. And then he was gone, and the flying demons with him. Only the stench in Sophie's nostrils lingered.

"Thank you. Thank you, Jesus."

The Demoniac

"I can hardly believe they would let us into the hospital to do this." Detta was on the phone with Sister Ellen from her prayer group.

"Well, it is a Catholic hospital. They believe in spiritual oppression and deliverance. And Jonathan has a relationship with the psychiatrists over there. They trust him." Ellen hummed for a second. "Not that everyone in the hospital would be comfortable with what we're gonna be doing in their group therapy room."

Detta pulled her index finger away from her teeth, checking her nail and noting that it was mostly still intact. She reached it behind her back, hiding it from herself. "You really think it's safe to have Sophie there?"

"You know her best. But from what you say, I think she's coming to faith. She may not be all the way there, but she says she's ready to take sides. And she trusts you and trusts her own gifts. She could be very helpful. And maybe this experience will boost her faith even more."

On the phone with Sophie later that evening, Detta tested her young friend's resolve one last time. "He may just be mentally disturbed, but usually there's also a spiritual part to that. So we can't be sure what all we'll see. But what if it's really bad, something really evil? Are you ready for that?"

Detta could hear a deep intake of breath over the phone. Sophie made a noise like the start of a word and then paused. "Well, it won't be like the other night in my bed. I won't be alone. So that makes it way better already. And I've been seeing stuff all my life, and not just the pretty stuff or the easy stuff. Creepy and scary are just more of the same for me. No matter what you say, I'm not worried about that part. I'm more worried that I might screw something up for your group."

"Oh, don't even think about that. You just follow the leaders. Jonathan and Ellen are gonna lead. You and me and the others just have to contribute what we have when we get it. I know you can do that."

"Thanks. Your confidence in me makes it seem possible."

It wasn't as much as Detta expected for herself, but for Sophie, *possible* was probably enough.

On a Friday evening between Thanksgiving and Christmas, Sister Ellen arrived at the same time as Detta and Sophie. They walked together from the parking lot to a group therapy room in St. Ignatius Hospital. Sophie seemed to be dragging her feet a bit.

"What's up, Sophie?" Detta asked it low and easy, so Ellen might not hear.

"Uh, it's just the hospital. It's a different hospital, but it reminds me of when I ... you know, was a patient."

Detta stopped. She turned from Sophie to look at Ellen. The easy smile on Ellen's face was as real as could be. Sophie could surely see that.

Sophie rested her eyes on Ellen, absorbing some of her confidence, perhaps. "I'm good. No problem. This is different." Sophie grinned at Detta. "I'm different."

"You are. Yes, you are." Detta repaid that smile and watched Ellen pat Sophie on the back.

Detta was still laughing over Sophie's obvious surprise at first meeting Ellen. "When I call her *sister*, it's not because we have the same natural mother." Detta had explained that while forcefully ignoring Ellen, who had her hand over her mouth and mischief in her eyes.

"Uh, I know that. I just thought the folks at your church were all part of ... members of ... people of color." Sophie had blushed a deep pink color in the harsh light of the hospital entrance.

"Well, that's mostly true. But the prayer group has folks in it from three different churches." Detta shrugged a little.

"Oh. I didn't know that." Sophie had seemed to push past her embarrassment until that little glitch about her history of hospitalization.

But she was back on track. The three of them entered the group therapy room.

Jonathan Chalmers, a clinical psychologist Detta had never met, welcomed each of them into the room. With him was a pale young man he introduced as Freddy McGuire.

Freddy sat sullenly on a low couch, watching the others from below his heavy brow. He wore hospital scrubs and soft clogs on his feet.

Detta and Sophie removed their coats and draped them over the backs of chairs facing Freddy in a rough circle.

Two gentlemen arrived soon after them. They were Jim Bates and Raymond Dubois. Jim was a hefty middle-aged man with pasty skin and big pink lips tightened into a tense smile. Raymond was even heftier and a bit taller than Jim. His shaved brown head reflected the ceiling lights in shiny squares. He greeted Sophie solemnly, maybe a little suspiciously.

Detta had met these gentlemen before, and she knew Jim and Raymond were included for at least a couple of reasons. Their size was one asset. Everyone had heard of the violent escape Freddy made from the police before turning himself in.

And they also knew stories of supernatural strength in the spiritually oppressed. But the presence of two men who looked like football linemen was more about show than intent. No one was there for a physical fight. It wasn't a battle against flesh and blood, after all. Detta had prayed and worshipped with these two gentlemen during and after another ministry session earlier in the year. They were men of faith. Big men of faith.

On a table along one wall, Detta helped Ellen arrange water bottles and snacks. Not a stockpile to last hours and hours, the way some of these ministry sessions had gone in Detta's past, it was just acknowledgement that they would be there for a while. There were snack bars, water bottles, and a few pieces of fruit—similar to what they used to have at the halftime of Anthony's rec league basketball games.

Jonathan called the folks to attention. "All right. Everyone get comfortable. Let's go around and say our names again, if you don't mind." He was standing next to Freddy, who still hunched on the couch, patches of red on each cheek.

Detta turned her head from Freddy to Sophie. The two were about the same age. Right now they were staring at each other. To Detta, Freddy didn't look like someone who was there voluntarily. And he seemed to be sinking into the couch as if he were being absorbed by a giant sponge.

Sophie was on the edge of her chair, her eyes occasionally shifting. Clearly she was seeing something, or probably lots of things.

Each person introduced themself. When it was her turn, Sophie's voice wavered slightly. "Sophie Ramos. I'm here to help however I can." She sounded more like a little girl than Detta had heard before.

Detta was hoping for some eye contact with Sophie, ready to let her know it was okay to change her mind, but Sophie was locked onto Freddy and whatever was going on with him.

Before Jim could introduce himself, the air in the room seemed to ignite. Freddy launched out of the deep cushions of the couch and rose unnaturally to a contorted standing position.

Detta and everyone around her jumped, except Sophie. She just sat up straighter, as if to adjust her line of sight.

Sophie glanced at each of the others, as if waiting for someone to take charge. When they hesitated, she spoke up. "These two creatures ... uh ... *spirits* have him lifted up there. Two big and threatening ones, acting like they're gonna take him away. They have these straps wrapped around his wrists."

Freddy started screaming, "You can see us! You can see us!" His eyes bulged toward Sophie. "You can't get away with this. I know who you are. I can kill everyone you care about!"

Detta wriggled in her seat and had to consciously slow her breathing. "*Just threats. Just the usual threats.*" Reassuring herself, she checked if Sophie needed those same reassurances. Sophie looked worried but not scared. Maybe a little distracted. Detta reached over and rested a hand on her shoulder.

Sophie turned and forced a grin. She didn't look like she was tempted to run for the door yet, not even to go and make sure her mother was safe.

"The names I hear are fear and shame." Ellen moved one step closer to Freddy, a couple feet from the couch.

Freddy twitched and writhed, suspended like a captive trying to break free from his guards.

Jim and Raymond were edging toward either end of the couch. Jonathan stood next to Ellen, holding his hands up to signal restraint to the others.

Detta stayed in her chair, intensifying her intercession for the whole group. That was her job, besides bringing Sophie and keeping an eye on her.

Sophie responded to Ellen's insight. "When you said 'fear and shame,' I could see each of them sort of highlighted. Fear is on Freddy's right, Shame on the left." Her voice was calm, only a slight waver.

Freddy growled and stared at Jim and then Raymond. Like an animal cornered.

From where Detta was sitting, she could see Ellen nodding confidently. Detta had been in quite a few sessions like this. Sometimes they knew pretty specific identities of the inflicting spirits. But she could feel the difference in Sophie's clarity and specificity. She expected that added to Ellen's confidence.

"Where does the shame and fear come from, Freddy?" Jonathan was directly in front of Freddy, who was still wriggling in the grip of his invisible captors, only one foot touching the couch.

Detta suspected that Jonathan knew the answer to his own question. He was probably just trying to get Freddy engaged with the visible world, to start him cooperating with his own liberation.

"No. No. *Nooooo*. Don't touch me there! You can't touch me *theeeeerrrrre!*" Freddy wailed.

"Uh, well, Shame is reaching for Freddy's … uh … for his private parts." Sophie cringed as she said it.

Jim put his hands behind his back, as if he thought Freddy was accusing him.

Raymond looked a bit confused and kept his distance too.

But Ellen and Jonathan stood firm, glancing briefly at each other.

Sophie spoke again. "I don't know if this is allowed, but it looks to me like the two gentlemen at the ends of the couch could just reach up and take ahold of Shame and Fear. The spirits seem intimidated by you guys."

Jonathan turned first, but eventually everyone was staring at Sophie. Even Freddy's eyes bulged toward her.

Ellen smiled. "It does sound odd, but I believe she's right. It's like Freddy has believed these two things are part of him, but they really aren't. And they pretend to be so powerful, but they really aren't. Sophie can see the truth. So we all just have to believe the spirits are liars. That they can just be pulled away from Freddy. He doesn't belong to them, and they don't belong to him."

"Don't listen to her. No. Don't do it. We'll kill him if you do." That was a different voice, not the whiny one. A deeper monster voice.

"That's just Fear talking with a different voice." Sophie spoke evenly, with no hesitation.

Jonathan was nodding. "I'd say, let's do it. Jim, Raymond, if you're willing, would you reach up to the space next to Freddy and let God's Spirit guide you from there." He waited for them to get in place. "And I say, Fear and Shame, you have to let Freddy go in the name of Jesus."

As Jim and Raymond pantomimed grabbing the invisible enemies, Freddy collapsed onto the couch.

To Detta, it seemed like real progress. She could feel a shift toward some bit of new freedom for Freddy.

Ellen nodded vigorously. "Shame and Fear, you have to go, as Jonathan said, and as Freddy wants. You are not part of him. Be gone. Go where Jesus sends you."

Detta noted a flush on Jim's pale cheeks. Raymond was huffing and puffing.

"You need to help them with those big spirits." Sophie lifted a hand toward each of the two large men.

Jonathan touched Raymond's back, and Ellen put a hand on Jim. They each uttered prayers for strength, peace, and protection. And both men seemed to relax.

Again, Detta felt an influx of hope. But she knew this was still early.

"Now there's this big thing wearing a dark hood. It's hovering above Freddy like it's overseeing all the little ones squirming in and out."

Jim and Raymond stepped back at Sophie's observation.

Freddy slumped into his seat, cowering.

"Death." Ellen seemed as certain about that name as Sophie did about what she was seeing.

"Yes." Sophie said. "Yes. And it's trying to kill Freddy now."

Exactly how that dark creature was trying to kill the young man, Detta could only imagine. She was used to threats and deceptions thrown in the way. She kept up her stream of prayers as Jonathan began to address that spirit of death.

Freddy's face flashed from pasty white to deep red and then back to white. And then he began to choke. His face turned red again. Deep red. He grabbed at his throat and squeaked and groaned, veins bulging in his neck. Then he collapsed to his side.

From where Detta sat, he seemed to have stopped breathing.

Ellen dropped to her knees and felt for Freddy's pulse in his neck. That response was no surprise to Detta. Ellen had been a registered nurse for most of her adult life.

"No pulse."

"What?" Sophie blurted that as Jonathan and Ellen exchanged alarmed looks.

"It's still just distractions and tactics." Jonathan was facing Freddy again, his back to Detta, but she could hear the conviction in his voice.

"Breathe, Freddy. I command your body to breathe." Ellen spoke forcefully.

"Spirit of death, you cannot have Freddy now. I declare life over him. Live, Freddy. We all want you to live. Jesus wants you to live." Jonathan hammered those words without allowing panic or pleading to take over his voice.

A gurgling sound from Freddy prompted Ellen to touch his neck again, checking for a pulse. Then Ellen lurched back.

Freddy roared and snapped at her with his teeth, like a mad dog disturbed from his sleep.

Ellen caught herself on the coffee table behind her and stood up. She wobbled for a second, clutching her hands across her chest.

Jim and Raymond both stepped forward protectively, but they seemed to be waiting for a signal to intervene.

With a gasp, Freddy started to pant.

Others in the room released a relieved breath.

Then Freddy was no longer roaring or threatening. He was shaking and sobbing.

Checking Sophie, Detta found her sedate but certainly not sedated. As far as Detta could tell, Sophie was as calm as anyone in the room. And it didn't feel fake. The natural slump of her shoulders, the slight tilt of her head, looked real. Sophie was watching, waiting for her next contribution.

Sophie opened her mouth, hesitated, and then spoke. "A shifting sort of thing is, like, flashing in and out. Like, behind Death, and sort of supporting him."

"Deception," said Detta instantly.

Jonathan seized that. "Okay. I bind the spirit of deception. Let go of Freddy. I break off your ties with Freddy and with Death."

Even after Jonathan eventually vanquished the spirit of death, with Sophie's confirmation, the spirit of deception kept its place around Freddy.

"It changed shape and is, like, half transparent. But it didn't leave." Sophie only provided that insight when Jonathan turned to her for help, as if he doubted that spirit had left when commanded yet again. During the struggle that ran well over an hour, Sophie's intelligence appeared to keep Ellen and Jonathan on track toward dislodging the spirit of deception and others linked to it.

Most of the spirits had generic names that Sophie confirmed when they reacted to being identified. She described them shrinking or changing color or fading from view. Often they would howl in agony, using Freddy's vocal cords. To Detta, the spirits were a bunch of drama queens. The worst kind of whiny children.

But one spirit seemed to have no single characteristic attached to it. Not shame or fear or lust. Yet it seemed particularly important.

"It keeps reaching behind it and pulling something up over its head—a cloak or hood or something—like it's trying to hide, trying to cover itself and Freddy." Sophie shrugged and looked at the two leaders.

For a while, Ellen and Jonathan addressed more recognizable enemies. But that nameless one repeatedly interfered.

Then Sophie gasped, right after Jonathan prayed for divine revelation about that spirit. "Its name is Agnes, I think. I don't know why. That just comes into my head as I look at it." She touched a hand to her lips briefly. "And as soon as I said that name, the cloak came off, and I could see clearly that it looks like a woman."

"Agnes, you have to go." Ellen spoke with authority, perhaps a bit of relief layered onto her voice.

Detta lost track of how long they struggled with the Agnes spirit. They figured out that its power came from an occult curse of some kind. Other lesser spirits flew into view, as Sophie reported, whenever the ministers seemed close to banishing Agnes. That was typical in a complicated deliverance—the ruling spirits throwing other smaller ones forward as a delay tactic.

As they closed in on Agnes again, Sophie sat up straight. "It's like she's weeping, trying to get us to feel sorry for her. She's begging not to be sent away, I think."

When the Agnes spirit spoke through Freddy, no one could understand what it was saying. It screamed and jibbered incomprehensibly. Jonathan persisted at silencing that strange tongue.

Then suddenly Freddy was cogent and calm. He leaned his elbows on his knees and labored to catch his breath.

Jonathan looked at Sophie.

She shook her head, certainly meaning that Agnes hadn't left.

When he turned back to Freddy, Jonathan reached out and put a hand on his shoulder. "You okay, buddy? I know this is hard."

Freddy was shaking his head. "I know who Agnes is." He was still panting. "A friend of my grandma's. She did something over me when I was little. My grandma took me to a psychic and to a palm reader, but there was also this friend of hers ..." His face contorted, as if someone were trying to tear him in half. He grabbed the collar of his cotton shirt and tried to rip it off.

Speaking with calm authority, Ellen stopped the antics. "Let him go, Agnes. We break the curse this woman put on Freddy and break all unholy power his grandmother still has over him."

Freddy cried out like he had burned himself on a stove. Then the cries became higher, a very realistic woman's voice. That voice threatened and cursed and then resorted again to speaking a strange language.

"She's calling other spirits onto Freddy." Sophie was watching the corners of the room like a flock of birds had gotten in at the windows.

Jonathan commanded an end to those calls for reinforcements and prayed for angelic protection around the room.

"Guardians are lining up all around, high and low. And more are still arriving." Sophie craned her neck to see around the room, her eyes wide and brows raised, more excited than during most of that stressful evening.

"I bless the guardian angels to do God's bidding and to protect God's children in this room." That flowed out of Detta loud and strong.

Sophie seconded her. "Yes!"

Then the Agnes voice wailed fearfully. "Oh no! Michael. Michael is here. The commander of the army of the host of heaven. Michael is here!"

When Detta understood those words, her hair stood on end. She glanced around the room, then let her eyes fall on Sophie. Everyone else was looking at her as well.

Sophie shook her head. "Just the usual guardians, as far as I can tell."

The others still gazed at Sophie. Detta wondered if Sophie could be mistaken. Would she know the angel Michael if she saw him? Maybe she just couldn't see the archangel for some reason. Or maybe she was being deceived somehow.

But Ellen broke into Detta's mental flapping. "Who cares if the angel Michael *is* here? We have the Spirit of God in us. The Lord Jesus Christ himself is right here with us. The angel Michael is only his servant."

That deflated the helium building up in Detta's head. She settled back in her chair and puffed a long breath she didn't even know she had been holding.

Sophie was nodding. She had a sparkly sheen in her eyes, a look of satisfied discovery on her childlike face.

That joyous glow prompted Detta to start worshipping. She allowed praise and worship to rise up in her, releasing it loud and louder. And the others in the room caught on to that elevating praise. Ellen started to sing hallelujahs. Raymond added his big booming voice, and Jim started shouting.

"There she goes. Agnes is outta here." Sophie almost giggled. She was breathing hard and smiling just as hard.

Aftercare

Sophie slumped in the padded stacking chair as Detta wound down her ecstatic shouting. A weariness lay on Sophie like a pile of quilts. But deep in her core, an energy pulsed. What was that? Hope? Belonging? Satisfaction? *"This is what I was made for. I am not a mistake. I am not a liar. What I have inside me is real. And it is powerful. And I have found people who know it and trust it."*

Detta had believed her since they first met, of course. But that could have just been Detta. Maybe she was crazy too, like Sophie. Of course it got real when Sophie helped banish that snake biting into Detta's chest, but her gift was out there, outside her relationship with Detta, or with Crystal, or Kimmy. She had seen it work in front of these people—strangers, really. And it worked well. Very well.

This room full of people trusted her gifts. Not just words. Not abstract acceptance. They acted on what she saw, what she said. Without doubt. No hesitation. Their acceptance had made a difference for Freddy McGuire. And it would surely make a difference for Sophie from here on.

She shook her head, rousing herself to join the world outside her head. In the room. Here and now. Sophie watched Ellen and Jonathan talking with Freddy. Freddy in his right mind. In that world outside of Sophie's head, she also watched a pair of angels standing at the ends of the couch where Jim and Raymond used to be.

Not until Detta patted her on the back did Sophie realize she had been sitting there shaking her head. She stilled herself and let her neck relax. She turned to Detta and let out a childish question. "You do this all the time?"

Detta smiled. She surveyed the other team members—Jim and Raymond talking quietly in one corner, Ellen and Jonathan talking to Freddy, praying for him, and holding his hands.

Freddy looked like a little boy, new to this school.

"We do ministry to spiritually oppressed folks every once in a while. But I've never seen anything *exactly* like this … ever." She beamed her most motherly grin at Sophie.

A long, slow breath relaxed still more parts that Sophie hadn't known were tensed. She stretched her feet in front of her from where they had been pulled under her chair and tucked together, almost fetal.

Freddy was crying now. His head rested on Jonathan's shoulder, one hand clasped to his own face. Small angels were carrying cups of golden liquid, pouring it on him and flying out of the room in turn.

For some reason, that made Sophie start to cry. And she didn't feel ashamed or embarrassed. It was like she was celebrating with Freddy and with those beautiful angels. Celebrating a prisoner being set free. Celebrating with tears.

She replayed images from the two-hour event, images of people fighting invisible beings that were fully visible to her. The faith of the folks who couldn't see what she was seeing wrapped around her like armor custom fit to her body. Their faith in her gift gathered into her a confidence she had never known before. Instead of the bitter disgust at the gap between what she saw and what others believed, she absorbed certainty that strengthened her very bones.

Detta patted her again. Wiping tears with her other hand, she was looking at Freddy too.

Sophie leaned into that strong hand resting on her shoulder. She studied Detta. What a blessing this woman had been to her. What a surprise. Like the stories of fairy godmothers from childhood cartoons. The power of Detta's faith and her love had lifted Sophie out of desperation and confusion.

Sophie smiled when Detta caught her staring. Detta scrunched her brow in consternation at Sophie's enamored gaze, but that only endeared her more. She didn't even know what a blessing she was.

Eventually Freddy was able to rise to his feet, tottering as if recovering from recent surgery. But Raymond hugged him athletically, no caution about stitches he might pop. Freddy laughed and cried at the same time now. Jonathan stayed close, a hand resting on Freddy most of the time. And Jim gave Freddy a big hug too.

Perhaps the best reason to have those two large men present that evening was for those fatherly hugs. A pretty good reason. Sophie could use one of those.

And that thought set free a different sort of tears. Not a celebration. Not relief at pain finally healed. Just an unnamed flow. A flow she allowed herself. Letting go. Hadn't she seen beauty come from someone letting go?

Voices rising at the other end of the room kicked her out of that emotional free fall. She sniffled hard and reached for her jacket where it hung on the chair behind her, hoping to find tissues in the pockets.

Detta handed her two clumped Kleenexes before Sophie could find anything.

"Thanks." She didn't want to look at Detta. She didn't want to explain what was happening to her. Or maybe it was that she didn't want Detta to explain it, to define it, to package it. Sophie could sense her friend holding back, looking at her and then away again and again. Holding her tongue.

Jonathan and Ellen were gathering everyone into a circle. Done with concentrating on the layer of spirits in the room, Sophie stood and joined the human beings standing and grasping hands.

"Let's bless God for what has happened here and pray for the good work to continue in all of us in the days ahead." Was Ellen looking at Sophie when she said, "in all of us?" She was including everyone in her gaze, each one in turn, but those words felt targeted.

Did Sophie have good work happening in her? Work? What kind of work? The kind she had seen Freddy going through?

Sophie allowed a smile to reflect the joy on the faces around the circle. Detta gripped her right hand, Jonathan her left. Across from her were Ellen and Jim, Freddy and Raymond on the sides. She tried not to look at anyone for too long.

Then the intensified glow of angels called her attention beyond the people. There were those two shining ones hovering over Freddy. They looked like they were ready to whisk him away at any moment, to carry him somewhere. To safety? Wasn't he safe already?

The two angels behind Ellen seemed fully satisfied. They appeared to be reveling even more joyfully than the humans in the circle. Both of Detta's angels were there as well. Big and glowing. Jubilant as much as vigilant just now.

Sophie could sense her own angel standing behind her. More clearly than before, she felt his blanket of comfort and protection for her. Her angel had her back.

Ellen and Jonathan led prayers along the lines Ellen had proposed. Detta added more forceful prayers for protection against the enemy's backlash.

That briefly distracted Sophie into speculations about how the enemy spirits worked. How coordinated were they? The enemies plaguing Freddy's life seemed organically connected to each other, some subservient, some ready to throw others under the bus. Were they organized in a way that could bring a retaliation? Retaliation against any of them, not just Freddy? Retaliation against her? Against her friends and family?

As soon as this fear solidified in Sophie's mind, Ellen started praying for her specifically. "I know she's new to this, Lord. So, answer her questions, calm any worries or doubts, and seal in your reward for her faithfulness with the gifts you have given her. Blessings and protection, in the name of Jesus, be upon Sophie and her family tonight and all the days ahead."

The soothing warmth of her angel at her back seemed to penetrate deeper with Ellen's prayers. The protection for which Ellen prayed seemed to be within reach right then. But the unnumbered days ahead seemed too long a stretch for such confidence. Sophie nodded, nonetheless, truly grateful for whatever protection might come because of it, especially for her mother.

For Sophie, there was no way to end that evening that wouldn't be awkward. She didn't really fit in this group, yet she had played a key role in the victory they had won. In doing so, she had discovered a sense of fulfillment and purpose that was new—and vulnerable. Rubbing elbows with the others on the way toward the door, she felt like she needed to pull her garments around her to conceal her nakedness.

Freddy stopped near the door, reaching a hand toward her.

She took that hand and shook it, a shy smile reflected from his face to hers.

"Thanks, Sophie. I really appreciate what you did for me. My life is changed forever." He appeared ready to start crying again.

She hoped he could hold off. She didn't want to slide down that fireman's pole again.

"Oh. I'm so glad. I'm … uh … glad to finally feel useful, ya know."

Probably he didn't know exactly, but he nodded and smiled more broadly. Maybe he got the feeling he had done her a favor in the process. And hadn't he? He had trusted her as Detta had trusted her, and Ellen and Jonathan.

Sophie could feel Detta's heavy hand on her back, the warmth coming through her jacket. She allowed that hand to ease her out of the room and into the hall. She glanced at her smart watch as she sleepwalked toward the big mechanical doors ahead of them. It was just past nine o'clock. Not so late for her on a Friday, but it was late for Detta.

"There's a good place to get some tea or coffee across the street. You wanna hang out for a little while?"

Smiling at Detta, Sophie briefly wondered if she had mutely requested that carryover meeting with the glance at her watch. "It's not too late for you?"

"It's a weekend. I can stay up a bit on a Friday night."

"What difference does that make when you're retired?" Sophie laughed, feeling the freedom in teasing Detta.

"Oh, it's just a habit, I suppose." She tipped her head with a smirk. "But I do sleep in a bit on a Saturday. It's kinda my Sabbath day, I guess. A day to rest up a little."

"Do you need extra rest after a night like this?" Sophie dragged heavy limbs through the mechanical doors toward the elevators. They had parked Sophie's car in the lot to the east of the hospital. The others in the group seemed to be taking a different route out of the building.

"Oh, I expect so. But it's nice to debrief afterward too. Kinda helps me get back to normal life, I guess."

Normal life? Sophie didn't say that. For her, there were five in the elevator. Three angels and two women. That was normal for her. But for now it felt more like a shared normal.

"Why do you think you have two angels? And so did Ellen. And there were two for Freddy at the end." Sophie stepped out when the elevator doors opened, but she kept her eyes on Detta.

"I asked the Lord that when you first mentioned the two guardian angels at my house." They crossed the lobby toward the automatic sliding doors that led out to the front driveway. Detta pulled her scarf closer to her neck and tucked it into the collar of her camel coat. "And I kinda thought I heard the Lord answer that there were some folks who weren't using their angels for anything." She shook her head and laughed briefly. "I don't know if that's right, but that's what I thought I heard in response to my question."

"Does God always answer your questions?"

"I expect he does." She was checking her footing. The sidewalk was clear. "You wanna walk over there and just leave your car here for now?" Detta gestured across the street.

Sophie nodded.

Detta continued. "I expect he does answer, but I'm pretty sure I miss the answer lots o' times. I'm not always ready to hear what he has to say. Or maybe I just don't understand what he's tryin' to tell me."

She led Sophie over newish pavement toward the corner where there was a stoplight and a crosswalk. The air was cold but not biting. The slight breeze smelled like approaching snowfall. "God is always available, Sophie. He's just waitin' for you to ask questions and hear the answers. You don't have to go anywhere to find him or ask anyone else to show you. He's there for you right now, as close as all those angels and spirits you see all the time."

Whether God was really so friendly and inviting as Detta claimed, Sophie felt welcomed by Detta. The old church lady was certainly inviting. Maybe she was even recruiting. But that prospect didn't bother Sophie so much as it used to.

She had heard people say they believed in God and in the spiritual world God occupied. That night she had seen people proving that faith was more than a religious word to them. Their faith had power. She could sign up for *that* kind of faith.

"Does it have to be Jesus? Is that the only way this works?" She surprised herself by voicing that dangerous question.

"For me it is. He's the one who makes all this possible. God seemed far off until Jesus made the way for us. Jesus is the one who gives us his Spirit and his wisdom to help someone like Freddy."

"Okay. Tell me how it's done. What do I need to do?" They were standing at the door to the coffee shop, the lights inside adding a golden gloss to Detta's face.

"I'd be glad to, of course. Let me get some tea, and let's talk about it."

Sophie nodded and followed Detta through the heavy glass door into the aroma of coffee, cinnamon, and hot chocolate.

The Girl Who Sees Angels

How to Start This Thing

Saturday afternoon, Sophie parked her car in front of her mother's house. When she climbed out, she noticed how dirty her blue hybrid was even though it was still early in the snow-and-salt season. Her train commute meant neglecting her car most of the week.

It occurred to her, as she was walking to her mother's front door, that she should have noticed the gray streaks of dried brine before. They had surely begun to obscure her shiny metallic paint weeks ago, at the first hint of snow. But back then she was still hooding her focus, trying *not* to see things. Today, there had been none of those surly riders in the back seat. Keeping her head up and her eyes open seemed less irritating now.

"Hello, my Sophia. You look bright and happy this afternoon." That was nothing like her mother's usual greeting, generally hesitantly inquisitive. Usually her mother sounded ready to apologize for something.

"I feel good, Mama. It's true. And I have important news about that." She had held onto her news last night. The urge to call her mother after her long talk with Detta had seemed premature, like announcing a pregnancy too early.

"Come in, come in. Let me take your coat."

Sophie locked eyes with her mother's angel and exchanged a smile. Something about her connection with him was new. A chill shivered her spine. She could feel that angel's approval. Acceptance. A sort of recognition that ran deep.

"Mama, I'm a Christian now." She couldn't even wait until her hands were both free from her jacket sleeves.

"You what? What do you mean?"

"I prayed with Detta last night and committed to following Jesus."

"Following Jesus?" Her mother's eyes dimmed just a half notch, but her angel radiated more brightly.

Sophie checked her own angel. He was close at her elbow without constricting her movement—one of the skills of angeldom, apparently. "I believe in all the things you taught me about Jesus, and the cross, and rising from the dead. I pretty much believed it all along. But now I'm not resisting it anymore. I love God, and I love Jesus. And Detta says I have the Spirit of God inside me."

Her mother stared with a sweepstakes smile on her face. She seemed to be swimming through the shock. Finally, she blinked hard. "Mija! That's wonderful news. I have prayed for you for so long." She grabbed Sophie in a tight hug.

Sophie heard her jacket hit the floor. She let loose a succession of sobs. Her mother's shocked hesitation had briefly freshened her fear about telling her. Her mother was usually awake later than Detta. Sophie could have called her after ten o'clock. But she had been uncertain what her madrecita would make of her daughter's conversion.

Sophie wiped her cheeks as she pulled out of the hug. "I don't think I've answered all the questions about how I feel about church and things, but I know how I feel about Jesus." She was still monitoring her mother's eyes. "Last night I saw the way Jesus gave people the power to do wonderful things for someone who really needed him. I could see that the Spirit of God is good, and is good for me. And I have been noticing how the other spirits fear God. I know they see things that people can't. And now I know it's all real." She hung onto her mother's arms.

Her madrecita nodded a growing affirmation—relief in eyes that loosened just a little, and a smile that relaxed a bit more. "You look so happy, my girl." She held Sophie's chin briefly. "This is such a relief. I knew you would find your way to God. And of course it had to be your *own* way, not just what others told you was right."

Surely Sophie still understood only a fraction of the difference between Detta's faith and her mother's, but that difference was dull now under the glow from the angels standing with them in the living room. Perhaps the churches and the traditions were very different, but her mother's angel was just like Detta's and like her own. And her mother's words of acceptance appeared to turn up the watts as the two angels stood smiling at the two women.

Was Sophie's angel really smiling?

For a second she remembered the man who appeared in her living room a couple weeks ago. That same smile had been on his face, or so it seemed to her now. At the time she was too freaked out to appreciate that smile, but she hadn't forgotten it.

Her mother wiping tears from her cheeks adjusted Sophie's focus.

"Thank you, Mama. Thank you for always praying for me and never losing hope."

Laughing, her mother stepped back. "Oh, I don't claim that I have never lost any hope at different times. There have been some very hard times for believing. But I always knew that you would fight through. You are a fighter, Sophie. You are a survivor."

Sophie ran her hands over both her cheeks again.

The primary purpose of this visit wasn't for Sophie to deliver her news. It was really part of a long tradition. Tears wiped, tissues wadded and deposited, they turned to the task of pulling the artificial tree and decorations down from the rafters in the garage.

As they assembled it all in the living room, the conversation was different from any year before. Sophie tried to describe to her mother the scene at the hospital the previous evening—the way the team gently surrounded Freddy and battled against the spirits oppressing him. She didn't know how much she was allowed to tell, so she kept the story generic and kept all the names out of it except Detta's.

"For me, the best part might have been being in the hospital without fear, without being a prisoner there. I was there to help. I had the power to do something. Being a patient had always meant being so powerless."

This prompted more apologies and more tears from her mother. But at least part of that catharsis was certainly relief over Sophie's newfound peace and freedom.

The lights wrapped around the tree and lit in the dimming of the day, Sophie saw the colors streaked through tears again and again. This decoration party required more hugs and tissues than any of the previous ones.

On her way home that night, Sophie got a call. "Priscilla, how are you doing?"

"Me? I'm not the one with the big news. When were you gonna tell me?"

There was only one headline in Sophie's life right then, but she hadn't expected the news to spread so fast, not even to one of her best friends—her Christian friend. "Uh, yeah. How did you find out?"

"Detta and my mother are really close friends, Sophie. Detta is just beside herself with joy. She had to tell someone.

I'm pretty sure she's not telling *everyone*, but I suspect she knew my mama would tell me too. You're gonna need support, girl."

"Support?"

"Of course. You're in the fight now. And the enemy is not gonna be happy about that."

Sophie was sitting at a traffic light when Priscilla said that. She pressed on the accelerator when the light turned green. But then she slammed on her brakes, allowing a black muscle car to *vroom* across in front of her on what must have been a red light for him. As that car roared past, Sophie spotted a large creature attached to it. Glowing green eyes lasered toward her.

"What was that?" Priscilla squealed.

"A guy just ran a red light. Nearly nailed me."

"Oh. Well, see? That's what I'm talkin' about. The enemy is gonna try to take you out now, girl. Well, oh my. You need protection."

"Really? Huh. Are you gonna be my bodyguard?"

Priscilla laughed. "No, girl. I'm gonna pray, and God is gonna send angels to protect you."

A golden glow at the edge of her peripheral vision made her turn her head. Her angel was in the passenger seat, which was new. And there was another glow. Someone else's angel? "Are there some angels that just do freelance, not assigned to be a person's guardian?"

"Ha. I don't know. That's your area. But I wouldn't be surprised. Why? What are you seeing?"

"Well, there's my angel in the car with me—"

"Sweet!"

"And there seems to be a guardian, or an angel of some kind, back at that intersection." Talking about it made her more aware of the spirit layer around her. But the rowdy crowd of creatures coming and going from various houses and bars along the street induced a wince. She turned down her sensors.

Priscilla sounded more subdued. "Okay. That's cool."

"But you make it sound like it was a bad idea for me to join up." Sophie settled back in her seat and gripped the steering wheel more tightly.

"Oh, no. Sorry. That's not right. I shouldn't say it like that. I definitely think it's a good idea. You just gotta know that there are no civilians in the world. We're all fighting on one side or the other. Some are just aware of it, and others not. At least, that's what my pastor says. Or maybe that's my mama's pastor. I think they agree on that though."

Sophie drew in a sharp breath. "My mom was weirded out by what I said about following Jesus. Her church talks about it differently, I think. And now I gotta figure out the difference between *your* church and your *mama's* too?"

"Uh, yeah. Sorry about that. It is pretty sad how it's all divided up. But we can't change that—we just have to make the best of it. It took my mama a while to stop buggin' me to get back to her church. She's okay with me going to Rescue House now. At least she stopped trying to drag me back. I think she's just happy that I go to church at all. My brothers are totally drifting."

"Wait, *Rescue House*? Is that the name of your church?"

"Yeah. I told you that."

"I guess I wasn't paying attention. Or maybe just not getting it. Why Rescue House?"

"Well, part of the name is to get away from churchy words. Like, my mama's church is called Bethany Temple. That's pretty religious sounding. Our church tries to reach out to people who aren't thinking of themselves as religious—at least not in the traditional sense."

Sophie let out another of those sighs. "So, *religious* is not good?"

"Some folks think so. I guess there's good religion and bad religion, really. And, of course, folks don't all agree on which is which." Priscilla echoed Sophie's sigh. "But don't worry. You don't have to figure it all out—not ever, really. You just gotta find a place where you can connect with people and grow in Jesus. After that you can let other folks do it the way that works for them, and then just try not to judge them."

"Okay. I'm glad I don't have to understand all that, because I don't."

"You wanna come to church with me tomorrow?"

As soon as that question reached Sophie over the Bluetooth connection in her car, two spirits grabbed the frame around her windshield, staring in at her. Her angel's glow cooled from gold to silver. The two outside glowed red and blue, but flashed white momentarily.

"Help me, God." She let that out automatically.

"What?"

"These two spirits just grabbed my car. I can't tell if they're good or bad."

"They just now showed up?"

"Yeah, when you asked me to go to church."

"Huh. And they don't look good or evil?"

"I don't know. I guess they're not evil. Not scary or threatening. But they're in my face." She lurched to a stop more abruptly than she intended when the light changed to yellow at the next intersection.

The two external passengers seemed to be waiting for an answer to a question.

"Sophie, what happens if you tell them to stop it?"

"Go away, and stop bothering my driving." Sophie spoke through the windshield, expecting the semi-transparent visitors could hear her through the safety glass.

"Did they take off?"

"Yeah, they did. But I don't know what that means. Do good angels leave when you tell 'em to? And would good ones get in the way of my driving?"

"Uh, this is past me."

"I don't know if they were trying to mess with me. I was just distracted. But maybe that's on me."

The light changed. This time Sophie checked for cross traffic before accelerating. "I should concentrate on my driving. This has my head spinning."

"Yeah. Sure. I understand. Sorry if I made it seem more negative than I should've."

"No worries. I love you, Priscilla. And now we can really be sisters." She snickered briefly, her own joke sounding corny to her.

"Ha. Yeah. I'll keep prayin' for ya. Blessings, Sister Sophie." Priscilla giggled as they hung up.

The Girl Who Sees Angels

A Quiet Sunday at Home

On Sunday morning, Sophie woke to a call from her mother.

"Do you want to come to church with me, mija?"

A half hour later it was Detta. "Sophie, you wanna come to church with me this morning? We can sit in the back in case it gets to be too much for you."

And a half hour after that, Priscilla. "Sophie, what do you think about coming to church with me? You wanna give it a try?"

Sophie was glad she didn't know anyone else who might invite her to church this morning. However, if Crystal had called to invite her to a drum circle, and Kimmy had invited her to a Narcotics Anonymous meeting, she wouldn't have been surprised.

By the time Priscilla's call ended, Sophie counted twelve visitors in her apartment. None seemed scary. Most were like the red or blue ones from the night before. Nice enough, but they seemed to be waiting for something. They made her nervous.

There were also new ones of those golden-guardian type. One was beautiful like Kimmy's angel. Graceful arms, smooth and shining, motherly eyes full of affection and the quiet confidence that all the guardians carried. Another golden visitor was more difficult to define gender-wise, but was clearly a warrior, sheathed in glowing armor. Intimidating, but not so intimidating toward *her*.

Emboldened by her experience of the previous evening, Sophie sent them all away except her usual guardian. "I hope that was okay, God. It was getting crowded in here." She glanced toward the ceiling as if that was where her prayer would meet God. She saw no visual evidence of that connection, just the usual traffic passing through her building and above it. When she allowed her X-ray vision to penetrate the walls and ceilings, her head teetered like she had stood up too quickly. She tried to shut that virtual vertigo down, but it was a struggle, like trying not to remember a traumatic image.

"Try *not* to think of pink elephants." Some therapist said that to her once. Maybe it was that kindergarten-teacher type with the wide eyes and whispery voice. When Sophie was twelve, she had liked that one, but she could only take so much of that cooing counselor. And the spirits crowded into her office had overwhelmed Sophie back then.

Had anything changed for Sophie on that score? Could she still see as much as she did as a girl? That was before she learned ways to focus on concrete things that dulled the spiritual layer. And now this was a new stage. There was something more. Sophie had signed up with God and his Son—and the Spirit.

"The Spirit." That part sounded extra weird. Spirits were familiar to her now that she realized they were what she had been seeing all these years. But God had a particular Spirit that was supposed to be in her life. Priests had mentioned him lots of times.

"And he isn't you, right?" She spoke to her guardian from where she sat on her sofa with a cup of coffee. A fleece blanket spread over her lap, she had her feet pulled up beside her. The floor was especially cold. She imagined the guy downstairs turning his thermostat down to fifty degrees just to freeze her feet. But she shut that accusation down when a pair of spirits from downstairs poked their heads in.

"Stay out of here."

That response to uninvited guests was part of her new stage—telling spirits what to do, as well as asking her angel questions.

But he wasn't talking. He didn't look mad, but he also didn't look particularly happy. He had lost that smile he flashed at her mother's house. He definitely didn't look confused, as if he didn't know the answer to her questions. But he always appeared to be waiting. Vigilant?

By lunchtime, Sophie was feeling stir crazy. She had to get outside, even if it was a gray December day with stints of precipitation alternating between gentle and nasty. The taco salad at the sandwich shop two blocks away invited her more persuasively than all the church ladies who had called her that morning.

"How was church?" Sophie was walking on the street, her phone held in a fingerless glove, the mitten top flipped open.

Priscilla spoke with a perky purr. "It was awesome. You should check it out online. You can see a video of the service—especially the teaching. I think you'd find it really encouraging. She was talking about identifying with Jesus instead of identifying with a political brand or even with a particular church. Very relevant to what we were talkin' about last night."

Something in that summary didn't sound right. "Wait, *she*? Did you say *she*? Your church has a priestess?"

A cackling, gasping laugh ended in a short coughing fit on the other end of the phone connection. Then a long sigh. "Oh, girl. I gotta tell that one to my friends at church. 'Priestess.' Ha. That sounds like we're some sorta New Age cult or something. Oh, girl. That's hilarious."

"Are you laughing at me?" Sophie slowed at the corner outside the sandwich shop.

"Oh, sorry. Yeah. I guess I got carried away. Uh, well, I should be serious, shouldn't I? Ha. Well, we have a couple, a husband and wife, who pastor the church. Co-pastors. No one around here is called a priest or a priestess. The Bible says we're all priests, but that's for another time." She paused. "Sorry I laughed at you, Sophie. You're so new to this, I just get caught off guard by how different it is for you."

"Okay. I get it." She shifted her weight left to right and back, peering in the restaurant window. "I'm ready to go in and order my salad. I'll visit the church's website when I get home. Rescue Church, right?"

"Rescue *House*."

"Okay, I'll check it out. Thanks, 'Cilla. Talk to you later." It was a hasty goodbye, but Sophie wanted to end the call before entering the restaurant.

She was noticing a guy in there, standing in line at the counter. A really hot guy. A hot guy who was obviously noticing *her* through the big window. Resisting the urge to pull her hat off and fluff up her hair, she slipped her phone into her jacket pocket.

The little two-inch step up to the front door tripped her, and she swallowed a curse at the klutzy entrance. In the romantic comedy she was writing in her head, that stumble was the comedy part. A short bout of pushing various spirits aside would have to be edited from that movie scene. This scene was just supposed to be about her and that guy, that very attractive older man.

Probably pushing forty, a bit of a crag to his face, certainly an outdoorsy type. Not really *that* much older than her. Perfect hair—no hat crunch in sight—dark and sleek, a bit of a wave, and stylishly cut. His eyes were blue. Yes, blue. He was checking her out with those gem-blue eyes. Smiling. And with perfect teeth.

Smiling right at her.

Oh, yes. Cue up the indie pop music, a bouncy, almost-love song, hope-filled chorus, and an easy dance rhythm.

The needle on that platter skipped and screeched when a hulking beast loomed over her dream man.

Deal breaker.

When she twisted her neck to get that creature in better focus, however, she realized that it was more likely attached to the slouchy guy standing behind her dream man. In fact, she could see no critters clinging to, or hovering over, the handsome man in the perfectly-fit leather jacket—a jacket a lot like the one she wore most days.

The crowd of spiritual occupants in the restaurant required Sophie to observe her target like a naturalist following a jaguar through a jungle. As far as she could tell, none of those alien arms, legs, and tentacles were attached to him.

No guardian?

She checked her own guardian. He had his arms crossed. Angel body language? She hadn't mastered that yet. At least he was there with her.

Sophie pressed through the spiritual vines into the order line. The handsome customer was ordering his lunch. Three other people were in line ahead of her. It was the midday rush. How was she supposed to meet this guy? Maybe accidentally bump him as he walked past? But he wasn't likely to pass her. The pickup counter was twenty feet away from the order counter. Could she think of a faster order that would boost her up the queue before he grabbed his goods and sauntered seductively out of the place?

She felt a snicker close to her ear. Felt it more than heard it. Something was making fun of her little romcom fantasy. Her guardian was there, but he wasn't laughing. He seemed to be waiting for directions. Could she order him to slow that guy down, or slow down his sandwich prep so she could catch up? She guessed not.

Finally reaching the front of the line to order her taco salad, she watched the hot guy receiving his sandwich at pickup, wrapped to go.

He glanced over at her and then opened the white bag to check on his order. He read the slip of paper. "This is a taco salad." He spoke to the guy working behind the pickup counter. "I ordered the muffuletta sandwich." His complaining voice was ironic and almost amused. Nice.

Wait. He got the wrong order. He got what Sophie ordered.

"I'll take that. I ordered a taco salad." She was looking at the guy, but realized she had to pretend this was just business. So she turned back to the girl at the cash register. "I could take that taco salad since he doesn't want it." Her voice thinned and cracked.

A spirit behind the cashier was smacking itself in the head. Sophie hoped the girl wouldn't follow suit.

"Uh. Well, I don't …" The cashier looked to an older guy who was turning from the order slips hanging in front of the kitchen.

"What?" That older guy was just entering this drama.

"She ordered a taco salad, and this gentlemen received a taco salad by mistake."

They all looked toward the hot guy, who arched his eyebrows in bemused suspense. Then they all looked at the guy behind the counter.

"Who was the taco salad for?" The older guy, who might have been the manager, asked the pickup counter guy.

"I don't know." He rummaged through a line of bags, glancing at the tickets stapled to them. "I don't see an order here for taco salad."

"She just ordered that." The cashier practically moaned it.

Sophie wanted to comfort the girl. And she didn't want to look like she was trying to cause trouble. "It's just a coincidence, I guess. I just noticed him ..." She glanced at the attractive guy and got hung up for an extra second. "I ... uh, that man ... that guy." She pulled out of the nosedive just in time. "I just thought it would save you some trouble, since you already made a taco salad. If it doesn't belong to anyone else, I could take it." Was she sounding frantic? While frantically trying *not* to sound frantic?

"Sure. Okay. Go ahead." The manager made a ruling. There was a growing line. No one wanted a congressional inquiry into the matter.

"Sorry. Didn't mean to butt in." Sophie sashayed toward her dream man. Was she sashaying? Not staggering? "I just thought ..." Of course he knew what she thought. She should stop talking.

"Yeah. Makes perfect sense to me. I'll just wait for my muffuletta."

"Ah. Muffuletta. Is that New Orleans?" That was all she knew about muffuletta sandwiches.

"Yeah. I love it down there. The food, the restaurants, the clubs." He nodded, grinning at some memory or other. "And they make a pretty good muffuletta here." He was smiling at her now, looking down from over six feet. Tall. Broad-shouldered. Gorgeous.

"Nice. I've never been there. But I hear it's ... nice." *Nice? Really? That's the best you could come up with?*

"It *is* nice. But I like it here too."

"Yeah. This city has lots to offer." She opened the white sack containing the taco salad, just glancing inside. The handsome guy and the pickup clerk had checked already. She didn't really need to check. But where else was she supposed to look? Looking into those definitely-blue eyes was like when she checked out the levels of spirits above her apartment. Dizzying.

That guy hadn't lost his grin. "So, are you carrying out? Going to meet someone, maybe?"

"Uh, no. Just gonna eat at home." How embarrassing. All alone. Poor her. Pitiful.

"Well, me too. Wanna stick around and eat here? I did get you a pretty quick taco salad."

She laughed. Relief. Hey, it wasn't a bad thing that she was alone. She was available. "Oh, yeah. I guess I owe you." She tried to sound ironic. Clever. He was that. All that.

"Good. Wanna grab us that last table?" He raised his eyes toward a pair of seats by the front window. He was lifting his face from looking at her, from looking into her eyes. Deep.

"Uh, okay. Sure. I'll go grab it." Sophie just missed crashing into a woman and a toddler and avoided banging into a metal railing guarding the counter area. Sprinting to that empty table wouldn't be cool, but what would happen if someone got there first? She had cash. She could bribe them.

There was no wrestling match for control of that table, no need for bribery. And Sophie didn't make a total fool of herself while having lunch with the handsome stranger.

Brent. That was his name. Not really a stranger anymore. Still handsome.

She Can't See His Angel

Anthony stopped by his mother's house to drop off the new Christmas lights he'd bought on sale. He was trying to get her to convert from her ancient incandescent lights, a fire hazard for sure.

Sophie was there. "Wait, this isn't your day, is it?"

He grinned at her standing by the fridge, looking like she was at home and pretty happy about it.

"Just dropping off, not crashing your dinner."

"You have plans, dear? You could eat with us." His mother took the boxes of lights from him. "Thanks for these. We'll see how they look."

"They're not the same, but they're way safer than your old ones. That Christmas tree is drying out more every day, and those old lights could spark or get too hot."

"Yes, dear. I understand."

She was just humoring him. He would have to switch the lights himself to be sure she did it. But she had asked another question. "Uh, no. I can't stay. I'm gettin' together with someone tonight. Kind of important."

"An important date? When are you gonna bring her home to meet me?" His mother was bending to check the chicken he could smell roasting in the oven.

"Never. I'm breakin' up with her tonight. That's why it's important." He hadn't planned to spill that. His nerves about breaking up with Jasmine diminished his defenses.

"Oh." Sophie looked disappointed. "I'm sorry to hear that."

"I'm not. I'm breakin' up with *her*. She's not someone I can bring home to meet my mama, so we got no future."

"Why? Why can't you bring her home to meet me?"

"She doesn't understand spiritual things. You should have heard what she said when I told her that Freddy guy was set free from his demon possession." He shook his head at the dank memory of that conversation.

"Hmm. She's skeptical, is she?"

"Yes, Mama. She's skeptical. And maybe not so bright. I don't know." He huffed. "Let me switch your lights for you and then get goin'."

"Sophie's got a boyfriend now. She was just telling me."

The slicing look from Sophie said she regretted his mama speaking so freely.

He headed for the living room. "Oh, yeah. When did that start?"

"Uh, well, maybe it hasn't even started yet. I put the brakes on after one lunch. I don't really know much about him."

"Where did you meet him?" Too many questions? He cringed at himself as he pulled open one of the boxes of lights.

"I met him at a sandwich shop by my place. We sorta bumped into each other and just shared a table. He's very ... interesting."

She probably meant he was very hot. He could see that deer-in-the-headlights look in her eyes. Sophie was interesting. She was pretty cute. But she wasn't really hot. Not like Jasmine. Jasmine turned heads wherever she went. She had turned Anthony's head, of course. Sophie was really more of an acquired taste. But maybe she was more than that for some guy in a sandwich shop. "He works in that restaurant?"

"No. He owns an architecture firm in the city. Green building, energy-efficient and carbon-neutral residential buildings." She sounded like she was quoting a website.

Anthony had more questions, but he had to get moving. He pulled his mother's old lights off the tree, having to displace a dozen ornaments she had already hung even after he'd asked her to hold off. As he worked, he listened to the women talking in the kitchen.

"Did he say anything about going to church?" That was his mother—a question she would ask, of course. Anthony didn't know how Sophie felt about that now that she had decided to become a Christian. She still wasn't like most of the church members he knew.

"He goes to that really big church out in the suburbs sometimes, he said. I don't even remember how that came up. It's not the sorta thing I would bring up."

"Oh, that's good. He brought up church. And you checked him out for ... you know, anything hanging around him?"

That was a new question. Anthony was pretty sure he had never heard his mother ask anyone that before.

"I was looking, of course. I didn't see anything. Not even a guardian angel."

That made Anthony wonder if *he* had a guardian angel. Did Sophie see his guardian angel? He wouldn't ask her that, of course.

"Hmm. No guardian angel. Well, you probably just couldn't see it for whatever reason."

"I don't know. It seems like I usually do see guardian angels, especially if I want to. The other kind can hide from me sometimes. It's hard to know if I'm seeing everything, of course. I don't have anyone to compare notes with."

"Oh, that reminds me—Sister Everly is coming to visit before Christmas. She'll be at prayer meeting. She sees angels. You could compare notes with her."

"Sister Everly?"

"She's as old as Moses. She helped start the church and started our prayer meeting before she was called to start a church in Ghana, where her people come from."

"Sounds like she's good at starting things. Does that come from seeing angels?"

Maybe Sophie was seeing her future. Anthony couldn't imagine her starting any of those things, however.

"Oh, it's not necessary. I've heard of plenty of people who start churches and such without sayin' they see spirits. And I've known folks who discern spirits but just use it for other ministries, not apostolic work."

"Apostolic?"

"Apostles start things, like churches."

"Oh."

Anthony tried not to laugh. He had a hard time keeping up with his mother's religion, and Sophie was a few decades behind him.

"How are you doing out there, Anthony?"

Had his mother heard him smothering a snicker? "Good. Just plugged in the white lights. You can come see 'em while I wind 'em around the tree." He settled a bundle of the green wire midway up the back side, lights clustered together like glowing grapes, and walked around to reach for it from the other side.

"Oh, those are bright. Not so much like candles."

His mother was probably being polite with company around. She didn't like the new lights. But he had expected that. He hoped she would get used to them. And maybe the colored string he'd brought wouldn't bother her so much as the white ones.

Sophie stopped next to the tree and stood with her arms crossed. She wasn't looking at the lights, she was looking at the angel perched on top of the tree.

That was an angel Anthony could see. Not the real kind.

"What does it mean if I can't see someone's guardian angel?"

"I don't know that I can tell you that." His mama was standing in a similar posture to Sophie's, but she was watching Anthony.

"What about mine?" He blurted it. He was hungry. The aroma of his mother's roast chicken was like truth serum.

"Your angel?" Sophie looked just over his head. She was probably stalling, not studying some big guy with wings and such.

He shrugged and draped the strand of lights up the front, toward the top of the tree.

"I guess I can live with those whiter lights. Or bluer, is it?" His mother was changing the topic, probably giving Sophie cover. They were clearly a team now.

"Maybe I have to do something to activate or initialize my angel or something." What was the right term? Even his mama might not know that one.

"Like calling an 800 number and giving 'em your pin?" Sophie practically winked at him.

Anthony coughed a laugh. That was the best joke he had heard from her. She wasn't that shell-shocked pagan girl anymore. "That must be it. I lost the angel mailing with the 800 number on it." He twisted a grin and glanced at her from the corner of his eyes.

"Okay, you two. Some things are holy, after all. Not everything is a joke." His mama had a little grin at the corner of her mouth nonetheless.

Sophie sobered. "I wonder about Brent. I just wonder if he's too good to be true. Just too perfect."

"You doubtin' yourself, Sophie?" His mama turned toward Anthony. "She's an attractive girl, isn't she Anthony?"

Despite the mother-induced awkwardness, he answered willingly. "Of course she's attractive. Everyone can see that." *Let's not make this personal.* "But maybe she's doubting something else, maybe doubting a guy who doesn't keep his guardian angel nearby."

Sophie was looking at him with those penetrating eyes. If anyone had penetrating eyes, it was Sophie.

And his mother was drilling holes in his head too.

He pretended not to notice. The string of colored lights came on when he plugged it into the white ones.

First Real Date

"Sharing a table at a sandwich shop isn't a proper date."

"Listen to you, 'proper' all the sudden. Are those church people getting to you?"

Sophie snorted. "Yes. They are getting to me. And you might just hear about me going to church sometime soon. Maybe I'll go with Brent. He told me about the big Christmas Eve service at his church."

"Uh-huh."

Her doorbell buzzed. "Okay, he's here. Gotta go."

"Have fun, Sophie."

"Thanks. You too." After she hung up, she rolled her eyes at herself. Crystal was home alone tonight. "You too" made no sense.

"Hi, Sophie. So, this is your place." Brent leaned in the door as if testing the ropes at the edge of a boxing ring. How far would they stretch?

That image was confined to her head, of course. "Yep. It's a mess. Maybe you can see it another time." Not a total lie.

He nodded and fixed her with those sapphire eyes.

For just a second, Sophie lost focus. His face blurred. What was that? Something other than tired eyes? Was something else there with Brent?

Maybe that was Brent's angel. Maybe his angel was right on top of him, right in the same space. She glanced at her guardian and noticed two others behind him. They looked familiar. One in armor, one a beautiful queen. That delayed Sophie from pushing her arm through her sleeve.

"Did you forget something?"

"Uh, no. I don't think so. Can't think of anything. Ready to go." Would all three of those guardians go with her? Would any of them merge with her? Get right into her personal space? Was that a thing?

Brent drove his luxury electric sedan to the north side of town, Sophie sinking into the leather passenger seat. Her increased awareness of her angels and of others around her seemed a liability for the first time in a while. She burrowed her mind into the conversation and the ride. But she did try to catch another glimpse of those other eyes she had seen layered over Brent's. Such revelations often came more easily in her peripheral vision. She spent a couple minutes trying to look at him out of the corner of her eye—until she started feeling walleyed.

"How do you like your work?" Brent was being a guy on a date. He was acting normal.

"Uh, well ... I like the way it allows me to stay focused on a task, to solve problems, and to feel like I created something." It was a standard answer, a job-interview answer.

"That makes sense. I could see that. I did a couple coding classes in school. I just found I didn't have the patience for it." His voice rose slightly at the end of the last sentence. Was he asking a question?

"Yeah. It's not for everyone. Sometimes I wonder if I could do something else."

"What about managing a small design team for a company website?"

"Managing a team? I don't really have personnel management experience, just managing my own small projects."

"Don't sell yourself short." He turned and smiled warmly at her.

276

He was pretty normal all evening, especially if averaged between a date and a job interview. Whether he was always looking for his next hire or just targeting Sophie, he seemed to be recruiting her. Recruiting her as what? A website project manager, or a girlfriend?

Was she interested in being his girlfriend? He was so attractive. But could they really have a long-term thing? *"Out of my league"* was a refrain playing as background music to her thoughts about Brent. But maybe he wanted something else. Something other than a long-term commitment.

Over the main course, he started talking about his past relationships. "I don't feel ready to settle down yet. I feel like I need to keep discovering things about myself. Spending time with a variety of people has helped me do that."

"Have you ever been engaged?" Sophie reached for her water glass. She was mostly ignoring her glass of wine—expensive wine.

Brent held the stem of his chardonnay glass. "Nope. Not engaged. Lived with a few different women over the years, but never bought the rock."

Not because he couldn't afford a big rock, judging by his clothes, his car, and the restaurant. The waiter stopped by to check on their satisfaction with the meal. Brent just nodded.

"It's very good, thanks." Sophie glanced at the waiter and stalled over the appearance of a very old woman clinging to his back.

"What about you?" Brent sipped his wine and set the glass back on the table. He was at least going slow on the alcohol. He probably wasn't going to need her to drive his luxury car home.

Sophie was still recovering from seeing that thing on the waiter. "Me? Uh … Oh. Engaged?"

Brent stopped chewing and nodded with his head tipped to the right.

Sophie may not need to worry about a future with Brent. She was clearly blowing it. "Well, no. I've never been engaged. Never lived with anyone either, really. Just a few boyfriends. Of course, I'm thinking now about how my faith will affect all that." *Awkward.*

"So you're *new* to faith?"

"Christianity has only gotten personal for me lately. I'm just now working out how that changes things."

"The answer to that depends on who you talk to. You could go hardcore with abstinence and all that, but that's not really necessary these days. Not so many rules as there used to be."

"Really?" Sophie wondered how Detta would respond to that. She talked about freedom and grace a lot. And one of the sermons Sophie sampled on Rescue House's website was about that too.

"I mean, we should be good to each other and honest and all. But there are lots of folks finding freedom to just be natural with each other, not having to do the whole celibacy thing. Too legalistic. Too Old Testament."

"Old Testament?" Here was another of those nuances. Was the Old Testament bad? Wasn't it part of the Bible? That was where the "Thou shalt nots" were, right?

The grin Brent had been offering since they met seemed almost fatherly now, patient. "I wouldn't worry about getting all of it straight. People have carried all kinds of old traditions into the modern church. It should mostly be about getting with like-minded people and serving humanity. It's about community."

Sophie resisted repeating yet another of Brent's incomprehensible statements. But she was thinking it. "*Community?*

That sounds good. But what does he mean by that? Does he want community with me?"

As he finished his steak, Brent described how he had taken part in various charitable activities at his church, and how he was able to tie his business into some of those. "It's good PR at the same time that it helps people in need."

Was he recruiting her to join his church now? His mission? *And* his business?

She shifted to asking him questions about his firm. Hearing him talk about church stirred a crawly sensation in her gut. When she wriggled slightly—imperceptibly, she hoped—Brent's face had gone blurry again. It was like a double-exposed picture, his eyes duplicated ... sort of.

But he turned the questions back toward her pretty quickly. "Tell me about yourself, Sophie. What do you want out of life?"

She was sure she didn't want dessert after this meal. But for her whole life? What *did* she want? "Uh, I'm probably a late bloomer, I think. My life is still ahead of me, mostly. And maybe I don't know all that I want out of it yet."

"What about relationships?"

She shrugged. "I do want love and commitment and a future with someone, someday." She hit that last word a touch harder than she'd intended. Trying to figure out Brent's smudged eyes was leaving only a fragment of her brain to answer his questions. She was giving him some placeholder answers.

"Well, in the short term, I hope we can spend more time together. I'd really like to get to know you, Sophie." The way he said her name was like silk on silk. It slipped from his lips and caressed her heart.

What would it be like to have such a charming and handsome man devoted to her? For much of her life she had looked for guys who could tolerate her—or at least ignore her giant oddities. Tonight she was just nodding at Brent's sales pitch. And she expected her response was uninspiring.

After paying the bill and walking to his car, Brent delayed opening her door for her. He pinned her against the cold side panel instead, and slid a hand around her waist. It was aggressive but smooth. Pushy but not violent. Practiced.

She didn't resist the kiss he planted on her lips, though she was pretty sure her response to that kiss was also uninspiring. She wasn't sure she wanted him to kiss her, but she was fascinated by how skillfully he pulled it off. Then came that crawling sensation again.

When Brent did open the passenger door for her, Sophie noted her guardian and the two others waiting, as if hoping for an invitation. She didn't literally wave them into the car, but internally she was all invitation—to the angels, that was. She wasn't inviting Brent to anything.

Her noncommittal reply to his offer to go to a club after dinner certainly finished off the evening.

After that he suddenly remembered he had to make a call, so he dropped her off at the front door of her building. He didn't even try another of those sneak attacks, and she was glad he didn't.

She waved at him as he turned to walk to his car. "Thanks for dinner. Have a safe drive home."

"I think I blew it." She was sitting on her couch in sweatpants and a fleece pullover. "He kissed me, and I didn't kiss him back." She shifted the phone to her other hand, set to speaker.

"You weren't ready?" Crystal was probably snuggled down on *her* couch too.

"I don't completely trust him."

"And it's a weeknight, anyway. You have work tomorrow. No sleeping over tonight."

Sophie had tried to limit her liaisons with Peter, from work, to the weekends. Crystal knew about those. "Yeah. That reminds me—I gotta get to bed. But thanks for talking."

"Sure. Thanks for sharing the next episode to the soap opera. Couldn't sleep without it."

"Ha. Well, he seems like a guy in a soap opera—not quite real."

"Too good to be true?"

"Something like that."

Intimidation

Sophie lay awake in bed for a long time, rolling from left to right to left. Switching which leg was pulled tighter toward her chest. Fluffing her pillow. Lifting her head at odd noises.

Mostly she was thinking about Brent. Something about him was wrong. Maybe just wrong for her. Of course she had no interest in a tall, handsome, charming, rich guy. The thought drew a grunting laugh from the back of her throat. Brent certainly qualified as her dream guy, but maybe not as her real-life guy. Not a friend, perhaps.

Brent wasn't friend material. That was her last waking thought.

A rustling in the dark alerted her. Woke her?

A hum in the air. Electric? A swarm of something?

Every inch of her skin sizzled. Wide awake.

"You cannot change. You have no reason to expect something better."

Were those words? A voice? Or just thoughts? Just in her head?

A struggle. Wrestling. Darkness. Intense darkness.

A huge figure covered the ceiling, black with glowing edges like embers of a dying fire. Even the red-orange glow seemed to darken the room.

She breathed relief that it wasn't the severed head of Maxwell Hartman.

Was this real?

"*Ssssssoooophieeee*," it hissed. That voice oozed over her. Seeped into her mind like poison. "It will be better for you to keep your head down. Don't cause trouble, if you know what's good for you."

The Girl Who Sees Angels

Words spoken, or just thoughts?

She tried to sit up. Her arms and legs wouldn't respond. She was pinned. But that dark figure wasn't touching her.

Then a bright hand slashed through the thing hovering over her bed, like a person reaching through a theater curtain. An arm followed that hand. And a face.

A shining man hung just above her now. His eyes radiant, his hair white, with electricity arcing out of the ends. He was beautiful. His skin was like mother of pearl. His face was lovely as a woman and yet strikingly masculine. And he looked deep into her.

Sophie relaxed.

Then she tensed. An acidic burn flared in her stomach.

"Don't worry. I can take care of you."

That specter above her was speaking directly into her head. The bright one was. Was that dark creature still there? Backing him?

"Who are you?" She thought it. She might have said it aloud.

"Light. An angel. Of light."

"Angel?"

"I have been and am and will be. I am light. I am everywhere. I am in all things on the earth."

She closed her eyes and saw his image burned inside her lids. Was she awake? She opened her eyes. She was awake ... probably.

He ... *it* ... was still there.

"Who are you?"

"I am the ruler of this world, the prince of the air. I am above all others. And I am available to you." His breath seemed to fill the room. An odor. An odor like nothing she had ever experienced before. But maybe tinged with sulfur like the breath from Hartman's decaying head.

"Who?"

"I am the god of this age."

"Not *the* God?"

"I have the power to give life and to take it. I want to give you a life."

"I have a life."

"I can give you more. I can give you riches. I can give you … Brent."

"What?"

"Wealth and prestige, glamour and influence. I can give you more. Always more."

"You're not Jesus?"

"I can give you everything you need. I can save you from suffering and pain."

"But …"

What was this? Not a dream. This thing was real. This thing was happening.

That sudden certainty froze her.

She needed help. She couldn't move. She couldn't speak.

I don't want this.

"You haven't tried it. Give it a chance. See what I can do for you."

"No. I … I don't …"

He began to sink toward her, blue and purple current branching from his fingers and toes like lightning. His skin flashed and shimmered. His eyes seared into her.

"No! Help!"

"Don't be afraid. I will be gentle with you."

"No! I … Jesus!"

"He can't hear you."

"Jesus, help me!"

His voice deepened. "I won't ever let you go. I won't ever stop coming after you. You cannot escape me." His eyes flamed red. Arrows launched toward her from behind him. Cords attached to those projectiles wrapped her limbs.

"Please, Jesus. Come. Help me."

A wave like the ocean in a storm swept through. Flooding her room.

That shining man dimmed, flashed brighter, cringed, and rose away from her. But his eyes stayed locked on her.

Those thin cords around her began to snap one by one.

Sophie closed her eyes. She wanted to see Jesus and no one else.

The room tipped. The bed lifted, rising on a wave and thumping back to the floor. She opened her eyes. The ceiling bulged upward and something fell from the shelf near the windows.

"*Call on my name.*" It was an internal voice.

"Jesus. Jesus. Come to me, Jesus. Help me, Jesus." Her voice became less transparent, gaining substance, gaining strength.

The shining visitor was gone. The dark one remained.

Then a golden sword sliced that black figure, cutting him in half. It was a shining golden sword. The ceiling shone through that huge gash.

Where was the light one? The angel of light?

Three angels appeared. One swept into that space above her paralyzed body. It looked like her guardian. The armored angel was the one wielding the golden sword. And the feminine one landed by her side, eyes filled with compassion.

"Jesus!" Sophie cried his name again, and the three angels glowed brighter. Their skin seemed to illuminate, and the joy on their countenances intensified. Smiles on all their faces, beatific smiles. Real joy.

"Are you real? Is this real?"

The female angel nodded reassuringly. She stroked Sophie's arm, and electricity spread across her skin again. A cooling touch.

Sophie was soaked in sweat. A refreshing calm replaced the feverish heat she hadn't even noticed until now. A deep breath. She took in fresh air, new air. "Am I okay? Am I safe?" She might not have actually spoken aloud. It didn't seem to matter.

That internal voice answered. "*I am with you. You are safe.*" And she felt the truth of it, even if that assurance echoed words from that angel of light.

"Who was that?"

"An enemy."

"My enemy?"

"And mine."

"Are you the Spirit of God?" Her eyes were closed. She was trying to focus on that voice inside.

"Yes. And the Spirit of Jesus."

She took a deep breath and let it shake its way out of her chest. One cough. "I have to get up. I have to get out of these wet clothes." She was soaked as if that wave that rocked the room had been real.

Her three angels faded from view, though she sensed she could reach them easily, could see them if she wanted. Instead, she resigned herself to the mortal task of removing her sheets and changing her clothes. The whole damp pile went atop her laundry bin, whether that was the best thing to do with them or not.

During that shivering chore, she kept thinking about how this nighttime attack had been different from the last time she saw the head of Maxwell Hartman. In that previous encounter, she had felt truly alone. That earlier struggle seemed more in doubt, like it could have gone either way. The outcome of this contest was more sure. She was more secure.

When she finally pulled her fresh blankets and clean sheets up to her chin, she noticed a message alert on her phone. It hadn't buzzed because of the late hour, but she must have bumped the table and woken the phone.

"**Are you all right I woke up feeling like I should be praying for you**" Detta was clearly overcoming her discomfort with texting. And she was praying for Sophie.

Sophie let out a sob. Then a raspy chuckle. The message from Detta was less than a half hour old. Sophie answered her. "**Was under attack. Jesus came to rescue. Two more angels. Somebody wasn't using theirs.**" She snickered at herself as she hit *send*.

"**Amen. Hallelujah.**" That was Detta's reply when Sophie had settled her head on her pillow. The perfume of her fabric softener seemed fitting for thoughts of Detta—a sweet, homey odor.

"**Thanks for praying.**" She set the phone on her nightstand and touched the lamp to turn it off.

"And thank you, Jesus."

Now she sounded like Detta.

Visiting Church

"Priscilla?"

"Sophie. What's up?"

"I think I wanna try church with you this weekend. Is that okay?"

"Of course it's okay. You want me to pick you up or meet you there?"

"I'm not on your way. We can meet there."

"Sure. Of course."

It was like pulling off a Band-Aid. Sophie did it quickly before stopping to think about how much it might hurt. The truth was, she didn't know how much this whole thing *would* hurt. She had driven past churches full of people. They tended to be full of other things too. Flocking flyers of all sizes, shapes, and colors crowded around houses of worship. She had never carefully analyzed that traffic. She just knew she wanted to stay away from it.

She didn't expect Priscilla's church would be free from all that. She did know Detta's church was different than Priscilla's, and she worried about the battle lines that would be engaged in that "holy roller" service. Whatever "holy roller" really meant. Better to start with Priscilla's church. What had she said it was? "Seeker sensitive?" When Sophie looked that up, she had to figure out if Priscilla's was also a "megachurch." That sounded like a church crossed with a discount warehouse, but it probably meant it had a lot of people. And that would be good for Sophie. Anonymous in a crowd.

On Sunday, she took twenty minutes deciding what to wear before texting Priscilla. **"What am I supposed to wear to this church?"**

"Supposed to? Well, clothes. Nudity is generally banned. Other than that, just wear what you wear to work. Not a date."

Sophie wore jeans and her leather jacket most everywhere. If she had a date, she might wear a blouse in place of the long sweaters she wore to work this time of year. She compromised, dressing the way she used to on cold days when she expected to leave work with Peter. Work and a date all in one. High-heeled boots instead of Doc Martens. Her newer jeans. Her nicest long sweater, one that hung well over her form-hugging pants. Stylish and modest. Not sloppy, but casual.

This was too much work. She was tired by the time she left the apartment. She almost locked herself out before coming back inside for her keys.

Deep breath.

The church—mega or not—was out in the near suburbs. It was less than a half hour drive from Sophie's place. Priscilla had a similar drive from her apartment in the city. And Sophie guessed that some folks drove farther than her to attend Rescue House. She wondered about Brent as she neared the destination displayed on her GPS. His church was definitely "mega." She wondered if they called themselves "seeker sensitive."

Was she a seeker? She was a newbie, that was certain.

The flow of traffic seemed to thicken as she drew closer to her destination—traffic including cars. In an idle moment at a streetlight, she let herself focus on the flow of multicolored beings sweeping through the sky or hovering over vehicles that turned toward the church, now just a couple blocks away.

Maybe this was a bad idea. Would she be able to block out all those otherworldly beings? Could she relax and not have to figure out which ones were good and which were bad?

That shining nighttime visitor came to mind. He had been an effective evangelist for church attendance, as it turned out. Would the angel of light be here? He claimed to be everywhere. But she doubted a lot of what he had said, as Detta had fervently confirmed.

A few cars waited in the turn lane ahead of her. She was on time. The parking lot was filling up, but she could still see available spots. This church was only about fifteen minutes from her mother's house, but her mother would never come to a church like this. She never said anything about going anywhere besides her Catholic church.

Just before Sophie turned into the parking lot, she reached up to touch the silver crucifix her mother had given her. That she had hung it from the mirror in her car wasn't something she was anxious to tell her mother. She would deal with it the next time she gave her madrecita a ride somewhere, no doubt.

She parked her car at the end of a long row and climbed out. As had always been the case, any flow of humans toward anything—from public transit to shopping malls—happened on multiple levels for Sophie. The people were solid. Less solid, but fully visible, were passengers riding on those people. Not everyone had a visible rider, and not all riders were visible all the time. She thought of Brent now, wondering if he was carrying a rider or two that stayed out of sight—mostly. That shining nighttime tempter had mentioned Brent like Mr. Rich-and-Handsome belonged to him.

Distraction. A distraction from the distractions. Sophie kept her head down and watched the pavement, blocking out the spiritual traffic by blocking out the human traffic. Mostly. So many things about her life seemed *mostly* true. Would that ever change?

"Sophie. Sophie, over here." Priscilla was waving and bouncing.

Sophie had rarely seen her tall, athletic friend so excited, outside of a basketball court. As Priscilla jumped and waved, a bright figure seemed to launch upward from her. That called Sophie's attention upward. And *up* was where her attention got stuck.

One of those large creatures loomed over them. Not a monster. Not clawing or leering at her. A tall angel, probably. Very tall. It seemed to be standing in the church building. Up to its knees in what looked like a rehabbed warehouse.

She stopped her progress toward Priscilla and stared for a moment before breaking free.

"You see something?" Priscilla turned toward the building, shading her eyes from the morning sun.

Sophie just nodded. How could she describe all that she was seeing to someone who had never seen anything like it?

Priscilla was staring at her now.

"Just the usual." She shook her head and grinned weakly.

Hooking her hand around one of Sophie's arms, Priscilla shrugged before turning them both toward the front doors.

Being towed into the building was good. The rush of people and their accompanying angels stirred Sophie's vertigo. Head down was the safest posture. Did she look like she was praying? Reverent, at least?

"Let's sit toward the back. We can find a seat there, I think." Priscilla was still towing as they passed through the wide lobby.

Sophie followed mutely. She felt antisocial avoiding eye contact with everyone, but this was just her first try. Awkward was the best she could do on a first try.

"Are you all right? Can I get you anything?"

"Um, water, I guess. Is that allowed?"

"Yep. We can bring anything into the auditorium these days. No restrictions. Though water was always allowed. I'll see if I can get you a bottle."

As soon as Priscilla turned to go, Sophie wished she hadn't. Here she was alone among a mass of strangers and their spirits. She sat down in a padded seat. Focus. That always helped. Focus on something.

She was reaching for a pamphlet in the little holder on the back of the seat in front of her when a voice landed on the top of her head. "Hello, I'm Nola. Are you new here?"

Sophie raised her head halfway and her eyes far enough to see the petite caramel-colored girl with a knee on the chair in front of her. She was extending her small hand with long pink fingernails.

"Uh, yeah. I came with Priscilla. My first time."

"Great." Nola kept her hand out, apparently optimistic. "So good to have you here."

Sophie finally got her right hand to cooperate and lifted it to take the offer.

"You're gonna love it. I have a feeling about that."

"Really?" Sophie wasn't as skeptical as her response sounded. She bounced her eyebrows once to communicate that—sort of. When she didn't say more, Nola finally let her go.

"Well, welcome to Rescue House. We all need some rescuing at one time or another."

Was that, like, the church motto? Corny. But still, Sophie could relate. Being pinned by an evil spirit in her bucking bed came to mind. "Thanks. Good to meet you."

Priscilla returned with two water bottles and a blond guy with long bangs. "Sophie, this is Austin. Austin, this is my friend, Sophie."

Austin held out his hand.

Sophie was quicker to take up the offer this time.

"Welcome. So glad to have you join us. Just sit back and let it happen. That's what I figured out when I first came here."

"Really?" That sounded sort of cultish. Sophie realized she had responded to Austin exactly the way she'd responded to Nola. Surprised. Doubtful, maybe. But she wasn't as doubtful as her automatic reactions implied. "Thanks for the advice." She hoped that sounded sincere to Austin.

He just kept smiling.

Then someone struck a guitar chord up on stage. Sophie had missed the arrival of a full band up there. That was the sort of thing that happened when she kept her head down. Austin, and a glowing white being with him, distracted her for a second more before she turned toward the stage.

The glow over that stage was almost blinding. As soon as she allowed that complaint—not really a whiny one—the glow softened a bit. Did she turn it down, or did someone filter it for her eyes?

As soon as the singer at the center mic started the lyrics of the first song, a flock of colorful creatures swooped across the audience and over Sophie's head. She followed that flight and smiled at the trail of light they left, like sparklers spinning in the hands of a dozen children.

She stood when Priscilla did and even followed her in raising her hands above her head. It seemed a fitting reaction to all that music and magic.

Priscilla got bouncy again, dancing and pumping her hands in the air. And she apparently did that without seeing the entwining formations of angels filling the top half of the big open room.

For a moment, standing there with the sparkle and splash of sound and sight—so many colors, such glorious light—Sophie was *glad* she could see it. She even wanted to share what she was seeing. She wanted the world to see, to know how beautiful it was. But that desire to share called her back to the crazy girl she had always been—the lying girl, at least in the eyes of most people. Even if she was going to embrace this gift, if she was going to consider herself *not* the crazy girl who no one believed, but the girl who sees angels, she still had to keep it to herself.

Priscilla bumped her shoulder and grinned at her.

Sophie would keep it to herself and a few of her friends, of course.

"You're seeing, aren't you?" Priscilla's eyes sparkled, as if reflecting those explosions of light and color that Sophie could see.

She nodded a bit deliriously, and then she looked up again. The song was about a great and awesome king. A king who loved everyone. A beautiful and generous king. And Sophie let the words soak in. When she did, the lights above her arranged into a triangulating network that seemed to pick up some greater light beamed down from above, absorbing it and firing it onward. And all those rays of light focused together in one place. They coalesced into a light more intense still.

That great light expanded. Sophie raised a hand instinctively to protect her eyes. But, of course, it didn't really hurt her eyes. She wasn't seeing it with her physical eyes. So she let her hand drop. And out of the confluence of those lights, a cross began to form. A bright white cross. And then that cross took the shape of a person, a human being with arms outstretched. A man. A glowing man.

For half a second Sophie winced, remembering the bright angel that tried to seduce her and intimidate her. But the fear from that nighttime encounter evaporated just as quickly.

The shining man in the center of the light from those angels was smiling. Smiling at her. Happy to see her. Happy to see her here.

Her neck was hurting from the strain of looking up there, so she let herself lie back. Several hands helped her sink to the floor so she could see that shining person better. That loving man. The light collector.

When the music stopped, more hands helped her to stand. She didn't recall wanting to stand, but she didn't fight it.

Priscilla helped her to settle back into her seat.

Sophie relaxed. Slumped. Drunken. She couldn't see that shining man anymore. Unless she closed her eyes. Then she could focus on his image burned inside her. She wobbled even sitting down.

Priscilla reached a hand to prop her up.

Sophie tried to nod a thanks. Her whole upper body seemed to nod with her head. She tried to speak, but could only communicate internally. *"So, this is church."*

Learning How to Steer

Detta held a finger poised above her phone. "I'm gonna try this thing that Anthony showed me. Call me back if I accidentally hang up on you." She settled her phone on the corner of her kitchen table and hit the picture of the little speaker. "Can you still hear me?"

"Yes. I can hear you. Did you put your phone on speaker?"

"Yes, I did. Is that all right?"

"You're at home alone, so it's all right."

"Yes. Of course. So, tell me how your first visit to church was."

Sophie might have giggled, or maybe she just cleared her throat. "I don't know if they're gonna let me come back. I kinda went nuts on 'em."

"Nuts? Like how?" Detta was pulling the broom and long-handled dustpan out of her closet while still leaning toward the phone to project her voice toward Sophie.

"There were so many angels. I got carried away watching. They were flying all over above the crowd and, like, making this light show. And ..." Sophie paused to laugh breathily. Then a longer silence. "Well, I remember you mentioning people falling on the ground at your church."

"Yes, but I don't think they do that sorta thing at Rescue House."

"No. Apparently they don't. Good thing Priscilla was there to let 'em know I wasn't having a seizure or dying of something."

"Sure. That is a good thing. But I'll bet you were havin' a good time and not really lookin' like you were having a heart attack."

"I was having a great time." Her voice coasted. "And I don't remember much about the sermon. I could hardly focus on what the guy was saying. You know, with all the angels. They didn't go away just 'cause the music stopped."

Detta spoke off the top of her head. "You gotta learn how to use your gift and not let it use you." She pulled a second chair out and swept under the table.

"I what? What do you mean?"

"Now that you have the Spirit in you, you should be able to get more control on your gift. I'm not talkin' about shuttin' it down, just learnin' how to slow things or get things out of your way. You should be able to listen to a good sermon. I know Jesus wants that."

"I guess I should. I just never expected to be able to control it, really. Avoid it, maybe. Ignore it, sometimes. I did plenty of that. And I can turn it up, looking through things and seeing more. But I haven't always been good at seeing less."

"The Spirit can help you. It's a gift. You don't have to let a gift take over your whole life. Some folks do real well with their gifts and still act like normal people most of the time."

"You mean *normal* like you." Sophie snickered.

"Now you watch out, girl. Careful what you're sayin' there." She chuckled back. Then she remembered something. "I told you about Sister Everly, didn't I?"

"Old as Moses, you said."

"Well, that's true, but that just means she's older than me. And that's not the real thing about her. She's a person who sees in the Spirit, and I think she can help you know how to handle what you see and help you use your gift."

"That sounds good. Where does she live?"

"Oh, she's down in Louisiana these days, come back from her mission to Africa. That's what I heard this week. But she's coming to our prayer meetin' on Tuesday. You think you can get to that meeting? I could introduce you, and she could lay hands on you."

"Lay hands on me?"

"It's a thing we do in our church. It's from the Bible. It's for blessing and for passin' on gifts and such. She can give you more of God's Spirit, if you're willin' to take it."

"More of that voice that talks to me from inside, the peaceful voice?"

"That's the one."

"That's what saved me the other night when the bright angel-demon thing came to my bedroom."

"Jesus saved you, dear. He just keeps on savin' us."

"That shining creature said *he* would save me. He said he was the god of the world and king of the air or something."

Detta stopped her sweeping. "Prince of the air?" Her voice caught in her throat.

"Yeah. Something like that. A bunch of hype, right?"

"Umm, well, maybe. I don't suppose the devil hisself came to your bedroom, though I expect he gets around. But Jesus and the apostles called him those things—god of this world, prince of the air."

"Oh. So I should have known who he was. If I read the Bible."

"That would be a good thing to start doing, if you haven't already."

"Okay. But explain that to me. How can the devil be the god of this world and all that?"

"Oh, it's the oldest story of all. When Adam and Eve gave up their place ruling the Garden of Eden, they gave it to the devil, the Serpent. That was how the devil appeared to them in those days. He comes as an angel of light these days."

"He does? An angel of light? That was one of the other things he said about himself."

"Sounds like he was sorta makin' fun of you for not reading your Scriptures. Mocking you. That's his way—a mocker from the beginning. And always trying to tear at the image of God that's in you and me."

"Image of God? How do you mean?"

"Read the book, honey. It's loaded with useful stuff. And come to prayer meeting Tuesday night. Sister Everly will pray for you."

"How many people will be there? I got overwhelmed with the big crowd at Rescue House."

"There won't be near so many people at our prayer meeting. Though Sister Everly will increase the attendance, no doubt. And I expect we'll have an extra big lot of angels." Detta snickered at herself, but only a little. She wasn't really kidding.

"Huh."

What else did she expect Sophie to say?

"Even if you come, you don't have to do anything. Just see what you think." From years of raising Anthony, Detta knew that a hard sell didn't usually work with this generation.

"Okay. I'll give it a try."

"Good. I should text you the address, right? Isn't that the way that works best?"

"It is." Sophie laughed. "You're really getting into the texting thing."

"I'm tryin'. There's folks I wanna communicate with that seem to only do it this one way."

"I, for one, appreciate your effort." Sophie breathed a laugh again, but the gratitude sounded real.

"I care about you, Sophie. It's worth a little effort."

"Or a lot of effort."

"I haven't been straining myself."

"Not worrying about me like you had another child?"

"Oh. Well, maybe a little of that. But that's on me. I'm not supposed to be worrying about anything or anybody. Not Anthony, and not you."

Sophie was silent.

"Anyway, I'll send the address. May take a couple o' tries. Then I'll see you Tuesday night at prayer meeting."

"I'll try to get there."

"I'll be prayin' for you."

They said goodbyes and ended the call.

"Why does it feel like there's gonna be a big fight for Sophie to get to that meeting, Lord? Am I just imagining that? I fear something's gonna try to block her from coming."

Hinderances

Tuesday at work was like battling a forest fire. Sophie was used to the cliché about tech work involving putting out fires. This thing seemed to be fanned by high winds and went uncontained for hours.

"I don't know how this happened. I saw your code, and you demonstrated it perfectly. How could it be so screwed up now?" Janice's gaze fell toward the floor, her head shaking on the way down. If she kept going like that, she would be prone on the carpet in a few seconds.

"They must have uploaded the wrong version—probably that test code we were using to prove Charlie's idea about mobile browsers."

"Oh. Huh. Yeah, I guess that's possible."

This conversation came after five hours of fighting that forest fire. It took Sophie that long to come up with her theory—and to come up for air. The forest fire analogy hadn't been a borrowed cliché for her. The office literally looked like it was on fire if she raised her eyes above her monitors and tuned into the spiritual layer.

When Janice shuffled back toward her office, Sophie turned to her guardian. He looked concerned, or at least stern. Was she just layering her mood onto his generally stoic demeanor? *Can you do anything about all this? Can you, like, call in the cavalry?* Keeping her question internal required a conscious effort.

The guardian raised his face toward the ceiling.

Was the ceiling going to collapse next? No, he was probably looking past that. When Sophie let her mind penetrate the walls and roof, she saw one of those giant beings that loitered around the building. This was a new one, or maybe one of the others had taken on a new look. Fireman. But not in the good sense of the word. Not a first responder. More like an arsonist.

She checked back with her guardian. Apparently his neck and shoulders weren't nearly so tight as hers. He was really bending his head back. His eyes glowed with a churning light. Yet the peace that covered his face was nothing short of heavenly.

Sophie didn't know a lot about heaven, per se. "Oh. Maybe I should …" It took her a second to remember to keep her thoughts on mute. *"Uh, God. Uh, Jesus. We need your help down here. Please put out the fire or defeat that flamethrower guy. Or whatever you need to do. Yeah. Do whatever you need to do to protect this place and these people who work here … including me."*

That was when her guardian launched a golden beam toward the sky. Then he began to expand. He grew until he had to bow his head to keep it under the ceiling tiles. And then there were three big angels. That warrior one swooped in, landing in a squat on top of the cubicle wall momentarily, like a bird on a fence. And that other one, the pretty one, slipped up next to Sophie.

The fire didn't go away immediately. The monsters surrounding the building didn't leave. But Sophie could sense that God had heard her and had done something. At least God was working on doing something. That was comforting. The little squad of angels she could see was comforting.

As soon as she touched that feeling, a more distant shimmer caught her attention. Glancing around to make sure no one was watching, she cocked her head back almost as far as her guardian had. It wasn't just a little squad of angels now. It was more like a platoon. And they were above the building and in it, coming toward her and soaring around the whole floor.

"Okay. I'll take it."

"Take what?" Charlie had just returned from a late lunch after the morning code disaster.

Sophie sighed. "I was just praying for help, and I was starting to feel it coming." She didn't look at Charlie to see his response. One advantage of working with socially awkward people was the expanded definition of acceptable behavior.

"Not a bad idea. I'm glad it's working for you." He ducked into his cube like a prairie dog escaping a coyote.

By five o'clock, it looked like she would be able to go home relatively soon, not be stuck recovering from the website failure much longer. Things were back to normal, and she was documenting what had happened. Then Sophie remembered Detta's invite to the prayer meeting. A moaning sigh squeezed out of her at that recollection.

Then her phone buzzed.

"You wanna go get drinks tonight?" Kimmy sounded her usual combination of weary and cheerful. "I have stuff to tell you about this angel thing." She had lowered her voice for that part.

"Wow. That sounds interesting. But I'm supposed to go to this …" Sophie lowered *her* voice "… prayer meeting."

"Really? Instead of drinks?"

"Uh, yeah. How about tomorrow?"

"Okay. Maybe. I'll have to get back to you." Her tone deflated. It seemed to be a quick leak.

Less than five minutes later, Sophie's phone buzzed again.

"Sophie, how have you been? I would love to see you tonight." Brent. Smooth-talking Brent.

She had decided not to see him again, but just then she didn't remember exactly why. She was tired, but she felt drawn to the prospect of those clear blue eyes ogling her. Rich compensation for a crappy day. "Uh, well, I have other plans tonight." She rehearsed that answer aloud, not yet sure it was her final answer.

"Oh. Maybe you could postpone those plans. You and I should probably talk. I think we may have misunderstood each other. I'm hoping to get another chance." His version of sincere sounded ... pretty sincere.

But Sophie remembered that horrid visitor who offered Brent as a prize for her loyalty. Was that real? Was Brent at the disposal of that deceptive angel? Or maybe that was just one of his lies.

Either way, Sophie had promised Detta. The urge to show Detta that she could count on Sophie tugged against Brent's invitation. "No. I have to go tonight. And ... I've decided not to see you anymore. No need to schedule another time. I don't think we have a long-term future."

"Really? Oh. I'm sorry you think that." His voice sagged under the weight of utter disappointment.

She had broken his heart. Hot Brent. Sophie had broken his heart. That counted for something. She took that little ego pill and said goodbye, ignoring his renewed pleas.

By six, she was out of there, amazingly early given the disaster scene in the office most of the day. She was thinking about where to stop for some food before driving to Detta's church.

Crystal called. "Hey, Sophie. I need some help. Can you meet with me tonight? I'm in trouble."

Sophie restrained a curse. The day, as it scrolled down her screen, read as a warning. Someone didn't want her to go to that prayer meeting tonight. But the phalanx of a half-dozen angels escorting her to the train assured her that there was also someone who wanted her to attend.

"I'm on my way to a prayer meeting. If you're really in crisis, Crystal, maybe you should come with me. But I have to go. I know it's important for some reason. I really have to be there tonight."

Crystal was silent for a few seconds. "You think it's an important meeting?"

"I do. I think this whole day has been one big effort to keep me from going to it. And I really need to go. I'll stay on the phone with you all the way there if you want, but I'm definitely going. Or at least trying to."

"Huh. I feel sick. I think I'm gonna have to call you back." Then silence.

"Crystal?" Sophie pulled the phone away from her ear. Call ended.

Standing on the train platform, Sophie rocked from heels to toes. She looked at her phone. Forty-five minutes until the prayer meeting was supposed to start. What if she got there late? How long would it take to stop at Crystal's place before going to her apartment and getting her car? She tapped on the address Detta had sent her. North and west. She could take public transportation, but she wanted to drive, expecting the meeting to run late.

"What should I do?" On the train platform, she could pray out loud. Who would notice? Half the people looked like they were talking to themselves, probably talking to their phones.

Her phone buzzed again. She assumed Crystal was done throwing up or whatever.

The Girl Who Sees Angels

But it was an unknown number.

If she hadn't just prayed for direction, she would have let the unknown caller go through to voice mail. This could be something. "Hello?"

"Sophie, this is Anthony. How ya doin'?"

"Anthony. I didn't recognize your number."

"Yeah. I hope you don't mind. I got your number from my mother." He paused. A long pause. "I thought maybe we could get coffee ... or a drink, or maybe dinner ... sometime."

Was that an invitation? An apologetic invitation?

"Uh, yeah. We could do that. Sure. But tonight I'm struggling to get to this meeting at your mother's church."

"You're going to her prayer meeting?"

"I think I'm supposed to be there, like it's important. But I've been running into roadblocks all day."

"Huh. Whoa. I just got the chills when you said that. Like I could feel that it *was* important for you to be there. Does that make sense?"

"Makes sense to me." A train was approaching. That one would get her close to Crystal's place. "I just prayed for help deciding what to do."

"About the prayer meeting?"

"About my friend Crystal calling me with some kind of crisis." On cue, Crystal's name came up on the phone with an alert for an incoming call.

"Huh. And she's, like, one of the roadblocks, maybe?"

"Could be. I told her she could come with me to the prayer meeting, but she's not interested in church."

"What time does the meeting start? Seven?"

"Yes."

"I don't think my mama always gets there on time. I think it's okay if you're late. But I don't know. I feel like it may be, like, strategic for you. Is somethin' special happening there, like a guest speaker or something?"

"Yes. This Sister Eisley, or Easley or …"

"Everly?"

"Yeah. Her."

"She's pretty cool. Oh, hey. She sees spirits and such, or at least claims to. Seems possible when you hear her talk." He sounded like a guy adding up a bill. "Yeah. That might be why this meeting would be a big deal for you." He stopped talking abruptly. Then he was back. "Is there any way I can help? I thought I was just calling to see if you wanted to get together, but maybe it's something else. My mama has stuff like this happen to her all the time."

"Stuff like what?"

"Like supernatural forces moving things and moving people to get some mission accomplished."

Without consciously deciding, Sophie had gotten on the train that would stop close to Crystal's apartment. "You think you could meet me at Crystal's to see if she really needs help, and then drive me to the meeting?" That would save time and would bring in reinforcements. Human reinforcements. But she didn't know where Anthony lived. "Are you on the north side?"

The number of angels surrounding her was up to eight. A few had embedded in the top of the train car like her guardian did in her cube at work.

Anthony hesitated a few seconds. "Yes. Is Crystal a northsider?"

"Yes."

"Okay. I can do that. I just got home. I'll get my car out of the parking garage while you send me your friend's address."

"Your mother sent me the address to the prayer meeting by text message. She's so cute with her digging into new tech."

"Ha. Yes. That's funny. I tried to get her to do things like that for a long time. Glad you finally got through to her."

"It was a team effort, I think. Okay, I'll send Crystal's address." She paused. "And thanks, Anthony. I really appreciate the help."

"No problem. Glad to be part of the mission." He might have chuckled. Then they were disconnected.

At Crystal's apartment building, Sophie was feeling her lack of food. She had stayed in the office all day, only venturing to the snack machines in the break room. Too much caffeine and sugar and too little real nutrition. She leaned on the doorframe while she waited for Crystal to buzz her in.

By the time she reached the top of the stairs outside the third-floor apartment, Sophie's head was floating. Was that about more than just missing lunch? She braced one hand on the dark wood framing Crystal's door.

Her friend pulled the door open and looked at her sheepishly. "Sorry I got you over here. I think I'm okay now. False alarm."

Sophie wavered when she noted two large greenish things hovering behind Crystal. They didn't even have faces or defined appendages. Green blobs, really. They squeezed together like one was trying to hide behind the other.

Sophie felt angels pushing in next to her. *This is a raid. Get your hands ... get your blobby things up.* She smiled at the obvious intimidation from her angel squad as the green things quivered like toxic Jell-O. She was kind of quivering herself.

"You okay, Sophie?"

She realized then that she hadn't said anything since Crystal opened the door. "A little light-headed. I haven't eaten all day."

"Oh dear. Come on in, and I'll get you something. Almond butter sandwich, gluten-free bread?"

"Okay. Sure. That would probably help." It wasn't the kind of sandwich Sophie would have preferred, not what she had in mind for supper, but she was desperate.

Then she remembered the bigger context of the evening—the mission. "Anthony Washington is coming to pick me up here to take me to that prayer meeting."

As soon as she said that, the two green blobs absorbed into Crystal, and she ceased her advance toward the kitchen. When she turned, she was looking ... pretty green. Then she bent forward and vomited on the floor, just missing Sophie's shoes.

Sophie's weak stomach offered to contribute to Crystal's fouling of the rug. But she turned her head away and locked eyes with one of the angels—that beautiful feminine one. That angel had a friend with her, similar in appearance, but a bit more serious. Was that Crystal's angel? Sophie had forgotten exactly what she looked like. "Can you help us? Can you get rid of those green things in Crystal?"

That other beautiful angel nodded at Sophie and then thrust her hand toward Crystal, just coming short of poking her in the head.

Sophie got the message. "Uh, green blobs, you get out of Crystal right now." She glanced at the angel. "In the name of Jesus."

Crystal flipped backward and slammed to the floor. But the two-headed green thing vaulted toward the ceiling and away.

Stepping around the fouled rug, Sophie dropped to one knee. "Crystal! Crystal? Are you okay?"

Opening one eye, Crystal reached up to her skull. "Banged my head." She looked at her hand. No blood. "I guess I'll live." She opened her other eye and frowned at Sophie. "Green blobs?"

Sophie tipped her head to one side. Before she could reply, her phone buzzed. She stood up and checked the message. Anthony was downstairs.

"Are you gonna be okay? Do you need to go to the hospital? Maybe Anthony and I can take you on the way to the meeting." A brief review of what she was saying added a new level of regret and incredulity to what this day had become. But she was at full gallop toward her goal, her mission.

"No. No, I'll be okay."

Crystal's apartment door was still standing open. The entryway door downstairs clicked open, and a muddled conversation rose in fragments up the stairs. Sophie and Crystal exchanged frowns. The sound of someone striding up the stairs kept them both listening in silence.

Sophie started to calculate how awkward it would be if that was Anthony coming up the stairs. She looked at her phone to see if he had texted her back after her "**OK.**" She turned her head just in time to see Anthony fill the doorway.

He looked at Crystal on the floor in her flannel robe and then at the mess on the rug. "What the hell?"

To Sophie, that seemed an appropriate question.

Not Sure What to Call This

Anthony drove Sophie toward the prayer meeting. Some air freshener, a breath mint, something like that would have been really good right then. He resisted checking to see if her shoes were clean. He was glad Crystal had agreed to bag up that rug and count it a loss. He had gone way beyond the call of duty by that time in his brief visit to her place.

"Call of Duty." He said it aloud without meaning to.

"Why are you talking about a shooter game right now?" Sophie looked more amused than mad. She also looked pretty pale. Crystal's sickness might not have infected her, but it did stop her from eating the food her friend had offered.

He laughed. "I was just thinking out loud, I guess. But that's not totally irrelevant. You're like a walking war zone."

She snickered and kept her eyes forward. Hopefully she was watching out for incoming attacks that he couldn't see in the headlights. A light snow was just starting to fall.

Shaking her head where it leaned back against the seat, she released a groaning breath. "I hope you're wrong. Maybe this Sister Everly can make things change."

"Change? Probably. But I doubt she's gonna get you out of the war zone. Going to this prayer meeting is probably *not* the way to do that." He was riffing. He had no idea what was supposed to happen at this meeting. But he did know his mother and her friends were serious about their spiritual warfare.

"My life has been one long mess. I've probably been in the war zone the whole time. Most of the time it was out of my control. I don't think it could get worse than that."

"So, your friend getting these things on her that made her sick and knocked her to the floor, is that the same or worse?"

He wasn't arguing, just trying to help her work this out. He would be interested to know if she *did* work any of it out.

"Wait. Look out!" Sophie grabbed for the steering wheel but stopped just short, her seatbelt probably limiting her reach.

Anthony let up on the gas and touched the brake pedal. He didn't see the threat at first, then the snowplow coming the opposite direction turned in front of him. He stomped the brakes, and that dull antilock brake thing happened. They stopped just short of getting plowed.

"Help us, Lord," Sophie muttered.

"Amen." Anthony took a deep breath. "I think I saw a Bruce Willis movie like this once." He snorted at himself.

"With Mos Def?" Sophie was turned toward him in her seat.

He blurted a laugh. "Yeah. You know what I'm talkin' about." Then he woke to the fact that they were still sitting in the intersection. He started the wipers and checked his mirrors before pressing on the gas.

She nodded with a small grin on her face. "Bruce Willis had to get this witness just sixteen blocks, but all these bad guys were trying to get Mos Def 'cause he knew something." Sophie got more serious. "What do you think it is that *I* know?"

He was still settling his heart rate back toward normal. "Maybe what you know is that it's all real. That the spiritual war is real. You see it. Maybe you're supposed to tell people that it's real. To be a witness." The longer he thought about his answer, the more he liked it. And that tickling sensation up his spine was back. Apparently that chill was part of being in Sophie's battle zone.

The Girl Who Sees Angels

A man in a long coat was pulling the front door to the church building open when Anthony parked his car on the street just up the block. The parking lot looked pretty full. It was a small lot. They were late. Probably later than his mama usually arrived at this meeting.

Sophie huddled close to him as they entered the building—as close as she could without clutching his arm. Closer than he would have expected under normal circumstances. They might have looked like a couple if folks noticed the two young people entering the back of the sanctuary. But they weren't really even friends. Or they hadn't been until tonight.

The roar of worship filled the sanctuary. Some familiar young men were behind the instruments on the stage—electric piano, bass guitar, lead guitar, and the drum kit. And there were three women behind microphones. One was Delilah Little. She still looked fine—tall and slim, big shiny eyes. Mostly her eyes were closed as Anthony waded into the worship and looked for a seat.

They sidestepped their way into a row closer to the back than the front. The room wasn't full. This was the advanced meeting. Not everyone in this church was ready for the Tuesday night prayer gathering.

He glanced at Sophie. She was acting really strange. She seemed to cower one second and then grin the next, hunkering down like they were being attacked by eagles and then smiling up at those eagles. They weren't eagles, of course. What were they? Angels? Demons? Aliens? Anthony wasn't a hundred percent convinced of the answer to that last string of questions, but he was convinced that Sophie was seeing *something*.

Three or four minutes after they arrived, Anthony could see Sister Everly consulting with Brother Wilkins. He usually presided at the prayer meeting even if Reverend Porter was around. Anthony respected that about Reverend Porter. He didn't seem obsessed with holding the controls all the time.

Brother Wilkins peered up the aisle. He always looked like he was preparing to scold somebody.

Sister Everly was craning her neck at Anthony. No. She was looking at Sophie. What exactly she and Brother Wilkins were talking about became less fascinating when Anthony sensed a rush of something. Not a rush of air, not a bunch of people charging toward the foyer. But *something* rushing at them. At Sophie, probably.

Anthony sat down hard. This was the closest he had ever been to really knowing this stuff was real. He had felt things before—chills up his back, a warmth in his chest, an intoxication during worship. But this was bigger. This was more powerful. This was more real.

Sophie was in a half crouch now, like the weight of the building was coming down on her. But she insisted on standing. Why not just sit down? Or fall down? Or something. He reached toward her, but didn't seem able to get his hand into that dimension she was occupying.

Brother Wilkins spoke into the microphone. "This is Sister Everly, as many of you know. Go ahead, Sister."

"God's blessings on all gathered here." She waited for the *amens* to fade. Sister Everly was still an erect woman with salt-and-pepper gray hair, but the years had carved deeper lines in her face. "I must interrupt this beautiful worship to reach out to a young sister who brought her own little spiritual battle with her this evening." She was staring right at Sophie, stretching her neck to see past the folks right in front of Anthony and Sophie. Sister Everly was a tall woman, but Sophie was crunched low. "Sister? Are you willing to come forward? I believe God wants me to pray for you tonight. You fought your way through a hell storm to get here. Now God wants to bless you."

That was when Anthony first caught sight of his mother. She was craning her neck and smiling big.

Then Sophie was on the ground. Anthony thought she had ducked behind a pew to avoid being seen. But that was a stupid thought. Sophie wasn't hiding. She was out.

"I'm comin' back there." Sister Everly turned to Brother Wilkins. "Just go ahead with more worship?" She handed him the mic and didn't stick around for an answer. She strode down the three steps off the platform and onto the blue carpet in the aisle.

As far as Anthony was concerned, Sister Everly was a migrating force of nature. Dignified, articulate, confident, and charismatic. At probably eighty years old, she was still vibrant. She was certainly someone who brought her own army of angels, if anyone did.

He tried to scramble out of the way, but Sister Everly caught his arm. "Help me get her laid out more comfortably." She was bent slightly over Sophie's crumpled form.

Sophie looked like a marionette with its strings clipped. Anthony tiptoed over her bent limbs to get to her head. He was thinking he should get hold of her by the shoulders to stretch her out straighter. But as soon as he touched her, he was down on his butt. Exactly how that happened, he had no good idea. Neither could he figure out why he was crying. He just was.

Sister Everly's deep, motherly voice, massaged him. "All right, brother. You just rest there. God has business with the both of you young people, I can see."

Seeing So Much More

What Detta had said about Sister Everly led Sophie to expect a wild-eyed character, a wizened woman with a strange accent and boney fingers she aimed at people. The tall, dignified woman who called out to her from the stage was none of that. She could be a lawyer, a doctor, or a school superintendent. She didn't look the part of the wild-eyed missionary. That was a revelation. Detta had said that Sister Everly could see angels just as Sophie did, and yet this woman looked normal. Healthy. Admirable.

Sophie could be like that.

And that was when she hit the carpet. The furious flush of angels back and forth over the meeting had weighed her down like a ton of baked goods. Sweet and soft, but intensely heavy when all piled on. Angels were dropping that heavy sweetness, special delivery from ... where? Heaven?

Even as she lay paralyzed on the floor, she was fully aware of what was happening around her—probably more aware than lots of people there, including Anthony. She could hear him crying forcefully.

Sophie could feel a twist in a half-dozen joints, pressured by the odd configuration of her arms and legs on the floor. She could see the tide of angels rushing back and forth like a video of ocean waves taken from under the surface. These waves were golden, however, not blue. She could see them with her eyes closed.

The light around Sister Everly was purple, though Sophie didn't open her eyes to look at her either. Maybe that purple was her aura.

How was Crystal doing, by the way? *"Lord, protect and bless her."* Sophie wasn't even mimicking Detta with that prayer. It just came out. She was sure she hadn't spoken aloud.

Sister Everly was speaking. She was praying. Not everything she said was clear. Why was that? Just another mystery Sophie didn't need to solve right away.

As she lay there surrendered to forces beyond her control, she felt like she was being levitated off the floor. Two angels, her guardian and that beautiful one, had grabbed her under the arms and were lifting her. They were taking her away.

Am I dying?

The answer, wherever it originated, was no.

Then an elaboration. "Not in the way you're thinking."

A qualified *no*. This was a *sort* of death.

The effortless flight landed her in a bedroom that was just like the one she had when she was seventeen. It was her room when Hector died. She was in that room with herself. The grown-up Sophie was looking at the teenage version. It was a room in her past. And it was a room inside her.

"I'll never survive this. I'll never even finish growing up." Her teenage self was speaking aloud, speaking to herself or complaining to fate. And then teenaged Sophie looked squarely at each of the angels that had carried her grown-up self into that room. "Go away. I don't wanna see you anymore."

Sophie remembered saying things like that fifteen years ago—half her life ago. And she remembered the golden people leaving. Around his death, she'd associated them with Hector. Had he sent them? She hadn't seen those ones before the bike accident. They didn't seem to ever do anything for her, so she sent them away. Kicking against the universe. Now, in the present, the adult Sophie remembered all this, like seeing a home video for the first time in years.

Then she slipped out of that bedroom, swept away by the two angels. They carried her to a different bedroom. This was the one Sophie shared with her little brother when she was small. She was six or seven.

The weeping girl in that room had just lost her father. A toybox was shoved against the door, and little Hector was pounding on the outside. Grown-up Sophie couldn't see him. She wanted to. She wanted to see Hector so badly. As a girl, she had locked him out of their room that time. And she could remember locking him out of her life lots of times.

Her mother had scolded Sophie for telling Hector stories about the visions she was seeing. Her mother was afraid of Sophie infecting her little brother with her insanity. Eventually, so was Sophie. That was why she shut him out. Not because she was mean. She was trying to protect him, trying to keep him from her craziness. The craziness that had driven her father away.

That thought changed something. Out of that old bedroom, they traveled to a dark place. Outdoors. An alley, perhaps. Unfamiliar. She could hear water lapping. Was that a canal? A river?

And there lay her father. He was drunk. She knew how he was when he was falling-down drunk. Here he was, inebriated and alone.

Around the corner of a building, coming to the edge of the river, a man flipped a knife blade open. He squatted and began to rummage in her father's pockets.

Her father roused and tried to fight him off spinning himself toward the water's edge.

The stranger stuck his knife into her father's neck.

The victim on the dirty ground writhed only briefly as the man again rifled through his pockets.

The man pulled a battered leather wallet out of her father's pants and shoved it into his jacket. Then he kicked the crumpled body toward the edge of the water. And he ran away.

Her father hung on the rusty edge of the canal. Moaning. He breathed words in Spanish. "My Isadora. Oh, my Isadora. I'm so sorry." He gasped and tried to push away from that edge. His voice faltered on. "My Sophie. I'm so sorry. I didn't know what to do for you. Oh, God." He groaned bitterly. "Hector. My Hector ..." He stopped. He lay still. Then he tried to push himself up again. His hand slipped. He cursed and rolled over that ledge. He fell with a shout. A splash. And he was gone.

Her father was sorry. And he had never had the chance to tell his family how sorry.

Seeing the death of her father shook Sophie's body like a person waking from a falling dream. But she didn't open her eyes. She didn't sit up. She felt like she could choose to pull out of this ... this ... whatever was happening to her. But she didn't want to. Not yet.

Someone was speaking. A mother's voice. Detta? Sister Everly? "You thought you were crazy because almost everyone told you it was so. But you were never crazy. You weren't the crazy girl. You were the girl who sees angels." It was Sister Everly, though Detta seemed to be there too.

Not the crazy girl. Not the girl whose insanity had ruined her family. Had driven her father away. Had killed her brother.

She was back in that first bedroom. She stood from the bed, the teenaged Sophie leading the way out of that room and out of the house. She emerged into her old neighborhood, just like she remembered it. But there was no sound. It was a silent film from her youth.

Young Sophie led her to the street, to the very corner where Hector had died. And there he was. Still alive. He was shaking his head at two boys older than him. One of them showed him a gun and said something harsh, vile, threatening.

Hector lunged at him and knocked the boy down. Then he straightened his bike and jumped on the pedals.

The two older boys shouted after him. Hector looked back at them just as he jumped his bike off the curb.

"Hector! No! Look out!" Grown-up Sophie reached toward him just as she had reached for the steering wheel in Anthony's car. But she couldn't get to him.

Hector didn't stop.

She saw the car, but heard no squeal of brakes, no crunch of bones on metal. She couldn't hear any of it. But she felt it. She felt all of it. Deep in her heart.

It was not suicide. Not even careless, really. Just desperate. A desperate escape. That's what had ended her little brother's life.

Sophie inhaled deeply and sobbed that breath out a hundred times. She was back on the floor of Detta's church, under a pew. Flat on her back now. Through a tight squint, she could see faces bowed over her like she was the one struck by a car, like she was the one stabbed by a robber. But she wasn't. She was alive.

She was Sophie Ramos. Alive and well.

Surrounded by Family

Her mother insisted that it was her turn to host Detta and Anthony—an early Christmas celebration at her house.

Sophie greeted the Washingtons at her mother's door. She forced her hands to stay away from her freshly washed hair when Anthony looked at her and smiled. She hoped he wouldn't laugh at her for wearing a dress. It wasn't really a dress, only a long sweater over her yoga pants. The sweater was an early gift from her mother. It felt like a dress.

"Good to see you on your feet. It wasn't so easy for you to stand up last time I saw you."

"Anthony! Behave yourself." Detta hip-bumped her son, her hands full of something in a casserole dish.

Sophie and Anthony shared a private smile. Without hearing any of the details of what had happened to him, she knew what he really thought about that prayer meeting. It had been a place of bending universes and linking dimensions.

Her mom laughed at the teasing and took the casserole from Detta, gripping the Pyrex handles between a finger and thumb. She probably didn't know what all the joking was about. Sophie had told her mother little about what had happened at Detta's church. She told her even less than the fragment of it she understood herself.

"I like the Christmas tree. I'm jealous of the needles that stay where they're put." Detta grinned toward the fully decorated artificial tree in the corner, next to the manger scene on the old sideboard.

Anthony thrust his head forward just slightly, like he was waiting for his mother to say something more. Sophie suspected it was about those Christmas lights. Her madrecita had the old golden glowing kind. Not the cold, modern lights Anthony had imposed on his mother.

The golden glow reminded Sophie of the guardians. She tuned in to the angels in the room and counted six. No, seven. A full house with the four mortals.

"Come on in and get warmed up. I have some hot apple cider on the stove. Would you like some?" Her mother looked at Anthony.

Detta and Anthony both accepted enthusiastically.

Sophie watched her mother steer the casserole toward the kitchen. "Can I help you, Mama?" She made one step to follow.

"No. Stay and enjoy our guests." Her sparkling voice was uniquely worry free, it seemed.

Sophie hadn't told her mother about the visions of the past she'd seen at Detta's church, but she had told her that she was more at peace about the deaths of her father and brother. If her mama needed to know more about how they died, Sophie assumed God would arrange for that.

"So, I'm still waitin' to hear all of what Sister Everly said to you at the service the other night. You said you'd tell me someday. I'm hopin' I don't have to wait until I get old." Detta raised her head to look through her glasses, which had slid halfway down her nose.

"She said so many things." Sophie sorted how much she could say to Detta and Anthony. She noticed that she was more worried about her mother overhearing, but she didn't want to let that stop her. "She said she didn't need to teach me a lot of things, because I have all the resources I need to learn in good time. I'm pretty sure she meant you."

"Me? A resource? Well, I've been called worse."

"And she probably meant other people too." Sophie tried not to rest her eyes on Anthony for a whole second. She wasn't sure how he would feel about being a spiritual resource for her. She still hadn't told him about his angel, which had become visible to her after that prayer meeting.

"And she said I have permission to not see angels and bad spirits all the time. It isn't wrong for me to want to focus on regular people just like everyone else—at least sometimes."

"Like I told you." Detta followed Sophie's inviting gesture, and she chose an armchair with an ottoman, the spot Sophie would have picked for her even if it wasn't exactly like her recliner at home.

Sophie nodded. "I'm practicing. And I'm asking for help."

"From your resources?" Anthony was still standing. He was examining the old ceramic manger scene her mother had acquired from a rummage sale twenty years ago. Most of the pieces were still intact.

She snorted a laugh. "Resources that are invisible to most people."

"Angels?"

She nodded. "And that voice inside. I'm starting to hear that voice better."

"Prayer is a weapon. Listening for God's voice is learning how to aim your weapon." Detta nodded with her face raised toward Sophie.

Anthony made a noise. Probably not a laugh. More like a version of "Aha."

The placid faces of her angels assured Sophie that she didn't have to understand everything about what Detta was saying. But she got the feeling that she should figure it out at some point. If she was going to go on being the woman who sees angels, she needed to know a thing or two about weapons and fighting, apparently.

"But that wasn't the best part of what happened." Sophie looked at her mother, who was carrying a tray with four cups of steaming cider on it.

"I put your casserole in the oven to warm up a bit." She spoke to Detta and then looked at Sophie, as if releasing her to continue.

Sophie knew her mother was curious about what had been happening to her. She appreciated her restraint—no interrogations. Now she was glad for her mother to hear what she had to say. "She said that I would go on seeing the messengers, the angels. But she said I would also get to see the one who sends the messengers." She stopped to wriggle a chill up her back. "And, while Sister Everly was praying for me toward the end, I could hear that voice inside me, and I could see a man standing behind her, even with my eyes closed. And I knew it wasn't just an angel. He wasn't just ... an angel."

Did everyone know what she meant? They all stared at her. Holding their breath, maybe.

Anthony started to clarify, perhaps. "It was ..." He stopped himself, as if reminded of something.

Sophie paused to wonder what had happened to Anthony while he was on the floor. She still hadn't teased him for all that bawling. She probably never would.

"Thank you, Jesus." Detta was smiling at her son.

"Yes. *Gracias, Dios.*" Sophie's mother reached a hand to touch Sophie on the shoulder.

Looking around at the softly glowing faces—on the people, and not just the angels— Sophie knew that she was surrounded. Not only surrounded by a myriad of strange beasts and glowing messengers. She was surrounded by family. At last. A family that accepted her with all her strangeness. A family that would insist she accept herself as well.

"Mm-hmm."

That humming affirmation sounded like what Detta always said. But it came from behind Sophie.

She turned to see which of the angels had spoken. And she raised her eyebrows.

The girl who *hears* angels now?

Book Two in the series is available for download here: https://www.amazon.com/dp/B09JDJT944

You might also like *Seeing Jesus*: https://www.amazon.com/dp/B00D8KZH0M

Sign up for our newsletter if you're interested: Subscribe | jeffreymcclainjones

Thank you!

Printed in Great Britain
by Amazon